THE DUKE'S UNTAMED DESIRE

AMY JARECKI

OLIVER
HEBER
BOOKS

THE DUKE'S UNTAMED
DESIRE

AMY JARECKI

Edited by: Scott Moreland

Published by Oliver-Heber Books

0 9 8 7 6 5 4 3 2 1

THE DUKE'S UNTAMED DESIRE

AMY JARECKI

To Bob.

Chapter One

16TH MAY 1818

❧❧

Georgiana Whiteside gaped at the actor while her dreams crumbled about her feet like an overdone pound cake. "You cannot read?"

Mr. Walpole winced, tugging on his neckcloth. "Ah...no, madam."

Could things grow worse? Left with few options but to hire Palmer Walpole, Georgiana had already made too many mistakes. Yesterday during his audition, his soliloquy had been flawless; he'd also seemed quite sober. Though this morning the actor had shown up smelling as if he'd slept on the floor of a tavern.

Now it was too late to find a replacement. Moreover, if she, a mere woman, summoned the courage to stand on a platform at the Southwark Fair and hold forth about her late husband's steam pumper, she'd be laughed off the stage and carted to an asylum.

At least Mr. Walpole looked the part—a bit of gray at his temples, a contemplative expression fixed on his face, which might be due to the effect of stupefaction brought on by imbibing in too much gin. Nonetheless, all the man need do was recite from the script she had prepared listing the attributes of the new steam-powered fire engine. Except he couldn't read.

Dash it, she should have thought of such a conundrum.

The actor held the parchment within an inch of his nose and examined it upside down. "You didn't say you needed me to study lines."

"No?" she asked, doing her best to contain her frustration. "How else would you know what to say?"

Mr. Walpole rubbed the back of his neck—not a good sign. Goodness, he'd performed at Covent Garden. Yet, of all the questions she'd asked him yesterday, the ability to read hadn't been one of them.

Georgiana drew the list from his fingertips. "How do you usually manage to learn your part?"

"Someone reads me my lines and I memorize."

She glanced to the machine. Everything was ready. This was her chance to find a financier. The moment she'd been waiting for. Biting her bottom lip, she gave him a once-over. "If I succinctly relay each important point, can you commit my list to memory in ten minutes?"

Though his mouth was agape, he uttered no sound for at least five seconds. "All that in ten minutes?"

"This has the workings of a disaster." She threw out her hands. "But you've done demonstrations at fairs before."

"Oh, absolutely. All manner of acting and dancing—fairs, the Garden, Vauxhall. I sing as well as play the violin."

"I'm sure a delightful waltz will help draw investors," she said dryly, looking to the skies. This was her due for hiring an unknown. Well, she couldn't back down now. "Here's how we'll proceed: I'll stand behind you and whisper your lines whilst you act as if you are the most renowned inventor in the world. Can you manage that?"

Mr. Walpole smoothed his fingers down his lapels like a distinguished gentleman. "I most certainly can, madam." At least his ability to perform was never in question.

"Very well." With a bit of improvisation, the demonstration might be a success after all. "The most important thing to remember is the steam pumper is far superior to any fire engine in use today. Every town and estate ought to have one. It pumps two hundred gallons per minute—far more than a hand-operated pump, and—"

"A moment, please." The actor cleared his throat. "That enormous contraption is a steam pumper did you say?"

Good glory, I am doomed. "Yes." She gestured to the iron engine on wheels—the culmination of six years of tireless work, the last of which she'd accomplished alone without Daniel—the true inventor and scholar. "The most important fact to remember is this new *invention* is a fire engine powered by steam."

"Does it work?"

"As long as there is a water supply nearby—" At Walpole's blank expression, Georgiana's explanation abruptly halted. For this man to understand the significance of her husband's design, she must make things clearer. "The current manual-stroke pumps tire the strongest of men in five to ten minutes. Correct?"

"Ah...yes, yes you are correct, madam."

"Excellent. Now picture this: The steam pumper does not require manual labor at all and shoots more water farther than its hand-stroked counterparts. Is that clear?"

Mr. Walpole smiled—not precisely a smile, but more of a grimace. "Perfectly."

Why wasn't she convinced?

"Are you ready, mistress?" asked Roddy, the errand boy she'd brought along to light the fire and keep it burning. With an intelligent glint in his eye, Georgiana was convinced the lad of fourteen would be a far better spokesperson than Palmer Walpole, who had already insisted on half his wages up front.

She looked to the fire engine and back to the young man. "We'll need to make a slight adjustment for the demonstration. Remember when I showed you how to throw the lever?"

"I sure do."

"Well, it turns out I'm required on stage, so you must do it." She grasped the boy by the shoulders. "Once you engage the engine, you'll need to be quick. It is imperative that you assume control of the hose immediately and douse the flame. Can you manage that for me?"

"You're allowing me to throw the lever?" Roddy threw up his fists like a champion. "Yes, mistress. I can do it. You can depend on Roderick Toombs for certain."

"That's exactly what I like to hear." If only Mr. Walpole exhibited half as much confidence, the roiling in the pit of Georgiana's stomach might ease. "How long has the coal been burning?"

Roddy held up the pocket watch she'd given him. "A good twenty minutes."

"And the holding tank is full?"

"Yes, mistress. Double checked it myself."

"And there's more coal at the ready?"

"Aye."

"Very well. Remember to keep the fire hot while Mr. Walpole is talking."

"I will. And I've piled the wood for the demonstration. It is ready to set alight when you give the word."

"Excellent." With his vigor, the boy certainly had all the qualifications to succeed when he reached his majority. "Tell me, Roddy, can you read?"

He puzzled. "Read?"

"We shall discuss such a virtuous and important skill after we return to the town house."

She smoothed her hands down her black mourning gown. Daniel had been gone for over a year now, but she still wore black from head to toe. She tugged her poke bonnet lower on her brow to ensure her hair was secured beneath. After adjusting the spectacles she'd purchased to provide a modicum of disguise at the request of her father, Georgiana gave the actor a nod. "A good opening might be, 'ladies and gentlemen, gather round—'"

"Not to worry, Your Ladyship. That's the easy part."

To Georgiana's surprise, Palmer Walpole became a different man onstage. To the tune of the engine's gentle pops and rumbles, he introduced the steam pumper as if he were an expert on the subject of fire engines and, as she whispered key attributes, he held forth with gusto. By the time a good-sized crowd had amassed, she gave Roddy the cue to start the wood fire for the demonstration.

"We are looking for venture capital. Someone to partner with us in the manufacture of the Whiteside steam-powered fire pumps," the actor repeated as she whispered the most critical information. "Fires will be snuffed before a building can be badly burned, saving lives, livestock and cherished family heirlooms. No town or estate should be without—"

"That's all well and good, but where does the water come from?" asked a man from the crowd. Wearing a beaver hat and an exquisitely cut tailcoat, the gentleman pushed through to the front of the dais and stood with his fists on his hips.

Though the expression on his dark features was quite arresting, butterflies en masse swarmed through Georgiana's stomach. The man had asked a very reasonable question and, by his commanding presence, he was completely engaged. Further, he looked like he was exactly the financier she needed. A real magnate—a man of money.

Bless the stars. At long last, she stood on the precipice of realizing her dreams.

Walpole's jaw dropped. "Ah...there's a reservoir?" he asked as if hadn't a clue.

"Yes, but the reservoir is only the beginning," she shouted in a whisper while smiling at her potential partner. "The engine draws the water from a source, like a well or a pond."

The man stroked his fingers along his square jaw, turning a critical eye. "Is the woman speaking for you?"

"Ah...er...noooo."

Georgiana's pulse raced. Good heavens, an obviously wealthy gentleman was showing interest in her machine and the accursed actor decided now was a brilliant time to grow tongue-tied? She gave Roddy a nod to start the wood fire then, adjusting her spectacles, she moved forward and held forth about the various options for the water source.

As she spoke, the magnate looked her from head to toe as if she'd descended from the moon. When she stopped to take a breath, he addressed Mr. Walpole. "What about the hose? Will it not burst under such pressure?"

"Not at all." Squaring her shoulders, Georgiana nudged the dumbstruck actor aside and continued, "Whiteside hoses are reinforced with copper-riveted seams. Moreover, they are coupled every fifty feet. With estimated pressures of one hundred pounds per square inch, pumping a distance of, say, seventy-five feet is entirely possible."

"Seventy-five feet? Now I know you're telling tall tales." With a snort, the man batted his silver-tipped cane through the air and turned on his heel.

Georgiana tugged Mr. Walpole forward while the crowd began to dissipate. "We're losing them," she growled through clenched teeth.

"Do you know who that is?" the actor asked as if the performance had come to an end.

"This is no time to stand about discussing who is who," she snapped, thrusting her finger at the steam pumper. "Now, Roddy!"

The boy threw the lever and ran around the front to man the hose.

Except he wasn't fast enough.

Under extreme pressure, the line came to life, whipping through the air like a serpent and sousing everyone within fifty feet. Men and women shrieked and ran while Roddy grappled with the hose, taking a whack to the face in the process.

When the lad at last managed to wrap his fingers around the nozzle, he leveled the spray straight ahead.

Lord, no.

Within the blink of an eye, Georgiana's potential investor was completely doused. Saturated. Deluged. Extinguished. The gentleman's hat flew off as the blast of water struck him directly in the center of his well-cut, beautifully tailored tailcoat. How he managed to remain standing was only a testament to his robust stature.

When all two hundred gallons finally emptied from the tank, the man whipped around with fury in his eyes. A bit of steam rose from his shoulders while he homed his gaze on Georgiana and shook his walking stick as if he might be about to strike her with it. "Women have no business tinkering with machines, especially something as powerful as a steam engine. Take this monstrosity and throw it in the Thames!"

Could a person wilt? Perhaps not, but she might crawl under the dais and hide for the rest of her days. Georgiana didn't have the resources to travel about the country in hopes of finding financial backing. She'd only come to London because her parents were in residence for the Season and, though the Baron and Baroness of

Derby hadn't approved of her marriage to a poor inventor, they had agreed to allow her to store the steam pumper behind their mews while she organized demonstrations in London—and that arrangement had taken all but an act of God. Papa wanted nothing to do with steam power—or *anything* that had interested Daniel Whiteside.

Having managed to remain completely dry, Mr. Walpole stared at her as if in shock. "Do you know who you just drowned with two hundred gallons of water at one hundred pounds per square inch?"

She splayed her fingers. How would the man's throat look with her hands wrapped around it? "Now you choose to commit such an important tidbit of information to memory?"

"That..." He pulled out a snuff box. "Was the bloody Duke of Evesham."

A duke?

Perhaps wilting wasn't enough. Perhaps Georgiana ought to throw herself in the Thames along with her *monstrosity*. Of course, the well-dressed, very handsome dandy was a duke. Prickly heat spread across her skin. Why couldn't he be a visitor from the Continent or a sea captain scheduled to set sail for the next decade?

"Aye." Mr. Walpole sneezed. "And he's the wealthiest, most notorious rake in London. I reckon every woman within fifteen miles of Town would recognize him. He's in the papers often enough. I'm surprised you didn't."

"Perhaps that's because I've been living in a workshop in Thetford for the past six years. I wouldn't recognize the Prince Regent if he kissed my hand."

Georgiana wandered down the steps while tears stung the back of her eyes.

"I'm sorry, mistress," Roddy said, a bruise rising on his forehead. "I had no notion the hose would come alive like that."

"Oh dear," she exclaimed. "You have a knot on your head. Are you in pain?"

"It doesn't hurt. I just feel as if I've let you down."

She mussed his sandy hair. "'Tis no one's fault but my own. We needed more people—one to run the engine and one to man the hose...and next time, Mr. Walpole had best have his lines memorized."

That was if the Duke of Evesham didn't take measures to ban her from giving demonstrations within a hundred miles of London.

❧

SOAKING WET AND FURIOUS, FLETCHER MARKHAM hired a sedan chair to take him home. Normally, he'd enjoy a stroll across the old London Bridge on a fine afternoon such as this, but not today. Aside from being a tad under the weather from a late night at Whites' back-room card table, the incident with the damned steam pumper had all but burst his spleen.

It wasn't the first time he'd seen complete nincompoops try to bring something untried and utterly useless to market. Did they not know how important developing a functional steam-powered fire engine was? Dammit all, with the force of the water blasting from the hose, those idiots could have seriously injured someone. What if a child had been in the line of fire?

And that puritan woman stepping in front of the inventor and speaking as if she'd built the damned thing herself was bloody absurd. Obviously, she'd spent hours memorizing facts and figures provided by her stage-frightened accomplice.

He groaned. Fletcher was most likely as interested in fire engines as anyone in England. He had cause to be. At the tender age of sixteen, he'd been away at Eton when he'd lost his mother in a fire. God rest the soul of the only person on earth who'd ever given a damn about him.

After paying the two footmen for the lift, the door to his town house swung open. "Your Grace, I didn't expect to see you return this early," said Smith, holding out his palm to take Fletcher's hat and gloves. "My word, are you wet?"

"Soaked to the bloody bone," he growled, marching through the entry. "Some henpecked steam engine inventor with no clue about dousing fires gave an abysmally amateur demonstration at the Southwark Fair."

"'Tis a shame," said the butler. "It would ease your mind a great deal to have such equipment at Colworth."

Fletcher shuddered. Though he might convince himself the involuntary action was due to being wet and cold, even after four years of dukedom, the name of the immense Tudor mansion still sounded like the foreboding castle where his father resided—the sprawling thirty-five thousand acre country estate upon which Fletcher had only gazed from a distance until the former duke was on his deathbed. Realizing his only son was still a bastard, the man who had ignored Fletcher for six and twenty years called for his solicitors at the last minute and had claimed his son as his rightful heir. Not only that, dear Papa's solicitors had falsified church documents claiming that the duke had married Fletcher's mother in secret and had not wed the woman who was suddenly referred to as his stepmother until after Mama's death. The records were all but written in stone and not even Fletcher could do a damned thing to retract them.

Father's dying words? "I'm sorry." But they were not spoken to Fletcher to provide an apology for his years of neglect, nor were they for his mother who'd died alone in a one-room cottage. The apology was to his weeping, childless duchess who was so heartbroken, she'd also passed away not long after.

Fletcher headed for the stairs. "Please tell the valet to draw a bath."

"Straightaway." Smith bowed. "Will you be going out as planned this evening?"

"Unless you have found a harem of women to occupy the second floor, yes."

The butler chuckled. "I shall never grow tired of your humor, Your Grace. I could predict your father's every word but, if you don't mind my saying, your clever wit surprises me each and every day."

The irony? Fletcher wasn't joking. He might have a title, but he'd been born a bastard and would always remain a bastard.

Chapter Two

"If you tug on the strings one more time, I am sure to expire." Georgiana clung to the bedpost, convinced the lady's maid tying her stays was a sadist. Did the woman haul buckets of water all day to acquire such inhuman strength?

Ignoring Georgiana's complaint, the maid gave another breath-defying tug. "Nearly done."

"Do not listen to her," said Mother, sitting beneath the curtains of the Grecian settee recessed into the window. The perfect baroness, Georgiana considered sending for an artist to paint a rendering right there. If only she could afford to pay an artist. It had taken nearly every last penny of her meager income to have the fire engine hauled to London.

"I for one am quite fond of breathing," she said, trying to inhale. "Besides, I do not see why you insist on dragging me along to this ball. You know I am a hopeless dancer. Even when I was a debutante, my lack of grace outshone everyone else."

"I am not dragging you anywhere. I am escorting you to Almacks at long last so that you may discard your notion of selling Daniel's ill-begotten machine and find happiness for once in your life."

"I *was* happy."

"You married a pauper and see what that got you. Not to mention he squandered your dowry on that enormous eyesore. And then he..." Mother pursed her lips. Thank heavens she didn't say it. The truth was unbearable without being uttered.

Georgiana still relived the accident every time she closed her eyes—the eerie sound of the chain being stretched to its capacity—the sight of the cast-iron cylinder dropping.

"Are you unwell?" asked the maid.

Snapping back to the present, Georgiana straightened. "I have no idea how I'll endure the night being laced so tightly."

Mama unfurled her fan and cooled her face. "Stays always feel too tight until you move around a bit. By the end of the evening, you'll hardly know they're there."

The maid held up a new gown of lavender tulle over ivory India muslin trimmed with lace. "This is lovely, mistress."

"It is." Mother continued to flutter her fan. "And that is because my daughter allowed me to choose her modiste as well as her fabrics."

Georgiana rolled her eyes as the dress slipped over her head.

"And not a word of thanks?" The baroness sighed loudly. "It is well past time you cast aside those dreary mourning clothes and dress yourself in some color. You look ever so lovely in pastels."

"She does at that," said the maid, lacing up the gown's rear seam.

"I must admit that since you were measured, I've taken the liberty of ordering you an entire new wardrobe." Mother snapped her fan closed. "You may thank me now, dearest."

Georgiana swallowed her urge to groan. Mother had exquisite taste, but black suited her daughter—at least it suited her mood. "Thank you. If only you were willing to help me find a financier for the steam pumper or introduce me to a few gentlemen who might be interested in placing an order or two I would be ecstatically grateful."

"I'd rather introduce you to a plethora of gentlemen who are able to support you in fine style for the rest of your days."

A sudden stabbing needled Georgiana's neck. "I do not need another husband, Mama."

"No? I disagree. I do worry about you out there in the country living in that hovel. It just isn't natural."

"Plenty of country women live in hovels."

"Not well-born daughters of barons."

"I suppose I am the exception, then."

"And you will be the death of me."

"I sincerely doubt that." At least it was likely dear Mama would not be crushed by a steam engine's cylinder.

Mother rested her elbow on the velvet cushion. "You were rather quiet when you returned from today's exhibition. I gather it didn't go as you'd hoped?"

Georgiana turned her back and busied herself straightening the tortoiseshell brush, comb and mirror on the toilette. "Not exactly. But I'll be better prepared next time."

"Hmm. Well, at least you'll be staying on with us in London, and I do like that. I cannot tell you how delighted I am to have you here to flit about Town with."

"Yes, Mama. But remember, I am six and twenty. Do not fill your head with ideas of parading me about the *ton* like a debutante."

Their agreement had been for Georgiana to accompany her mother to all manner of the Season's functions in exchange for room, board, and especially the storage of—in her father's words—the hulking, useless heap of iron. However, at every opportunity, she made it imminently clear she did not have an iota of interest in being flaunted about the marriage mart.

Still, Georgiana couldn't fault her parents for trying. During her one and only Season, she had hopelessly fallen in love with Daniel and had refused all other offers. The problem was she still loved him. And now that he was gone, she wanted to do everything in her power to see that his brilliance lived on through the legacy of the Whiteside steam pumper.

Yes, she'd been vague about the day's disaster because her parents cared not about her disappointment. Besides, what if she slipped and told them about the dousing incident with the Duke of Evesham? Mother would insist on a formal apology. Groveling most certainly would be involved. And then they'd all conspire against her. Papa's words rattled in her mind now: "A woman your age should be bustling about her home, fussing over children and menus, planning soirees, embroidering beautiful seat cushions and, most of all, keeping well away from anything mechanical."

IF THERE WAS ONE THING FLETCHER DISLIKED MORE than chatty debutantes, it was their chatty mothers. And Mrs. Finch had three daughters for whom she was seeking husbands, which made the woman prattle ad nauseum. Worse, in her desperation, she was gripping his arm so tightly his fingers were growing numb. Poor woman, if only she knew what he really thought of her unseemly brood, she'd never speak to him again. Though such an idea had its merits, deep down Fletcher pitied her plight. It wasn't easy for widows left behind with children or any woman trying to manage children alone.

So there he stood. To the tune of her chirping his mind wandered, first admonishing himself for making an appearance at Almacks that evening. Though his reason was sound. Sooner or later he must produce an heir and, when he did, the child damned-well must be legitimate. The problem was finding a suitable wife. Love did not have to play into the equation, but the woman must exhibit intelligence, talent in the arts, had to be reasonably pleasing to the eye, and must not have her nose so far up her backside to prevent her from understanding the privilege of wealth and the need for compassion for those who did not have it.

He'd met a handful of women who might have been suitable candidates. The problem was every female of interest who'd crossed his path was married. He'd even bedded one or two, but only by taking precautions. Fletcher Markham stood by his convictions. Any child produced from his loins would *not* be labeled a bastard.

Some things were worth enduring the punishment of pretending to pay attention to Mrs. Finch's high-pitched babble while prowling for a female who might suit. Perhaps a marriage of convenience was what he needed.

When the Baroness of Derby appeared beneath the archway, Fletcher's gaze came to an abrupt halt. Beside Her Ladyship stood an interesting specimen. And though the back of his neck tingled with recognition—in fact, far more of his body parts tingled than the back of his neck—he definitely couldn't place the woman.

Wearing lavender over ivory lace, the rather tall brunette looked on with an air of maturity. Was she married? Fletcher intended to find out—and by his own means. He wasn't about to ask for an introduction from Mrs. Finch. Asking anyone to introduce him would set the gossips aflutter. He wrested his arm from the woman's grasp and bowed. "Very interesting, madam. If you will please excuse me, I have a matter to attend."

"Have you heard a word I've said?" she asked, the matron's voice fading into the crowd.

Lady Derby and her companion moved toward a circle of mothers—a group of women from whom all unmarried gentlemen were wise to keep their distance. Circling the mob, Fletcher found a pillar partly concealed by a potted fern with a clear line of sight to the mystery woman. She posed a very interesting vision, indeed. Her expression was a tad blasé rather than anxious and overly eager as were the faces of the young ladies embarking on their first Season.

A faint hint of rose touched her cheeks—her skin flawless, satiny. Fletcher rubbed his fingertips together, imagining a silken caress.

She politely engaged in conversation, nodding, speaking softly. But as her lips moved, he heard her over the others. Her voice was sultry, womanly. And when she smiled, it was as if a ray of sunlight flooded the ballroom.

Oh, do that again, if you please.

Someone moved and blocked his view of the beauty. He inclined his head just enough to see her again. She stood oblivious to his attention, smiling, nodding, a soft chuckle here and there.

Not until she excused herself and headed away from the gaggle did he make a move and follow her out to the corridor.

GEORGIANA HAD DONE HER DUTY AND MADE A GRAND appearance at Almacks. It was surprising how quickly all the years of finishing school and training to be a proper lady magically returned. Mama ought to be proud. Georgiana hadn't uttered a single word of complaint, she had kept her expression engaged and thoughtful while gentlewomen of the *ton* expressed their glee at seeing her in lavender rather than black.

She had smiled at the right cues and offered a demure chuckle when the conversation commanded she do so.

When Mama was pulled away by one of her friends, Georgiana took the opportunity to excuse herself and flee to the lady's withdrawing room where she intended to find a cozy chair and spend the remainder of the evening reading the book she had hidden in her reticule.

She climbed the stairs, pushed inside, and stopped abruptly.

What have they done with the women's withdrawing room?

She stared across a dim salon, lit only by a wall sconce. Though Georgiana had an uncanny memory, it had obviously failed her as to the location of her coveted hideaway. However, since no plans had been set in motion to use this chamber, perhaps she might find a candle to read by and hide in here.

But then the door opened.

To Georgiana's horror, standing in the brilliant light of the corridor was none other than the Duke of Evesham.

She glanced about for another exit and found none. Could she run? Had he recognized her? Without the spectacles and her mourning gown, she hardly looked the same. But then he might be of those people who never forgot a face. A clammy chill spread over her skin.

Holy help!

He stepped into the salon, letting the door close behind him. "Sorry to intrude, madam, but I believe you dropped this."

Madam? Truly, he hadn't recognized her. And thank goodness the light was dim. "Ah..." To ensure he remained ignorant of her identity, Georgiana moved further into the shadows as she looked to his outstretched hand. She'd dropped her dance card? Blast it all, she should have refused the useless thing at the door.

She held up her palm. "I assure you, I will have no need of that tonight."

"No?" He made not a sound as he drew nearer. "A beautiful woman so finely attired should dance every set."

Beautiful? Prickles of warning fired up her nape. Daniel had been two inches shorter than she, but Evesham was taller. Dominating. He stood a good head higher—his eyes dark, his face far too fetching. Good Lord, Georgiana's hands trembled. He held out the card and grinned, his teeth gleaming white through the shadowy light. As she took it, her fingers brushed his. Warm. Rough. Strong.

Her palm perspired and stuck to the paper. She couldn't breathe. Never again would she let Mother's lady's maid tie her stays. *I knew I shouldn't have come.*

Georgiana pointed a slippered foot toward her escape. "I haven't danced in several years."

He neared and with him came a feral scent of spice and citrus. "Oh my, that is a shame."

She backed. "Not really." With a thump, her spine hit the wall.

The duke stood not but two feet away while his gaze raked down her body. No, not raked, meandered. A lock of black hair fell over one eye while those beautiful teeth scraped over his bottom lip. He studied her as if he were admiring a sculpture—a nude—a *female* nude. "I do not recall seeing you before. Are you new to London?"

Gracious! She missed her mourning gown and the brooch she wore pinned at her throat. The lacy affair clinging to her breasts was cut far too low and fit much too snugly. "N-no, though I haven't been here since... well, in a very long time." No use explaining her life's history to a notorious rake—a duke she was responsible for showering with two hundred gallons of water earlier that very day.

With one more step, he placed his hand on the wall above her head. "Are you as averse to Town as you are to dancing?"

Georgiana looked him in the eyes. *Mistake*. Even with poor light they glimmered amber like those of a predator—and oh, so very hungry. The room began to spin. Her breath came in short gasps. "Y-y-you might say that."

"I see. Well this seems to be a conundrum." His lips neared as he whispered, "Pray tell, what manner of persuasion brought you to Almacks this evening?" By the deep, sensuous tenor of his voice, he might have been uttering sweet words of passion.

Squeezing her palms against her ribcage, Georgiana took the deepest breath her stays would allow. "I-I'm here to appease my mother."

His Grace's minty breath whispered over her as his gaze dipped to her mouth. "Who is?"

By the queen's knees, if she didn't escape this very moment, the Duke of Evesham might actually kiss her. No wonder the man had a reputation of being a rake. Did he often follow unsuspecting women into darkened rooms and seduce them?

In a moment of sanity, Georgiana ducked under his arm and fled. "Please excuse me. I must be on my way."

Chapter Three

❧

As sunlight streamed in from a gap in the velvet draperies, Fletcher threw an arm over his forehead. Had he slept? After searching every corner of Almacks and being unable to find the mystery woman, he'd taken to the streets. She'd bloody disappeared, and he didn't even know her name.

He'd acted so cocksure. Had he misinterpreted her interest? But as he'd sauntered toward the woman, she'd practically been panting. And why the hell must he always skirt around the rules? He should have asked Mrs. Finch or any other woman in the hall to give him a damned introduction. But no, he wanted the chase. He wanted the thrill of following the beauty into the shuttered salon. And why the devil had she gone into a dimly lit room alone? Was she lost? Had she planned to meet someone there?

Groaning, he rang for his valet. Fletcher would solve the mystery once and for all. The woman had entered Almacks on the arm of Lady Derby. Was Derby the beauty's mother, the woman Lady Beauty was there to appease? He would call on the baroness this morning and put an end to this quandary.

Most likely the woman in question was married, or otherwise engaged. She didn't fit the bill for a debutante. Truly, she didn't fit the bill for anything except for that of a lovely matron, married to a country gentleman who didn't care much for balls. Once the mystery was put to rest, he'd stop thinking about their encounter and that would be the end of his torture.

An hour later, a butler answered the door to Derby's Mayfair Place town house.

Fletcher handed the man his card. "Evesham here. Is Derby in?"

"No, Your Grace. His Lordship is at court."

Of course he was—which was exactly the reason Fletcher had chosen this hour to make a call. "Unfortunate. Would I be able to gain an audience with Her Ladyship? It won't take but a moment."

"I shall inquire." The butler gestured inside. "Please have a seat in the parlor."

It took less than five minutes for the baroness to make an appearance in the exquisitely appointed parlor, painted in rich mauves and furnished in the latest Grecian style. "Your Grace, it is an honor to receive you."

Fletcher stood and bowed. "Thank you for seeing me at such short notice, my lady."

"Please do resume your seat." She gestured to the settee, every bit a well-bred gentlewoman. "I've ordered some tea and cakes."

"How very kind."

"Now tell me, what has brought you to Mayfair Place this morning?"

It was always a relief to dispense with the pleasantries and move on to the reason for his visit. "I saw you enter Almacks with a woman on your arm. I couldn't place her, but when I thought to ask for an introduction, she was nowhere to be found. I imagined she might be a matron, or a relation of some sort...?"

The woman beamed—her expression not unlike those faces of the mothers of the *ton*. "That must have been the fleeting moment when my daughter made an appearance. Please forgive her. Last eve was her first social engagement in some time. She spent nearly the entire evening reading in the women's withdrawing room."

"I take it she's averse to dancing."

"She's averse to socializing—though I aim to cure her of the malady this Season." The woman's lips pursed as the maid brought in the tea service. "Thank you, miss."

Fletcher stretched out his legs and crossed his ankles in an attempt to appear reserved and patient while Her Ladyship poured. Four years of dukedom had taught him not to reach across the table, shake a gentlewoman by the neck and demand answers. Truly, he'd never stooped so low as to shake any woman by the neck. He drummed his fingers on the armrest and looked toward the door.

"It must be very unnerving to have a daughter so lovely, yet so shy," he ventured.

Lady Derby handed him a cup and saucer. "I wouldn't say she's exactly shy, but Georgiana has led a reclusive life."

"Oh?" he asked with an incline of his head, willing her to tell him more.

"Six years ago, she married a poor scholar."

A lead ball sank to the pit of Fletcher's stomach. "I see." He did see. Every time he met a woman who remotely interested him, she was married.

"The man took her to the country where we rarely saw her. And to my dismay, Georgiana only grew more withdrawn. Why, just yesterday I convinced her to stop wearing mourning clothes."

The lead ball levitated. "Mourning, did you say?"

"Yes. Mr. Daniel Whiteside has been gone over a year. And it is high time Georgiana spent a Season in London and realize there is more to life than being miserable in a shabby cottage."

"Ah, so that's why I haven't seen her at any affairs in London before."

"Exactly. Hardly a soul has seen her in six years, the poor dear. And I intend to ensure she enjoys everything the Season has to offer."

"Including dancing?" he asked, recalling how Mrs. Whiteside had all but refused to take her dance card.

"Especially dancing, the theater, music, soirees, luncheons."

For a recluse? He swallowed his question with a sip of tea. "I'm sure the lady will be delighted."

"She will be."

"Is she here?"

SEATED AT HER WRITING TABLE, GEORGIANA nibbled a bit of toast as she read a paper delivered earlier that morning. Seeming to be a lady's journal from the fashionable rendering of an evening gown on the front page, the title was rather odd: *The Scarlet Petticoat*.

Halfway down the page, an article caught her eye:

"The Duke of Evesham has been caught exiting a sedan chair dripping wet. Our sources report he was doused during an exhibition of a fire pumper at the Southwark Fair and that a mysterious woman did the dousing. Has the ton's most notorious rake at last had his fiery lust extinguished by a shunned lover?"

She looked up in disbelief. Roddy had manned the hose and Mr. Walpole had given the lion's share of the presentation. How had someone targeted her as the culprit, let alone a shunned lover? The ridiculous article went on to prove the inaccuracies of news reporting. The only possible truth might be the subject concerning Evesham. He was definitely wet, most likely hailed a sedan chair for a lift home, and even Mr. Walpole knew of the duke's philandering reputation.

With a snort, Georgiana slapped the paper on the table. The pile of lies was naught but a miserable gossip tabloid fit only for the rubbish bin.

"Mistress?" Dobbs, the family butler's voice came through the timbers.

"Come in."

"The Duke of Evesham has asked to see you."

Sixty leaping lords bounded through her stomach while a lump the size of Gibraltar took up residence in her throat.

"Evesham, did you say?" she managed in a strangled whisper. *Oh dear, oh dear*. He'd realized who she was and had come to bury her.

"Yes, he's in the parlor with your mother."

Lord save me. Clutching her midriff, Georgiana sprang to her feet. "Tell him I've stepped out."

Dobbs threw out his hands. "Stepped out? But Her Ladyship—"

"Tell them I'm walking the dog. Where can I find Rasputin and...and his lead?"

"He's most likely in the kitchens. Are you sure you can handle a hunting dog?"

"Of course. I've walked a dog before." Georgiana snatched her new bonnet and gloves. "I'm off. Tell Mama I've already left the house."

As soon as she entered the kitchen, Rasputin bounded up to her, planted his paws on her shoulders and licked her face. Shifting her head away, Georgiana gave the Pointer a push. "Are you ready for a walk, chappie?"

With a display of enthusiasm, slamming his tail into every standing object in the kitchen and knocking over a stool, the dog dashed to the door and fixated upon the lead dangling from a hook.

"Right-o. You're a bright lad, are you not?" She snapped the clasp onto his collar. "Where shall we go? Green Park?"

Rasputin yowled. Only about a quarter-mile away, it was likely where Papa took the dog on their morning jaunts.

Lead in hand, she pushed outside into the drizzle. But a tad of rain wasn't about to stop her from a stealthy escape. Evidently, Rasputin thought the same as he scampered through the rear garden at far too fast a pace.

"Heel." Georgiana tugged on the lead. "We're not in a footrace. Has my father not taught you proper manners?"

Her question was met with a slap of his tail as the dog scrambled with long strides, tugging against his collar with such force the beast made choking noises.

Yes, Georgiana had walked a dog when she was still living at home. At the time, the family's beloved pet was an overweight Corgi who generally waddled up the street and back, after which he was ready for a long afternoon nap. But this year-old Pointer clearly took to the idea of a stroll in a completely different light.

Before Rasputin managed to pull her arm from its socket, she yanked him beside her with all her strength. "I say heel. What on earth does my father feed you, gunpowder?" She gave another hearty tug. "We are *walking* to the park, you four-legged ox."

Georgiana tried to stop and check for traffic at the corner of Stratton and Piccadilly, but Rasputin would have nothing to do with slowing the pace even in the face of certain death by an oncoming phaeton with a high-stepping team. She had naught but to grip the lead, blink away the rain, and cower while the dog dragged her zigzagging across the cobbles to the tune of more shouts and curse words than she'd heard at Southwark Fair the day prior.

Once they reached the path leading into the park, Georgiana tried to catch her breath and compose herself, but the Pointer had different ideas. Gurgling with ravenous snorts, he tugged on the lead as if he'd been starved for weeks and had homed in on a roast goose. The beast hauled her beneath sycamores dripping sloppy globules of water that slapped her in the face.

"Heel!" she shouted, having given up all semblance of a ladylike demeanor while she fought desperately to hang on, praying the dog wouldn't run roughshod over any elderly passersby.

Abruptly, the mangy mutt stopped. Thank God. Panting, Georgiana planted her palms on her knees and took in a deep inhalation. "Surely, you mustn't misbehave this badly with my father."

After creeping forward, Rasputin pointed. Left paw tucked up, head low, tail straight out like a ramming rod.

In the five minutes that she had come to know the animal, without a doubt, pointing meant nothing good. Not for a hunting dog confined in the midst of a city.

Quack, quack.

"Nooooooo!" Georgiana howled, her arm yanked forward while her feet pummeled the ground at a run.

Barking loud enough to alert every Bow Street runner in the city, Rasputin darted straight for the pond. A flock of ducks set to flight just as the bedeviled hound took a soaring leap. At the edge of the water, Georgiana released her grip, but the accursed leash caught on her finger.

Shrieking, she flung out her hands as she dove, face-first into a grove of lily pads. Murky water filled her mouth as she hollered for help, only to be choked to within an inch of her life. Engulfed by cold and wet, a simple stroll with a dog became a fight for her very breath while the weight of her skirts and petticoats dragged her downward. Her right shoe dropped as she battled against lake weed, stretching her feet toward the bottom.

With a rush of strength, her head broke the surface.

"Help!" Georgiana coughed and sputtered, gasping for air.

As if the hands of God had swept down from the skies, big meaty fingers clamped around her waist.

"I have you," growled a deep voice, one that made gooseflesh pebble her skin. Water whisked away as the man lifted her into his arms. Georgiana curled into his protective chest.

"Thank you ever so much," she said, looking to his face. If a woman could die from shock, this would be the moment. "Ah...Your Grace," she squeaked.

The Duke of Evesham grinned at her much the same as he'd done the night before but, this time, it was in complete daylight. The sun peeked through a gap in the clouds, making him look as if a halo encircled his black hair—his rugged face framed by a hint of fiery light. "Mrs. Whiteside, I presume?"

"How did you guess?"

Even his eyes sparkled beneath those fierce brows. Was it natural for a man's eyes to be so inordinately amber? "Your mother became quite concerned when the butler mentioned you'd taken the dog for a stroll."

"And now we both know why." She glanced toward the ground. "I believe it is safe to put me down."

"I suppose it would create a spectacle if I carried you to your doorstep." Chuckling, he gently placed her feet on the grass as if she were as light as a feather.

Georgiana felt anything but steady. Was she floating? The dog rubbed his wet body along her leg and sat wagging his tail while he smiled up at her, his tongue lolling to the side. "Now I know why my father named him Rasputin. This beast is the spawn of the devil."

Evesham gave the mutt a pat. "I think not. This fellow is just a pup. Pointers love running and need plenty of exercise. It is difficult for them to be in Town."

Was this the same man who'd practically seduced her at Almacks last eve? "You're fond of dogs, are you?"

"Love them. I have a pair of Gordon Setters."

"Setters and Pointers? We ought to have a grand hunt. The dogs would be overjoyed."

"They would."

The air swelled with silence. Unable to pull her gaze away, Georgiana's shoeless foot turned inward. There he stood, the same man who told her to throw the steam pumper in the Thames who was again dripping wet—at least to his waist—but he seemed completely unperturbed by his discomfort. Should she tell him?

Absolutely not!

"Ah...I truly am in your debt, Your Grace," she managed. "Thank you ever so much for coming to my aid."

She reached for Rasputin's lead. But the duke relieved it from the tips of her fingers. "No thanks is necessary, though I would not be fulfilling my gentlemanly duty if I didn't see you home."

Hugging her shoulders, she forlornly watched his hand wrap around the leather strap. Why was he being so nice? Where was the irate gentleman from the fair? Was he a chameleon? Irate to sensuous to kind? How many faces did Evesham have?

She nodded toward the path. "Very well."

"Your mother told me about your recent loss," he said as Rasputin walked at heel, pretending he hadn't just nearly caused her death. "Please accept my condolences. You must have thought me inordinately forward last eve."

"Thank you." Had he come to call to offer an apology? And why didn't her heart twist into a knot like it usually did when someone mentioned Daniel's passing? "Honestly, I didn't know what to think. It had been so long since I set foot in Almacks I'd forgotten where to find the lady's withdrawing room."

A droplet fell from his black hair onto his shoulder.

He didn't look entirely like a duke. He looked more like a Gypsy in duke's clothing—a very attractive, somewhat dangerous man of Romany descent. "Where you were heading to spend the evening reading, I've been told."

"I performed my duty and made an appearance with Mama to spare my father a dreary night out, mind you."

"It was very nice of you to accompany her."

"She does love the Season."

"And you do not?"

Georgiana shivered. "I abhor it."

"But why, especially now you are free to do as you please?"

Hmm. What she pleased was to find a financier and promptly return to her *hovel* in Thetford. "Ah, but my mother has other plans."

"And as the dutiful daughter, you have chosen to humor her?"

"Something along those lines." No, she definitely *never* would mention the steam pumper to His Grace.

Evesham stopped at the entrance to the alley. "Shall we take Rasputin in through the rear?"

"Positively not." Georgiana hastened her step. If the duke caught sight of the steam pumper, he'd throttle her for certain. "I cannot allow a man of your station to venture back through the mews. It wouldn't be proper."

He followed, thank heavens. "You mustn't think of me as being inordinately lofty. I haven't always been a duke."

"But you are now." She stopped at the bottom of the town house steps and held out her hand. "I think I can handle the dog from here. And thank you ever so much for coming to my aid. I truly am grateful."

A furrow formed in his brow while his gaze dipped to her lips...and perhaps a tad lower. Something deep inside came awake like a cat that had been sleeping for ages. "You'd best don some dry clothes."

Georgiana glanced down. How daft could she be?

Her bodice clung to her breasts. Worse, her nipples were as erect as Rasputin's tail had been when he'd spotted the ducks. Drawing an arm across her bosoms, she dipped into a hasty curtsy. "Good day, Your Grace."

She couldn't dash up the stairs fast enough.

"Good day, madam," his deep voice called after her, carrying a touch of humor. "And if you should ever decide to walk your dog again, please do send for me beforehand."

Too polite to ignore him, she cast a gracious smile over her shoulder and slipped inside.

Chapter Four

THREE DAYS LATER

❧

"Georgiana, is that you?"

Smiling radiantly, a dear friend from Georgiana's distant past approached with outstretched hands through the crowded vestibule of Covent Garden. "Eleanor? Oh, how lovely to see you!"

"My, you look absolutely stunning." The daughter of the Viscount of Lisle, Miss Eleanor Kent had been a dear childhood friend. "I had no idea you were in London."

"'Tis a bit of exchange, really. I'm accompanying Mama to her social engagements..." Georgiana drew in a deep breath. The opera was about to start and there was little time to explain all that had transpired in the past few years.

"And what are you gaining?" Eleanor asked.

Georgiana glanced to her mother, deep in conversation with a woman wearing a great many diamonds. "I'm trying to find a financier for Daniel's steam pumper."

"He finished it?"

"Not exactly."

"Oh dear, why do I have the feeling something horrible has happened?"

"Because it has. There was an accident. And...he's

gone." Georgiana whispered. Blinking away tears, she snapped open her fan and hid behind a flurry of fluttering.

Eleanor placed a gentle hand on her shoulder. "How awful for you. I am so sorry I wasn't aware—how on earth have we lost touch? Please accept my sincere condolences."

"Thank you." It seemed few people knew. Not that Daniel's death had made the papers in London. And Georgiana hadn't written anyone. After moving to Thetford, she'd fallen out of contact with her friends, even Eleanor. "It has been over a year since the accident, and Mama feels I need to reenter society."

"But it cannot be easy for you to be out and about, not after all you've been through."

"I have my motives, and it is nice to see Mama with her friends. She's such a social butterfly."

"She always has been." Eleanor nodded at a passing dandy. "Tell me, do you have any children?"

"No." Georgiana's gaze followed a man who winked at Eleanor over his shoulder. Was her friend flirting? "And you? I do not recall reading about your wedding."

"That's because I am far too busy running my father's affairs."

"After all this time, you're still taking care of him?"

Tugging up her gloves, Eleanor cringed. "Someone must keep the household afloat."

"I'm surprised the viscount hasn't received a war pension."

"He has—enough for his basic needs, but not enough to fill his coffers."

The bell rang, indicating all should take their seats for the opera.

"I'd better go." Eleanor squeezed Georgiana's hands. "I'd love to hear more about your steam pumper. We must have tea soon."

"I'd absolutely adore that." What a boon to find an

ally. And why hadn't Georgiana thought of her dear friend sooner? True, she had only been in London a week, but she needed a confidant and Eleanor would fit the bill quite nicely.

Smiling, she joined her mother as they ascended the stairs to their second-tier box.

"Was that Miss Eleanor with whom you were speaking?"

"It was, indeed."

"Are you aware she's still a spinster?" Mama whispered behind her fan. "'Tis a frightful shame. I've always considered her such a lovely girl. Her hair shines like copper."

Georgiana's shoulders tensed. "She has her hands tied, taking care of her father."

"Why must the burden fall to her? They have servants."

"I'm certain there is a good reason for it." She rubbed her neck. "Besides, I commend Eleanor for looking after the viscount."

"Hmm." Mother handed two tickets to the usher waiting at the top of the stairs. "Box five if you please."

"Yes, my lady. Have you seen *Don Giovani* before?"

"Not for years."

He led them down the corridor. "Then you are in for quite a treat."

"At theses exorbitant prices, I would hope so."

Drawing a hand over her nose, Georgiana snorted. Her parents were wealthy enough to buy the theater if they desired and yet her mother always managed to complain.

If the man was offended by her remark, he didn't show it as he opened the door to their box. "Here we are."

"Thank you," Georgiana said as she followed the baroness inside.

Though the box was spacious, there were only two

velvet upholstered chairs, festooned by red curtains with gold trim. When the door closed, Georgiana scoffed. "If you're so worried about the ticket prices, we could have spent the evening at home."

Mother took her seat and fluffed out her skirts. "'Tisn't the price that worries me, it is that Covent Garden sees fit to raise their fees by a quarter every year. And nonsense about staying home. No one remains at home in London on a Friday evening, especially when an opera by Mozart is playing."

"Papa isn't here."

"And he's not at home either. The card table at Whites was too tempting for him tonight." Mother raised a lorgnette to her eyes, primly peering across the parterre. "I see the Duke of Evesham has come—he's alone, mind you."

Georgiana didn't intend to look, but before she stopped herself, she spotted the man in the box directly across from them, staring her way. "Oh, dear."

Mother regarded daughter with an aghast cough. "I am still disappointed that you chose Tuesday morning to walk Rasputin. I think you may have caught Evesham's eye."

For her own well-being, Georgiana hadn't said a word to her mother about the incident in the park. And three days had passed without another altercation with His Grace. Clearly any attraction he might have harbored was doused in Green Park's pond. "You cannot be serious, Mama. Even I've heard of his philandering reputation.

"Hogwash." She snapped her lorgnette back to her eyes. "He's a single man. A very wealthy one, mind you —reported to earn over twenty thousand per year. What he needs is a stalwart woman with whom he can grow roots. Deep roots."

"Well, I wish him all the very best in his search."

"Oh, look there. I do believe he's waving at you, dear."

He was.

Georgiana gave him a polite nod, then stared at her folded hands until the overture began with a thundering cadence. All through the first act, the intensity of Evesham's stare made her skin fiery with awareness. Nonetheless, she wasn't fooled. Every time the soprano commanded the stage, she sang to the duke as if there were no other person in the audience. No wonder he was alone. He'd come to the theater to listen to his lover sing. In fact, by the time the curtain closed for intermission, Georgiana was convinced the soprano was Evesham's mistress and on the morrow *The Scarlet Petticoat* would contain an article stating the same.

The usher knocked. "Beg your pardon, my lady. You have a missive."

"Truly?" Mother asked, taking the note and reading. "Good heavens. How absolutely fortuitous, my dear— Evesham has invited us to join him in his box."

🐾

FLETCHER HADN'T EVEN LOOKED AT THE STAGE. Alternatively, aside from a fleeting glance, Mrs. Whiteside hadn't averted her eyes from it. No, he wasn't about to sit idle while the woman who had consumed his every thought for the past three days and nights ignored him.

That's why he'd addressed the invitation to Lady Derby rather than her daughter. The baroness plainly wanted to see Georgiana happy, and had been quite clear about her intentions during their discussion in her Mayfair Place town house. If Her Ladyship thought it was time to reintroduce her daughter to the marriage mart, Fletcher intended to be the first man at the trough. Mrs. Whiteside mightn't be the one for whom he was looking, but he planned to find out before some other sniveling nobleman showed up on her doorstep with a fist full of roses.

He stood when the usher opened the door. "Ladies, how lovely to see you this evening. I am delighted to have you join me."

"Thank you for hospitality, Your Grace." Lady Derby held out her hand, which Fletcher promptly kissed. "I am surprised to see you sitting alone this evening."

"Unless you have a friend in the cast," said Mrs. Whiteside, giving a polite curtsy.

The woman was astute. Indeed, Fletcher had come in hopes of meeting Signora Morella after the performance. Lying awake and frustrated over the past several nights, he'd thought the soprano might assuage his damnable lust. But as soon as the lovely widow had taken her seat in the box across from his, all thoughts of the woman he'd once enjoyed bedding fell by the wayside.

"I am a patron of the opera," he explained. At least that wasn't a lie. He rarely missed an opening.

Fletcher took the young woman's hand and bowed over it, breathing in her scent. She wore no perfume, but she smelled clean, and so very female. And though her hands were covered by kid leather gloves, he took extra care to impart a kiss equal to the blood thrumming through his veins.

By the woman's soft gasp, she wasn't completely impervious to him.

"Welcome. Please do have a seat." He held the far chair for Lady Derby, the one closest to the stage for Mrs. Whiteside, then opted for the middle.

"Compliments to your modiste, my lady. Both mother and daughter are among the most smartly attired women in the theater."

"How kind of you to say," said Her Ladyship.

37

Fletcher turned to Mrs. Whiteside. "And how is your dog?"

She silenced a snort with the palm of her hand. "Papa is undertaking a course of strict obedience with him."

"I'm surprised she made it home without incident," said Lady Derby.

Arching an eyebrow, he looked between the women. So, Mrs. Whiteside hadn't told her mother about her drenching at the pond? Interesting. But then the entire dog-walking adventure must have been mortifying for the woman. Still, it showed him she truly was a bit of a recluse—someone very private.

The orchestra began to play as the curtain rose, revealing a street scene and bloody, bedamned Signora Morella. But with such tempting fare beside him, Fletcher had no problem tuning out the music and Mrs. Whiteside in. Her evening gown was exquisite. Ivory embroidered with crystal jewels that sparkled every time she moved. Her hair was pulled up in a chignon crowned with a tiara and softened by chestnut ringlets framing her face.

Fletcher chose not to fight the sensation of champagne bubbling through his blood, the smoldering heat pooling in his loins. He rather liked this stage of an infatuation.

Dropping his hand to his side, he leaned toward her until his fingers met with folds of silk, his lips so close to her, he couldn't help but whisper, "You are the most beautiful woman in the theater this night."

A rueful chuckle slipped through her lips as she regarded him out of the corner of her eye. She shifted her seat, her hips nearer though her crossed ankles moved away. "Are you flirting with me, Your Grace?"

Through the silk fabric, he lightly brushed her thigh. "Isn't it obvious?"

She made no move whatsoever. "Then I feel it prudent to inform you that I am not yet ready to entertain a courtship."

"I see." He swirled his little finger, reveling in the wicked friction while the thrill of the chase emboldened him. "Such a goal will be near impossible for a woman as attractive as you. Unfortunately, during the Season, dandies are like flies to honey and you are the sweetest the *ton* has to offer."

"I am in no way to be measured among the multitude of young, inexperienced debutantes. Nor do I have any desire to be one."

"So true, and that makes you all the more alluring." Vaguely, Signora Morella's high C pierced the air.

Mrs. Whiteside clamped her hand around his fingers, rather powerfully for a woman. She deposited Fletcher's fist in his lap. "Tell me, are you planning to see the soprano after the performance? She seems quite taken with you and rather distraught with your present company."

"I—" Fletcher looked to the stage. Indeed, Signora Morella was shrieking and waving her arms, though while in character, her tirade was directed at him.

Before he had a chance to explain that he had no intention of rekindling an affair with the singer, Mrs. Whiteside excused herself and headed to the corridor.

Fletcher pushed back his chair and bowed to the baroness. "Excuse me, my lady. I think something I said might have been misunderstood."

Lady Derby waved her lorgnette through the air. "By all means, Your Grace."

He pushed out into the passageway. At least the baroness seemed to like him, even if her daughter did not. *Yet.* And why did it matter if he'd initially gone to the theater intending to spend one night in Caterina Morella's arms? He'd only done so to stop dreaming about the woman who'd just fled his box.

Fletcher found the object of his preoccupation alone in an alcove, her face to the wall. She sniffed.

His heart tightened. "I've hurt you."

Wiping her eyes, she faced him. "How could you possibly hurt me? I hardly know you."

"True." Not one to mince words, he opted for directness. "Please allow me to explain. You are right on one account. I did once have a tryst with Signora Morella, but it ended years ago."

"Then why is she giving a performance as if you are the only patron in the entire theater?"

"I have no idea." He stepped toward her, the scene reminiscent of the darkened salon at Almacks a few nights past. But this time, he intended to follow through. "I have no control over the actions of others."

Mrs. Whiteside backed to the wall, her lips slightly parted, the soft, supple mounds of her exposed breasts rising with every breath. Tempting him. Calling him. Begging to be caressed. The woman's eyes grew dark. Yes, this sweet, reclusive woman wanted him. She wanted him far more than she realized.

"But you have control over your own," she whispered, breathless.

"I do." Fletcher shifted a hand to the arc of her waist. "And right now I intend to kiss you."

Chapter Five

❧

For the second time since Georgiana arrived in London, she couldn't breathe. And it had everything to do with the Duke of Evesham. The man's powerful hand rested on her waist, rendering her powerless to resist his commanding presence. Long, black lashes fanned hungry eyes while moist, full, masculine lips neared.

Everything around them faded into oblivion.

Except for him.

The heat of his minty breath seared her, making a rush of fire thrum through her body. Georgiana raised her chin, every inch of her skin alive and tingling with want. She hadn't kissed a man in ages—not that Daniel had ever been terribly romantic—not like Evesham. No, Daniel had never made her feel like she did right now—wanton, wicked, insane with the hunger of lust. What was it about this man? His looks? His reputation? That his personality was completely opposite hers? That she could never have him—not ever, not in a million years? He was forbidden fruit. Untouchable. Yet, in this moment, his intention was unmistakable.

As his lips brushed hers, she sighed with the desire to taste him while her knees turned boneless. As if she'd uttered aloud her hunger, powerful hands slid around her back while the duke's tongue swept into her mouth. Delicious, soft and oh so naughty, he devoured her. Overcome with her own unexpected wildness, Georgiana sunk her fingers into his hips and held on. He plundered her mouth, taking it with urgent licks and sucks.

She gasped. Dear God, a blast of heat rushed deep inside her. Evesham growled, the sound rumbling through to the tips of her breasts. He slid his fingers to her buttocks and pulled her flush against him. She molded into his chest, her hips connected with his. Hard, virile and oh so very male, the duke had her pressed against the wall while Georgiana submitted entirely as if she were burning from the inside out.

A noise in the distance brought a flicker of lucidity. Georgiana opened her eyes and gasped. *What am I doing?*

There she stood in a public theater in the arms of the most notorious rake in London. Anyone could walk past. Her mother. Eleanor. A journalist from *The Scarlet Petticoat*.

She shoved her hands between them and gave him a hearty push. "Stop!"

Stepping back, Evesham looked stunned. "Stop?" he asked as his voice shot up.

"You, sir, have bewitched me, just as you must do to all your conquests."

"Conquests?" A furrow etched between his brows while he reached for her hand.

She drew her fingers away, recoiled, and slapped the rogue right across the face. "I do not care if you are a duke, everything the scandal sheets say about you is true!"

His mouth dropped open as Georgiana dashed past. How could she be so gullible? She wasn't a young lady experiencing her first Season. She'd been married for five years. Though Daniel *never* would have kissed her like that—especially not in plain view, while attending a theater full of patrons. Thank heavens they weren't discovered.

In no way could she return to Evesham's box, and yet her mother was still there.

She stopped an usher at the top of the stairs. "Please inform Lady Derby that her daughter is waiting in the carriage."

❦

MISS ELEANOR TOOK A SIP OF TEA, THEN thoughtfully placed her cup in the saucer. "I think you're looking at this all wrong."

"I beg your pardon?" Georgiana had just spent the past ten minutes explaining her plight. "If you have a better idea, please do not keep me in suspense."

"We women must make use of the opportunities available to us. I'm not telling you to stop searching for venues to demonstrate your steam pumper but, as you are aware, men with means attend all manner of social gatherings this time of year." Eleanor reached for a tiny cake. "And as an importer of fine items of haberdashery and the like, I have found there is no better place to make a business transaction than dazzling one's partner on the dance floor."

Had she heard correctly? Eleanor danced her way to her fortune? "If you hadn't mentioned business transactions, I would insist you were in collusion with my mother." Georgiana stretched out her leg and pointed her toe. "Please. I know it has been years, but surely you remember my clumsiness."

"You weren't that bad."

"No? In one very short Season, I managed to trip on

the Duke of Surrey's toes, fall in front of every courtier in London at Carlton House, spill raspberry cordial down the front of Lady Annabelle's outrageously expensive gown, not to mention slip and deluge myself in a quagmire of mud when walking with Mr. Dover in Hyde Park."

Georgiana selected a cucumber sandwich and nibbled. There was no use telling her friend about her most recent foibles with Evesham. Good Lord, how could she have let the man kiss her? No wonder he'd made so many conquests. It took a will of iron to resist him.

But Eleanor's expression only grew more engaged. "Yes, my dearest, but that was when you were a nervous debutante. You are older, wiser, and far more composed."

"You may be composed, but I still feel awkward, uncomfortable, and completely unsuitable when surrounded by members of the *ton*—especially in a ballroom."

"Hogwash. Do not forget you are the daughter of a powerful baron and you have every right to rub shoulders with anyone you please."

"Perhaps." Georgiana tapped a petite marble statue of an opera dancer on the table beside her, envious of the depiction of feminine grace captured in the small rendering. "But that still does not allay the fact that I always manage to trip over my own feet."

"I say, if you truly want to sell your machine, I suggest you take lessons without delay."

"Right. I can see myself bumbling amongst a gaggle of twelve-year-old children whilst the dance master beats the floorboards with his staff, shouting, 'Mrs. Whiteside, we are not mustering sheep!'"

Eleanor rubbed her hand along the velvet armrest of her chair. "I can teach you."

"You?"

"Yes, but we'll need a man for you to partner with." Eleanor drummed her fingers. "The problem is who."

"You're serious? You would take away from your busy schedule of appointments?"

"My schedule needs a diversion of sorts at the moment. Besides, I'd like to see you succeed. So few of our sex do."

"Or have the opportunity to attempt to do so." Georgiana considered her friend's proposal as she sipped her tea. Truly, she hadn't even considered using a social arena to garner interest in the fire engine. If she were to entertain such unconventional methods, she must be very discreet, else her parents would be furious.

Eleanor chuckled. "I can see you thinking."

"Yes." After setting her dish down, she reached across the table and grasped friend's hand. "If you are truly willing to endure my missteps, I think I might know just the person."

"Who?"

"The actor I hired to give demonstrations—an older gentleman, and he's an accomplished dancer."

"Perfect."

Finally at ease, Georgiana sighed, taking in the parlor as if she'd only just entered. The furnishings were new. Even the Oriental carpet looked as if it had no wear. She again ran a finger over the marble opera dancer, noting the intricate detail from the flowers in her hair to the way the skirts appeared to be in motion. "My, things have changed since I last visited. After speaking to you at Covent Garden, I assumed..." She looked away.

Eleanor popped a tiny cucumber sandwich into her mouth. "Yes, well, I do not make my success widely known."

"Oh my, I cannot tell you how happy I am to hear it. Would I be prying overmuch to ask how you've come into your success?"

"There's not much to tell, really. We had our Season together in 1812, remember?"

"How could I forget? 'Tis the same year I met Daniel." Georgiana raised her cup for a refill. "But do continue."

"At the time," said Eleanor as she poured, "war was rife and, as it turns out, I happened upon a small import business."

Before she sipped, Georgiana blew on her tea. "Truly? How do you mean happened upon?"

"A cousin of sorts—left no will, and my father was his only living relation."

"But your father—"

"Cannot manage a coop of chickens." Eleanor laughed. "But he is endearing."

"Truly, how is he?"

"Much the same since the war. Still in an invalid chair and refuses to entertain visitors."

"I'm so sorry. It must be a terrible strain on you."

Sighing, Eleanor looked to a portrait of her father—the viscount in an admiral's uniform. "I've grown accustomed to this life. And to be honest, after so much time I can no longer see myself constrained by marriage and all that goes with it."

"So, let me guess, you forwent your opportunity to marry Baron Strange and took on this import venture."

"I did."

"And may I also say it has kept you quite busy as well as provided for your comfort."

"It is lovely to have one's independence, though few in society would agree."

"Well, you have my admiration, truly."

"I always did like you, Georgiana."

"And I you, especially because you were the only one who didn't balk when I accepted Daniel's hand."

Clasping her hands, Eleanor scooted to the edge of

her chair. "So, when shall we schedule our first dancing lesson?"

"The sooner the better." Georgiana collected her reticule and stood. "Mother's taking me to Lady Maxwell's ball on Friday after next."

Chapter Six

H is fists high and tight, Fletcher circled, bouncing on the balls of his feet.

Opposite, Brumley Jackson did the same, throwing a jab now and again. But the boxing champion was merely testing the waters. For the past four years, they'd met on Monday mornings in the ring at Fives Court. A large man of Romany descent on his mother's side, Fletcher rarely came across anyone able to match him. But Brum not only had the muscle to beat him into a stupor, the champion had taught him a great deal about controlling his anger, knowing when to fight and when to walk away. And now the student had become a master in his own right, the two men sparring like stags.

Brum threw a left.

Bobbing beneath the gloved fist, Fletcher found a hole and thrust a jab to the chin, then another and another. But Brum didn't expose himself for long.

"Oof," Fletcher grunted, receiving a cuff to the solar plexus, almost grateful for the pain. Damnation, he had been too forward with Mrs. Whiteside once again.

Was the woman fickle? Hang it all, she had told him she wasn't ready to entertain a courtship. Why could he not let it pass? How on earth had she attracted him in the first place? She was a bluestocking—a wallflower.

48

Hell, she attended a ball and spent her time in the women's withdrawing room reading of all things.

In no way could Fletcher imagine spending eternity with such a woman.

"Oof!"

And she was too bloody perceptive. What man needed a wife who was observant to a fault? And why the devil was he so confoundedly preoccupied with the widow? When and if he was ready to take a bride, he'd just do it. The pox on courting. The only decent thing his father had ever done for him was make him a bloody duke. Now women from all walks of life clamored for his attention. He only needed to take a stroll through any ballroom in the kingdom, point his finger and the young lady's parents would be groveling at his feet, begging to make their daughter a duchess.

He attacked with a left then a right. Lunging forward, Fletcher threw his fists harder and faster. A jab to the nose, a hook to the temple, and uppercut to the jaw —all bloody blocked by the champ.

He would stop thinking of Mrs. Whiteside this instant. He would avoid balls and soirees. And if he happened to see her in passing, he'd bloody well pretend he hadn't.

Left, right, left.

Thank God he had that settled.

Nothing like a raucous spar to sort out a man's priorities.

"Oof!" he grunted, his eyes crossing with the vicious jab to his nose...and then an upper cut to his jaw. Fletcher tried to raise his guard as fists pummeled his temples while he staggered backward against the ropes, sliding down, down, down.

Flat on his back, Fletcher blinked to clear his vision.

"God's stones, Evesham, you're fighting like a maniac." Brumley offered his hand. "Is something amiss?"

Fletcher wiped the blood from his nose on the back

of his arm and allowed the man to help him up. "Nothing a good pummeling will not cure."

"Problems with women, aye?"

"Bloody oath, and one in particular will be the death of me."

"You? Since when could a filly find a way under that thick hide of yours?"

Fletcher unlaced his gloves, loosening them with his teeth. "She cannot, and I refuse to allow her to do so."

"Good to hear it." Brumley clapped him on the back —one of the few men bold enough to do so. "Women have a way of festering under a fellow's skin like a splinter of wood. Madam Bouvier is bringing a number of new ladies for entertainment in the upstairs suite of the saloon tonight. Why not call in?" The big champion grinned. "Gentlemen by invitation only."

Now why didn't Fletcher's blood stir at the offer? He'd have his choice of the tastiest morsels London had to offer yet he wanted to throw another jab. "That sounds like a summons I cannot ignore," he replied, ignoring the confounding voice in the back of his head.

Brum unfastened the hasp on the ropes and gestured for Fletcher to step through. "How are things at the home for unwed mothers?"

"Hold thy tongue." Fletcher made a show of checking over his shoulder. "Do you want to ruin my reputation? I am a silent benefactor."

"Very well, allow me to rephrase. How are things at the establishment where you are an anonymous patron?"

"As far as I know, well." Reaching for a cloth, Fletcher wiped the sweat and blood from his face. "They request funds for food and supplies. I comply as long as there are no extravagances."

"When was the last time you visited the... ah...facility?"

"Visit? No self-respecting duke would be caught dead there in the light of day."

"Right, and you just blindly write notes, paying countless pounds. I'll believe that when hell freezes."

"Last time my carriage happened to be in the neighborhood, the upkeep was adequate." Together, they headed for the bathhouse. "I never should have told you about that venture."

Brum gave him a sidewise smirk. "Why? Are you afraid I'll think less of you?"

"'Tis not your opinion that concerns me. The tenants do not need any more attention than they already have. Imagine if someone discovered I am their financier? Those poor, set-upon women would be the subject of polite society's scrutiny."

"Poor? Set-upon?"

Fletcher thrust the towel into the champion's chest. "Please. Not all young ladies who end up in the family way are evil debauchers."

"Forgive me if I insinuated they were." Brum bowed. "But you, Your Grace, you will never cease to bemuse me. The scandal sheets tout you as the *ton's* most notorious rake, yet they have no idea as to your true nature."

"Good. That is my objective. Never let it be said I am predictable or too kindhearted. I loathe being pigeonholed by either moniker."

❧

"WHEN IS THIS BALL, DID YOU SAY?" ASKED MR. Walpole.

Even with Eleanor beside her, standing in the vestibule of Covent Garden with the actor made Georgiana lose her nerve. She took a step toward the door. "Friday after next. Perhaps there's not enough time.

After all, I've never been very good at dancing. I doubt anyone could help me."

"Nonsense." Eleanor grasped Georgiana's elbow, not allowing her to take another step. "We have ten days. And with your keen mind, you won't even need that."

Georgiana gestured to her feet—both of them left, she was quite certain. "If only I were able to dance on my head."

"Miss Eleanor speaks true," Mr. Walpole said, ushering them toward the door. "Just a bit of practice combined with the will to learn, and I can have anyone ready to waltz in ten days—even gentlemen who have no sense of rhythm."

Georgiana looked back as they stepped onto the footpath. "What about women with no sense of rhythm?"

"Not to worry, Mrs. Whiteside. You have my word, either you will be dancing by Friday after next or I am not Palmer Walpole."

"That's what I'd like to hear." Eleanor offered her hand. "We'll see you at my town house on Mayfair Place at half past ten tomorrow morning."

The actor made a flourishing bow and kissed the lady's hand. "I shall be there with a fiddler in tow."

When he reached for Georgiana's fingers she curtsied. "Thank you for your kind generosity, sir."

As soon as he started off, she pulled Eleanor aside. "Every day for ten days? That will be quite expensive."

"You needn't worry, it was my idea and I will ensure the man is paid."

"But you cannot—"

Pursing her lips, Eleanor tilted her head with a flare of her nostrils. "I can and I will. And I'll entertain not another word on the topic."

The sound of a team coming to a stop accompanied by a deep "ho" and the screech of brakes drew Georgiana's attention to the street.

"Good afternoon, ladies. Are you in need of a lift?" asked none other than the Duke of Evesham. He gazed upon them with a halfcocked grin, commanding a phaeton with a perfectly matched pair.

Immediately shaking her head as well as her hands, Georgiana refused. "Thank you, but we are quite—"

Eleanor gave her a rather sharp poke in the spine. "Of course, we would be grateful for your assistance, Your Grace."

"Splendid."

As the duke secured his reins, Georgiana turned away from the carriage and glared at her friend. "We cannot accept a ride from him," she whispered. "We ought to take a hackney."

"Have you lost your mind?" Eleanor sidled toward the carriage. "One of the wealthiest men in the kingdom just offered to give you a lift and you deign to tell him to go hang?"

"Your inference is..."

"All set, ladies?"

"Yes, thank you. It is quite fortuitous that you happened along at this very moment." Eleanor stepped aside and allowed His Grace to help Georgiana aboard first so she'd have no choice but to sit in the middle —blast her.

This whole debacle wasn't fortuitous in the slightest. In fact, it was so unlucky, if she didn't know Eleanor better, Georgiana might have thought the pair had colluded to trap her into another altercation with the duke.

"Who was that chap?" asked Evesham, glancing over his shoulder. "I'm certain I've seen him somewhere before, but I cannot place the man."

As her heart flew to her throat, Georgiana's gaze darted toward the theater. Thank heavens Mr. Walpole had moved out of sight. "He's just a passing—"

"He's an actor we hired to give Georgiana a few

dancing lessons." Eleanor smiled as she took the duke's hand and climbed aboard the phaeton. "A lady needs a refresher now and again, especially since it has been ever so long since she attended a ball."

"She attended a ball not long ago," said His Grace before he headed around his team.

"But I didn't dance," Georgiana said, raising her voice loudly enough to be heard before Eleanor managed to bury her any further.

The duke climbed up beside Georgiana and grinned —amber eyes, made iridescent by the light. Good Lord, when he smiled, it looked as if the sun were made only to shine upon him. What was his ancestry? It was unusual enough to see a man with darker skin in England and even rarer to see a member of the gentry who appeared to be of Romany descent. He looked like no one she'd ever seen before—so very exotic.

Once Evesham climbed beside her and took up the ribbons, she continued, "I've arranged to take a few lessons so I don't embarrass myself."

"So, you've decided to embrace your mother's wishes and play along for the Season?"

"Yes." Georgiana shot Eleanor a stern look, pursing her lips and tapping a gloved finger to them.

But her friend didn't catch the gist of her dissent. Pointing behind her hand, Eleanor mouthed, "Tell him about your machine!"

"No!" she silently replied, slashing her hand through the air to demonstrate the strength of her conviction. Holy everlasting Father, if she told the duke that she was responsible for deluging him at the Southwark Fair, he'd stop his team and shove her to the cobblestones.

"How are your dogs?" she asked, her voice far too high-pitched. "Gordon Setters, aren't they?"

He glanced at her out of the corner of his eye. "Last I heard they were enjoying their freedom at Colworth. They're hunting dogs—not suited for Town."

"Ah yes. I have first-hand familiarity with recalcitrant dogs confined in London town houses."

The duke chuckled, looking far too amused. "And how is Rasputin?"

"Still knocking over everything in his tail's path."

"And his fondness for the pond?"

"Papa says he's grown quite the affinity for chasing ducks in the past week."

"Have you told him about your impromptu swim?" Evesham asked.

Georgiana drew a hand to her forehead, sure she had turned scarlet. "I think that tidbit of humiliating information might have escaped me."

Eleanor leaned forward. "This sounds interesting. Is this dog responsible for the pair of you being acquainted?"

"No," Georgiana said while Evesham replied with a yes.

They looked at each other and laughed. No matter how much she wanted to push the duke away and never see him again, he was diverting. And the memory of him pulling her dripping wet out of the lake while Rasputin wildly chased after the ducks was too comical to ignore. What would she have done if Evesham hadn't rescued her from the web of lake weed?

She glanced down at his gloved hands holding the ribbons securely. Big hands that looked as if they might be more at home in a smithy shop than in a duke's salon —or wherever the man spent his time. "What brought you out this way?" she asked, before she thought. And after all, why was he driving through the theater district in the middle of the day?

"I've been sparring with Mr. Jackson."

"Brumley Jackson?" Eleanor asked, sounding impressed.

"The one and only."

Georgiana glanced between them. "Who is Mr. Jackson?"

Eleanor patted her arm. "My, you have been shut away for a very long time, have you not, dearest?"

Evesham pulled the ribbons left for the turn, his arms flexing beneath his coat. "He's a boxing champion."

Watching the man's display of strength, Georgiana's tongue slipped to the corner of her mouth. "A large man, then?"

Her friend fanned her face. "Quite."

Evesham's muscles strained against his coat while Georgiana stared, unable to manage to shift her gaze aside. Goodness, judging by the way he'd carried her from the pond as if she weighed no more than a bushel of oats, he was far stronger than the average laborer. "Is this Jackson even stronger than you, Your Grace?"

His eyebrow arched along with the uptick of the corner of his mouth. "Brum is one of the few who can outmaneuver me in the boxing ring."

"Though I doubt he can manage a team as well," she blurted.

At the sound of Eleanor's snigger, Georgiana's face again burned. She quickly cast her gaze to the folded hands in her lap. The man beside her was the same rogue who had cornered her in the theater and kissed her—wildly, passionately, daringly...and oh so inappropriately.

This man was dangerous. And regardless of his fortune, he would never, ever, not under any condition, become a partner for her steam pumper venture. Moreover, keeping company with the Duke of Evesham was unwise and frivolous, and complimenting him in such a way would only serve to encourage his ungentlemanly behavior.

Fortunately, Evesham was preoccupied with maneuvering around a wagon filled with barrels, proving his prowess with the reins and, hopefully, missing Georgiana's comment. And after taking one more corner, they safely arrived in front of her parents' town house on Mayfair Place.

The duke helped Eleanor alight, then offered his hand to Georgiana. And though they both wore gloves, it was as if the warmth and power in his fingers seared her. Unable to withhold a gasp, she managed a pleasant smile. "Goodness, it seems I must once again thank you for coming to my aid."

"It was my pleasure." Once both of her feet were securely on the footpath, he kept ahold of her hand, though he did not kiss it. "I say, if it is a dancing partner you need, I would be happy to stand in."

Eleanor clapped. "Oh, that would be—"

"A disaster," Georgiana finished. "After six years, I'm afraid my dear friend has forgotten how poor my dancing is and, furthermore, I could never impose upon you to endure a single afternoon of such clumsiness."

His face fell. "Very well, though I daresay I can hardly picture you blundering your way through a waltz, madam."

"Indeed? And that coming from a man who dragged me from certain death from strangulation by a lily pad."

Chuckling, his eyes grew dark as he bowed and gave the back of her hand a gentle peck. "Well then, I bid you good day, ladies. And I look forward to signing my name to your dance card when we meet again."

"At Lady Maxwell's ball," said Eleanor all to eagerly. "Friday after next."

Georgiana waited until Evesham drove away before she faced her friend. "You mustn't encourage him."

"Are you serious? He's not only a duke, he's one of the wealthiest men in the kingdom. If anyone qualifies as your steam pumper's financier, it is he."

Thrusting her fists to her sides, Georgiana shook her head. "It is most definitely not he."

"Why?"

She gulped against the strangling sensation in her throat. "It is too mortifying to put into words."

"A moment." Eleanor gestured toward the street with a swing of her reticule. "Since I have agreed to help you with this endeavor, the least you can do is share with me the reason why the most qualified man in London is not acceptable to you because of some utter mortification? Of what trifle do you speak? Did you step on his toes at Almacks?"

"If it had been mere toe stepping, I would have agreed to his offer and sent a missive to Mr. Walpole cancelling his services."

"Well, then what is it? Something to do with the dog and the pond? The pair of you seemed quite amicable on that point."

As Georgiana closed her eyes, a clear picture of the fury on Evesham's face after the dousing crushed her. "The incident with Rasputin did cause a great deal of embarrassment, but I assure you it pales in comparison to my reason."

Eleanor looked to the sky. "It may start raining at any moment, but I assure you, if a cloudburst suddenly deluges us, we still will not go inside until you tell me this dark secret of yours."

She cringed, wringing her hands. "He was at the Southwark Fair for my first steam pumper demonstration."

"The one where you discovered Mr. Walpole couldn't read?"

"Yes. And though Evesham did show initial interest, he became irritated when he deduced that I was whispering the actor's lines—and then once the duke started asking questions which Mr. Walpole wasn't equipped to answer, I stepped forward to explain—and then when

Evesham started to leave, I gave the lad the signal to start the demonstration but we were short one person and the hose came to life as if it were a serpent from the depths of the sea and..." Georgiana took a breath for the first time since she started the abominable explanation. "And all two hundred gallons of water deluged the duke."

Eleanor drew a hand to her chest. "Oh my."

"Oh yes, and, in no uncertain terms, he commanded me to throw my monstrosity into the Thames."

"But surely he has forgiven you for the blunder. He seemed taken with you, and I'll even venture that he was flirting."

Georgiana's shoulders fell. "That's because he doesn't know I was the woman on the dais at the Southwark Fair."

Snorting, Eleanor gaped. "That's preposterous. I would recognize you from fifty paces or more."

"I was dressed in mourning black with a poke bonnet pulled low over my brow and a pair of spectacles on my nose—thanks to Father being adamant I needed some sort of disguise, else the duke would have let me drown in Green Park's pond."

"Good Lord, and I thought my life was complicated."

Georgiana grasped Eleanor's hands and squeezed. "You must promise me you will not breathe a word about this to anyone. To make matters worse, the day after I doused the duke, it was the premier story in *The Scarlet Petticoat*."

Her friend's expression softened as Eleanor gave Georgiana's arm a consoling pat. "Your secret is safe with me, and do not worry about that silly gossip sheet. 'Tis only good for a laugh—and everyone knows it."

"Yes, a laugh at a poor widow who is only trying to make something out of her late husband's invention."

"Not to worry, my dearest. There are plenty of other

men in London who will find your machine quite interesting, indeed. I have no doubt you will happen upon your financier or have a parcel of orders before the Season comes to an end. Mark me."

Georgiana grasped her friend's shoulders and embraced her. "Oh, by the stars, I hope you are right!"

Chapter Seven

━━━

"**E**vesham," said Brum, grinning and offering his hand. "Welcome. Though I'm surprised to see you took my advice."

Stepping inside Jackson's Saloon, Fletcher shook the man's hand, then gave his hat, gloves, and cloak to a footman. "I've had quite enough of the Season. Why not endure an evening in your den of ill repute?"

In truth, though the boxer's establishment was on the west end, it catered only to the elite. With a façade of respectability, it resembled Whites somewhat with richly upholstered wingback chairs arranged for reading and gentlemanly conversation and, on the mezzanine, card tables for gaming.

Brumley gestured to the door behind the maître d's podium—the one leading above stairs where only the most trusted, influential, and wealthiest patrons were allowed. "Madam Bouvier is entertaining a small gathering this evening. I'm sure you will find one or two of the new ladies to your liking."

"Excellent." After a bow of his head, Fletcher headed off. "I'll show myself up."

The stairwell was stark and poorly lit, but he'd ascended these steps many times in the past. Usually he was light of step, but this evening it was a chore to lumber upward. As he neared the third floor landing, deep chuckles and soft giggles came from beyond.

No other brothel in London matched the quality of this establishment. A gentleman didn't march in, point to a wench, and haul her to a dingy room with nothing but a soiled bed. There was an evening of parlor games first where guests were able to gain a flavor for the young courtesans. If someone caught a man's interest, he then would pass Madam Bouvier a note with a price and the name of the object of his desire. If the woman was satisfied with the man's offer, the courtesan would excuse herself after which the gentleman was given the room number where he would find his delight in a well-appointed chamber complete with a lavish bed, a settee, and a warm bath.

This evening, Fletcher almost preferred a house of ill repute with no speaking, no games, a fast release, and a faster escape. But Brumley had offered, and this was one of the few clubs a duke could attend without his name being in the headlines of the morning papers. Not that he cared about what the damned news reported about him.

He just didn't care to have Mrs. Whiteside read anything unsavory about his outings. She'd already accused him of an illicit affair with Signora Morella. Fletcher's hand paused on the latch. *Why in God's name am I thinking about the widow when paying a visit to the most exclusive brothel in London?*

"Your Grace!" Instantly rising to her feet, Madam Bouvier glided across the floor and took both of his hands between her petal-soft fingers. An unreal smile was fixed on her face like a painted marionette. "What a delightful surprise to have you join us this evening."

The back of his neck bristled. *Why?* His reaction most certainly wasn't caused by the lady's over-powdered translucent skin or the ample use of rouge or her heady perfume. In fact, the woman smelled like a field of lavender. Perhaps it was the earl, the baron, and the two wealthy bankers who looked on, their eyebrows raised. Regardless, Fletcher suddenly wished he hadn't come.

Madam Bouvier pulled his hand. "Come and sit between Agnes and Delilah. We were just starting a game of love leaf."

"Splendid," he mumbled as the two women who couldn't be more than eighteen years of age scooted apart, their smiles too eager. An even younger-looking maid promptly served him a glass of brandy. Fletcher took it and drank, eyeing the girl and wondering how such a frail child had landed at Jackson's.

If only he were able to save them all. And Smith had laughed at his harem idea. It wasn't all that preposterous. At least Fletcher might be able to save a number of foundlings from the gutter—feed and clothe them.

His stomach soured. *What the blazes am I on about now?* Not even the Duke of Evesham could take advantage of a young lady's unfortunate circumstances. His harem would turn into yet another benevolent society with a parcel of chatty girls taking over the privacy of his home.

He turned his attention to the present company. Fletcher endured the game where everyone receives four cards posing questions as to what is said on the "love leaf" with certain answers requiring a kiss.

He managed to avoid being coaxed into kissing the girls by lying about his cards. Most players lied in order to receive a kiss—he'd done so countless times in the past. But being deceptive so to abstain was an absolute novel experience. *Perhaps I am fevered.*

When finally all of the gentlemen had given penciled notes to Madam Bouvier and disappeared down the corridor, Fletcher scribbled a name along with a ghastly sum on a slip of parchment and passed it across the small table.

As she read, the woman's eyebrows arched slightly, she folded the note and looked to the two remaining courtesans. "Leave us."

Fletcher stood politely and waited until the ladies departed.

The madam affected a guarded expression. "You know I'm no longer *in service*, so to speak."

"I am aware." Not quite certain where he was going with his proposition, the last thing Fletcher wanted was to bed Madam Bouvier. But there was something wise about the woman—experienced, shrewd and, most importantly, feminine. And come to think on it, Fletcher didn't have any female acquaintances with whom he could engage in conversation, nor did he have any female relatives. In truth, he relied on his instincts when in the company of the fairer sex, something which, up until now, had suited him quite well.

He'd never found himself in a situation where he might consider what women think, or what they liked, or dreamed, or desired—aside from the usual: being showered with gifts after a night of sweaty passion...especially if the passion was rather enjoyable.

The madam waved his note. "Though with this sum...I might—"

"Before you utter another word, please allow me to explain." He stepped around the table and took her hand between his palms. "I was wondering if we might enjoy an evening of conversation."

Her expression blanked. "Conversation?"

"Yes. That would be talking. Perhaps savoring a brandy or two."

Releasing his hands, she opened her arms, looking from wall to wall. "Here?"

"Considering only the pair of us are present, here will be fine." He resumed his seat. "Agreed?"

The woman nodded while Fletcher sipped his

brandy and cleared his throat. "You are aware I was not raised a gentleman?"

"I am. Word is you were legitimized as your father was dying."

"That might be the only correct tidbit of information the papers have reported." He drummed his fingers on his glass. "I've never given it much thought, but now I'm rather perplexed."

"About what, Your Grace?"

Where should he begin? The whole debacle with Mrs. Whiteside had him completely flummoxed, though he'd admit the extent of his quandary to no one. "You see, generally, I state my wishes...ah...where a woman is involved and there are no questions, my desires are fulfilled, the woman is compensated in some way and we both part on congenial terms."

"Are you referring to women of easy virtue?"

"No, no, of course not." Bless it, he was making quite a shamble of this. And most of the time, the answer to the question would be affirmative. "It has come to mind that I am, perhaps, not the most gentlemanly behaved when amongst highborn women."

"Most of polite society may agree with you." Madam Bouvier collected a paper from a side table and handed it to him. "Though I'm not one to judge, *The Scarlet Petticoat* repeatedly refers to you as a scoundrel and a rake."

He read the headline in black and white above a rather poor rendering of him driving a phaeton. To his dismay the words below were troublesome. "*The Duke of Evesham was seen driving with the widow, Mrs. Whiteside who, six years past, married far beneath her station. It seems the widow is determined not to make the same mistake again. However, we are skeptical in her choice of suitor. Can this consummate bluestocking tame Evesham's lascivious ways?*"

He rubbed the back of his neck. "Right-o. I suppose I have earned such a reputation."

"I don't know about that. You are always courteous and congenial whenever you visit my rooms."

"That's not exactly how I would see it. We enjoy a few games, after which I have my way with a saucy lass and leave a happy man."

The lady examined her expertly manicured fingernails. "Isn't that what men desire?"

"Not always."

"So, what do you want from me?"

"How, would you say, does a man like me go about courting a woman without coming across as a merciless rake?" To Madam Bouvier's snort, Fletcher took another drink—a gulp this time. "You see, there is a gentlewoman with whom I might like to become better acquainted, but it seems my methods are a bit too forward."

The woman gestured to the scandal sheet. "Mrs. Whiteside?"

"Perhaps."

"Hmm." Madam Bouvier adjusted a velvet pillow at her side. "She is a widow, as the article states?"

"She is."

"But a bit of a recluse, I imagine."

"Most definitely. In my observation, she is very private."

The woman heaved a sigh. "A bluestocking is as foreign to me as one is to you, Your Grace. I wonder how passionate her marriage was?"

Not very, I'll wager. Fletcher preferred not to think about Georgiana's deceased spouse or anything to do with the widow's enjoyment of another man's attentions.

"Well, I'm not one to give advice about how to court a widowed gentlewoman, but I might suggest you allow her to set the pace. What activities does she enjoy? Can you enjoy such things with her?" The madam reached for a tiny bottle of perfumed salts and waved it beneath her nose. "Is she attracted to you?"

He had no answer to a single one of the woman's questions. Was Mrs. Whiteside attracted to him? Possibly. After all, she had turned molten when he'd kissed her. At least until she'd realized the impropriety of his advances...and he wasn't about to utter a word to the madam about stalking and kissing the woman in the window embrasure at the theater. "I believe so."

"Then, I say think with your mind instead of the part of male anatomy that always manages to take men astray." Fanning herself, Madam Bouvier looked him in the eye. "Though I cannot tell you how much I dislike giving such advice. It is a detriment to my profession."

"From your clientele this evening, it seems you are not soon to be out on the streets." Fletcher reached inside his coat and pulled out fifty pounds in notes—a fortune to pay for a mere conversation. "I trust this tête-à-tête will go no further."

She slipped the notes into the hidden folds of her skirts. "I have kept the confidences of kings, Your Grace."

"I thought no less." He stood and bowed. "I bid you good evening."

Chapter Eight

"The...r-red apple was...um..." Sitting in the kitchen, Roddy looked up from his book.

"Sound it out," said Georgiana, looking over his shoulder. "g-oo-d."

"The red apple was good?"

"Precisely!" She thumped the table. "I am impressed at how quickly you have taken to reading."

His mouth twisted as he reached for a biscuit. "I'd rather be working with the steam pumper. When is the next fair?"

"I have had some difficulty finding an appropriate venue, but there's a fete in Richmond Park in three weeks and I'm told it is quite well attended."

"All the way to Richmond?" Roddy closed the book. "It'll take half a day to drag the old engine that far."

"'Tis nine miles. We will need to leave by dawn for certain but, given good weather conditions, it oughtn't take us more than two or three hours. And if we arrive by mid-morning, we'll have the pumper ready to go by early afternoon."

"Very well, but if you want more people to see it, you ought to put it out in front of the town house or something. Mayhap set up your own demonstration in

Hyde Park. You could use the water from the Serpentine."

Shuddering, Georgiana pictured all manner of members of the *ton* being doused by an unsecured hose. And now that Evesham had made himself rather familiar, wheeling the pumper into the middle of the busiest park in London and holding forth with a demonstration would most likely see her dragged off to Newgate Prison.

She gave the boy a pat. "I do appreciate your concern but allow me to worry about finding the right financier."

Roddy popped the remainder of the biscuit into his mouth. "What will you do if you cannot?"

"Let us refrain from predicting doom and gloom so early in the Season." The standing clock in the corridor chimed twice. "Besides, I may meet the right associate in a ballroom."

"I beg your pardon?"

Georgiana pushed to her feet. "I must away to my dancing lesson. A dear friend of mine suggested I might fare better with the steam pumper if I tried to be more sociable."

Roddy scratched his head. "That makes no sense at all."

"You may be right." She pulled on her bonnet and tied the ribbons. "But my friend's opinion is opportunities for a woman to engage a wealthy gentleman in conversation are more likely to arise during a waltz than at a fair."

After collecting her wrap, Rasputin excitedly bounded alongside her while Georgiana dashed through the town house to the front door. With her hand on the latch, she focused on the Pointer. "You must stay. The last thing I need is an excitable dog underfoot."

At the earsplitting sound of the brass knocker, the dog launched into a barrage of raucous barking while

Georgiana clutched at her heart not knowing what had startled her more, the dog or the door. "Silence, you beast!"

"Would you like me to do the honors?" asked Dobbs, the butler.

Since her hand was already grasping the latch, she opened the silly door, which only served to make her heart fly out of her chest. At least it felt as though her heart were flying. Unable to think with Rasputin carrying on like a rabid hound, she swung the door shut.

In the Duke of Evesham's face.

Dobbs cleared his throat. "If you would allow me, madam."

Georgiana grasped the Pointer by the collar and stepped back, managing to breathe. "Very well."

"Good afternoon, Your Grace," said Dobbs as if he hadn't witnessed her behaving with unforgiveable impudence.

"Good afternoon." Evesham peered over the top of the butler's head. "It may have been my imagination, but I believe the door opened and closed."

She chanced a glance to the dog—could she find a way to blame him? Wagging his tail, the Pointer stood angelically with his tongue dangling to the side. "Forgive me," she squeaked as Dobbs opened the door wider. "I was headed out and when I saw you, I was afraid Rasputin might attack he was carrying on so." There, at least she sounded as if she'd thought before she slammed the door.

The duke's gaze flickered toward the dog. "And how is the Pointer, madam?"

At a loss, she shrugged. "How are you, Rasputin?"

He yowled and wagged his tail.

Georgiana looked up with a nervous smile. "It appears he's quite well."

"Was there a reason for your visit?" asked Dobbs.

Thank heavens someone was attentive to the fact that a guest had called.

"Indeed." Shifting his attention to Georgiana, Evesham removed his hat and bowed. "In truth, I was strolling past the house and thought I'd inquire if Mrs. Whiteside might enjoy joining me and taking a walk with Rasputin. I do hope he is being exercised regularly."

"Does any young dog ever receive enough exercise in Town?" asked Dobbs.

"Quite," Evesham responded, giving Georgiana a questioning look as one black brow arched. What was it about his eyes? They were so unusually expressive and prominent.

"Ah." She released her grasp on the dog's collar. "I am sorry, but I was just heading across the street for a dancing lesson. You might recall Miss Eleanor and I made arrangements—"

"Of course." The duke offered his elbow. "Then please do me the honor of escorting you there."

Dobbs smiled and urged her out the door. "I'll take charge of Rasputin."

"Thank you." What else could she say? And it was just a stroll across the cobbles. It wasn't as if he'd asked her to go riding in Hyde Park or to enjoy a romantic wherry voyage on the Thames at sunset. "How thoughtful of you."

Through the wool of his jacket, his arm flexed like steel. "Are you certain you do not need another gentleman for these lessons of yours?"

They started down the steps to the footpath, though Georgiana's feet must have been numb because she floated downward, envisaging what it might be like to dance with this man, to stare up into his fathomless amber eyes. To dance in an empty ballroom while elegant music swirled around them as together in perfect step, they waltzed—

"Madam?"

Georgiana blinked. Good heavens, they were already to the far curb. "Sorry, what was that?"

"I asked if I might be of assistance with your dancing lessons."

"Oh yes..."

His expression brightened. "Yes?"

Shaking her head, Georgiana stepped onto the footpath. "I mean no. Absolutely not...not that I do not appreciate your offer, but you most certainly cannot."

"Whyever not?"

"Ah...you are a duke...and, and, the last person who should see me stumble. Besides, you most likely are quite attached to your toes."

"True, though I am accustomed to bruising now and again."

Good Lord, she needed to find another tack. Clasping her hands, she stood firm and looked him in the eye. "Your Grace. I do appreciate your thoughtfulness, though I must be clear that your attentions are wasted on me. I am not a young lady on the marriage mart. I thought I had been clear."

"Quite clear." He bowed over her hand and kissed it, his lips searing on her bare skin.

Why did I not don my gloves?

"Regardless, I will be devastated if you do not allow me a dance at Lady Maxwell's ball." Straightening, he kept her hand in his fingers. "Promise me this one trivial thing, or I will sincerely think you despise me."

Oh, how far from the mark he was. "I do not despise—"

"Then you'll promise?"

"One dance." Georgiana held up her finger. "If and only if I feel confident enough to partake."

Grinning like the devil, he released her hand, stepped back and bowed again. "Agreed."

As she watched him stroll away, Georgiana's head

swam. Now she not only would be attending Lady Maxwell's ball to try to explain the benefits of her steam pumper, she would be fending off the advances of a very irresistible duke.

Help. But it was only one dance she'd agreed to, and there'd be dozens. If she fulfilled her commitment early in the evening, she'd then be free to move on to more important matters.

"There you are," Eleanor called from the doorway. "We're ready for you, my dear."

Standing at the bottom of the steps, Georgiana cringed. "I'd hoped it was all a bad dream."

"And miss my chance to entertain? Not on your life."

"Entertain?" She held her skirts aside as she ascended toward wallflower's hell. "This is a dancing lesson."

"True, but that doesn't mean I won't have Cook prepare cakes and tea." Eleanor led her down the corridor to the old ballroom they'd played in as children. It wasn't large in the way of ballrooms but since she'd last seen the chamber, it had been painted and bedecked with lavish new chandeliers.

Georgiana took a turn, admiring the display of wealth. "I say, your importing venture must be very profitable, indeed."

Eleanor gave her a sideways glance and a subtle smile. "Someone had to rescue Father's estate." She pressed a finger to her lips. "Shh. Remember, I prefer to keep such matters under wraps."

When Mr. Walpole turned from the violinist and smiled, Georgiana stopped herself from asking her friend why she wanted to remain anonymous. But it did seem rather peculiar.

"My dear madam, I hope you are ready to become the belle of the ball," said the actor, striding forward with open arms. Today, he looked like the man who had auditioned to perform the part of inventor, rather than the half-inebriated wastrel who had appeared at Southwark Fair.

She smiled, giving a polite bow of her head and admonishing herself for being overly critical. After all, being illiterate wasn't uncommon and Mr. Walpole had promised to be well-prepared for the Richmond Park demonstration. "Avoiding my dance partner's toes and managing to turn the right direction would be quite an achievement where I am concerned."

"Nonsense. You mustn't have had the right dance master in your youth."

Georgiana directed a dismayed sigh toward Eleanor. "Please tell him. Surely you remember me tripping my way through my first Season."

"You weren't all that bad. Only Priscilla Perkins was flawless and made the rest of us look like soldiers marching through a bog."

"Ha!" Georgiana covered her mouth to keep from bursting forth with laughter. "How dare you exhume her name from the archives."

"And why not? She may have been the belle of the Season and married well, but she and her husband now keep separate houses in Kent."

"You know this?"

Eleanor swayed in place. "You'd be surprised what I know."

"I'm beginning to believe you, most emphatically."

"Are you ready to begin?" asked Mr. Walpole

"May as well."

Georgiana smiled at the violinist as the actor made the introductions. "Initially I'd like to forgo the music," Mr. Walpole explained. "To understand the nuances of motion from waltz to a contradance, we must break it down into simple components."

"The most important being the feet?"

"Why, yes. One cannot add flourish until one can

stop thinking about one's feet." The actor took her hand. "Now we shall move forward in a straight line to the count of three."

Determined, Georgiana completed the feat, proceeding directly across the floor, managing to step and count to three at the same time. Rather than move on and make it more complicated, Mr. Walpole continued with the same three counts. She hadn't even noticed when the violin started to play, nor did she notice when Mr. Walpole let go of her hand. She continued waltzing around the room to the count of three until the music stopped.

"My heavens. You looked like a butterfly," said Eleanor.

"It seems I'm quite adept at dancing in a straight line."

"One must master the basic principles before one can move on." Mr. Walpole again offered his hand. "Allow me to introduce our first variation. We shall waltz forward twice, one two three, one two three. Can you do that?"

Georgiana demonstrated.

"Then step across your partner with your left foot, one two three, two more waltzes straight ahead, then step across your partner with your right foot, one two three, and stop right where you began."

She chewed her bottom lip. "Two combinations straight ahead, one to the left, two more straight ahead and one to the right?"

"Yes, madam. It is nothing near as complicated as your steam pumper."

She eyed him sternly. "So say you."

"Let us begin slowly."

"Slow is good."

It took a few tries but, with Mr. Walpole's patient manner, she managed to execute the pattern without stumbling.

Eleanor clapped. "You did it!"

"Once does not a virtuoso make." Georgiana grinned at the actor. "Shall we go again?"

"Yes, and this time we shall continue to repeat the pattern over and over."

"Repeat?"

"Just follow my lead and keep your eyes up. Your feet do not exist, only the movement matters."

By the time they had circled around the room twice, the violinist started again. And once the beautiful music took her away, Georgiana lost count of the number of times they danced past Eleanor, or the door, or the violinist.

One thing filled her mind which definitely had nothing to do with her feet: How glorious it would be to dance in the Duke of Evesham's arms at Lady Maxwell's ball.

Chapter Nine
LADY MAXWELL'S BALL

❧❧❧

"Oh my." Smiling, Georgiana crossed through the entry of Lady Maxwell's grand manse and joined Eleanor. "You must wear azure from here on out. I do not believe I have ever seen you looking more radiant."

Truly, her friend's gown was a stunning blue lace over a satin slip, the bottom of the skirt trimmed with a drapery of blond lace entwined with pearl and ornamented with pink roses in full bloom. The bodice was cut very low and accentuated a pearl and sapphire pendant. Red ringlets curled from beneath her matching headdress, trimmed with no fewer than five plumes of ostrich feathers falling to the left.

Eleanor grasped Georgiana's hands and kissed each cheek. "I'm not to be outdone by you, dearest. I believe your stifled-sigh pink puts every debutante in the hall to shame."

"Thanks to Mama, not that I'm trying to outdo the young ladies of the *ton*. But if it were not for her, I'd still at least be wearing half-mourning."

"I'm ever so glad you are not." Eleanor pulled Georgiana through the crowded corridor, awash in gossamer and lace. "I know you are here to find an associate, but have you given any thought to your own happiness?"

"I believe I am in the pursuit of happiness."

"Truly? Have you given no consideration to entertaining a gentlemanly companion? After all, you are a widow, the rules are somewhat eased for you now."

Georgiana stopped and pulled her friend into a window egress and whispered, "Good heavens, are you suggesting that I have a rendezvous?"

Eleanor blinked like an innocent waif. "The idea has its merits."

"How on earth can you think of courting at a time like this?"

"My dearest, seeking companionship is entirely up to you. 'Tis simply that at times you—"

"I what?"

"You come across as a tad frumpish."

With her gasp, Georgiana's hand flew to her chest. "I beg your pardon?"

"Look at it this way. You are only six and twenty and you are lovelier now than you were in your one and only Season. I oft see men's eyes stray your way and I'll tell you here and now they are not worried in the slightest about your grace in a ballroom."

"Wonderful. If only they were interested in dousing fires."

"They will be. But flirting never hurt a soul."

Flirting? Georgiana was about as talented at flirting as she was at waltzing. "Since you are being so free with your advice, may I ask if you are a consummate coquette?"

"Of course." Eleanor unfurled her fan with a beguiling air. "There is nothing more enjoyable than a nuance with a fan, the shift of the eyes, a well-timed smile."

"You?" Shocked to her toes, Georgiana popped her head out of the egress and looked both ways before she continued. "But you are a spinster."

"By choice, mind you."

"You've had offers, then?"

"Several."

"Then why are you not married? Have you never fallen in love? Surely there's a gentleman out there who would be sensitive to your father's care."

"Perhaps I haven't found the right one as of yet." Eleanor rapped Georgiana's arm with her fan. "Besides, I'm content with my independence."

"And why should I not be with mine?"

"Isn't that what I've been saying? Take a deep breath and enjoy yourself and stop being a—"

Georgiana whipped out her fan and cooled herself animatedly. "A frump? A bluestocking? A wallflower? A complete and utter bore?"

"Not my words."

She snapped her fan closed and pointed it under her friend's nose. "No, they're my words."

Eleanor gently pushed Georgiana's hand down. "I know you to be delightful and amusing. And I want others to see it as well."

"You and my mother."

"Lady Derby isn't as bad as you think. At least you have a mother who cares." Eleanor leaned out of the egress and looked both ways. "Come to think on it, where is the baroness?"

"Last I saw, she didn't make it past Lady Maxwell. The two are in cahoots planning some end of Season ball to exceed all balls."

"Good for her. At least she is enjoying herself."

"Exactly, and leaving me to your devices, so stop criticizing me and let us start filling our dance cards."

"And flirting."

Georgiana squared her shoulders and took in a deep breath. "If that's what it takes, then I shall do my best." Good Lord, if she made it through this night without mortifying herself to death it would be a miracle. Flirting? When was the last time she'd ever flirted with a man? Daniel had preferred her to be sensible, helpful, and bookish. He abhorred flighty young ladies who hid their giggles behind their fans while batting their eyelashes and speaking as though they had not a coherent thought in their finch-brained minds...*his words, of course*.

"Ah, Mr. Webster," Eleanor said to the very next gentleman who strode past. "How lovely to see you this evening."

"Madam." The man stopped and bowed. He was of average height with small eyes. "I was hoping you'd be in attendance tonight."

"Oh?" Eleanor gave Georgiana a look that said, "watch this". "Are you in need of a delivery of libations?"

Rubbing his chin, Mr. Webster gave Georgiana a curious once-over. "Indeed I am."

"You're in luck. A ship is arriving in a fortnight. Send a messenger with your order and I'll see it filled." Gesturing to Georgiana, Eleanor changed tack. "Please allow me to introduce my dear friend, Mrs. Whiteside. She's joining us from Thetford, newly out of mourning, she is."

"I am so sorry for your loss, madam, but ever so glad to make your acquaintance."

Georgiana curtsied. "Thank you, sir."

The man took her hand, but leaned in, a pinch forming between his brow. "Were you not married to Daniel Whiteside?"

"I was."

"Brilliant chap." Mr. Webster's gaze shifted aside. "I attended Cambridge with him."

"Truly?" Georgiana's heart thumped. "Were you familiar with the work he did on developing a steam-powered pumper?"

"I was." With a sniff, the man adjusted his neckcloth. "'Tis such a shame he passed before he could make something of it."

Eleanor leaned in, her ostrich plumes fluttering. "You'll be surprised to hear that Mrs. Whiteside was able to complete the testing of the prototype herself."

Mr. Webster's jaw dropped. "Astonishing."

"And it is quite functional." Georgiana smiled, trying to appear composed and not too eager. "I could arrange for a demonstration if you would like."

"Ah—I—um." Licking his lips, Mr. Webster glanced over each shoulder. "And did you say you have Mr. Whiteside's drawings?"

"I do, though I didn't mention it." She rolled her hand through the air. "Have them, that is."

Eleanor walked around the man, drumming her fingers against her chin. "I would venture to guess a fire engine such as a Whiteside pumper might be useful at your gaming hall."

He tugged on his neckcloth as if it had grown too tight. "It would be something to consider, though—"

Georgiana waved her dance card in hopes he might notice it. "If a public exhibition would suit better, I am giving a demonstration at Richmond Park on the twelfth of June. I do hope you can come."

"The twelfth, eh?" The man bowed, ignoring the card. "I shall make an effort to attend. Good evening."

Georgiana smiled at the man's retreating form. "That went rather well, do you think?"

"I think we may have been a bit too exuberant. There he goes fleeing to the patio." Eleanor patted Georgiana's shoulder. "Not to worry. He hides it well, but I suspect Webster is in no position to finance anything more than a delivery of rum barrels."

"But he knew Daniel. And he owns a gaming hall did you say?"

"Yes, but his saloon is hardly reputable. And they serve watered spirits I'm told."

Georgiana held up her dance card. "And he didn't ask to sign this."

"Give the man time to mull it over. If he is truly interested, he'll seek you out." Eleanor pulled her along. "Oh, look. There's Lord Hamilton. Now I know he's worth meeting. And this time, let's not bamboozle the poor chap with anything about your steam pumper."

"But I didn't even bring it up with Mr. Webster. He asked."

"And then he dashed away."

"Men. They're so unpredictable," Georgiana whispered under her breath, following. No matter how she felt, she was determined to take Eleanor's advice and act as if she was having a gay time. Several well-appointed gentlemen did sign her dance card and, every so-often...well, every opportunity to seize a chance, she scanned the hall, never once catching a glimpse of the Duke of Evesham. Had she been too forceful when she'd refused to let him help with her dancing lessons? Then again, she had slammed the door in his face. Though afterward, hadn't he asked to dance with her at this very ball?

She'd been so embroiled in her thoughts, once they reached Lord Hamilton she hadn't paid any attention to Eleanor's introduction.

The earl seemed not to notice as he offered his elbow. "Madam, I do believe the quadrille is next."

"Yes, my lord. You are quite right." Resolutely, she placed her fingers in the crux of his arm. "Tell me, have you estates outside of London?" she asked. If Eleanor wanted her to be subtle, then she would ask potential investors about their estates. Let them talk about how long a castle had been in their families. Talk about the priceless artifacts that had been collected by their ancestors through the centuries. Mayhap ask about past fires, and wooden floors, wall tapestries, draperies, hearths, coal, candles and wall sconces. Only after she had listened attentively, smiled graciously, managed a few bats of her eyelashes and, most importantly, established the invaluable treasure at risk, would she mention that she might have a solution to help put their minds at ease.

While they danced, she stole frequent glances across the hall, but Evesham was still nowhere to be found. Truly, she ought to be relieved that he hadn't come. Regardless of Eleanor's confounding advice, Georgiana was only there for one purpose.

Goodness, she had spent her entire adult life focused on her goals and working day and night, only sleeping out of pure exhaustion when unable to work any longer. Other people had fun. She had no need of it.

❧

FLETCHER NEVER ARRIVED AT ANY SOCIAL AFFAIR ON time. One of the benefits of arriving late was avoiding the welcoming line, though it oft irritated the hostess. Nonetheless, Lady Maxwell would be thrilled to have a duke attending her ball, even if Evesham was a sham of a duke, and as long as he behaved himself.

"An ice, Your Grace?" asked a footman with a tray full of silver dishes with half-melted red ices.

"Do you have something with a kick? Brandy, perchance?"

"I'll fetch you a glass straightaway."

"Good man." Fletcher stood amid the crowd and searched among the ladies and gentlemen lining the walls and, not finding Mrs. Whiteside, he turned his attention to the dance floor. The orchestra was playing a country dance and the ballroom was packed with two long sets of lines.

A splay of pink silk caught his attention. Chestnut locks curling beneath a stylish hairpiece trimmed with pink roses and ribbon. The dress was elegant with pink satin over a skirt of something lacy. The satin was gathered in such a way that it parted slightly at the bottom of the bodice, being swept aside as it tapered downward, revealing more and more of the lacy underskirts.

Rubbing his fingers together, Fletcher leaned forward. Was there a shadow of feminine legs he saw beneath all that satin, lace, not to mention layers of petticoats, or was it his imagination?

"Your Grace."

Fletcher's attention snapped away as the footman handed him a crystal glass half-filled with brandy. "Thank you."

"Evesham." Lady Derby fanned herself as she approached, her head held high, dressed in violet and looking like a queen. "Have you been here all along?"

He bowed before he sipped his brandy. "Just arrived, my lady."

The baroness gestured with an arch of her brow and an incline of her head, a command that demanded he follow, though he'd be damned if he knew why he obeyed. Continuing to fan herself, she casually strolled away from the crowd, stopping only when they had moved well beyond the gossips. "My butler tells me you stopped by not long ago."

"Indeed, I did."

"And you met with my daughter," she said, not posing it as a question.

Fletcher had nothing to hide from the baroness. *Why not play along?* He grinned, swirling the brandy. "I thought she might enjoy a stroll with Rasputin."

"The dog?" Lady Derby asked as if the idea were preposterous.

"I don't think there is anything wrong with the Pointer, my lady."

"I suppose nothing a good run in the country and a strong course of obedience won't cure. Though presently, Rasputin has no manners—he's a bit of a rogue."

"Perhaps I have a bit of a soft spot for such nonconformists and creatures which are not afraid to show their unfettered glee."

"Is that so?" Looking rather stunned, Her Ladyship smiled as Georgiana danced past. "My, it is lovely to see my daughter happy. I knew the Season in London would do wonders for her melancholy. The poor dear's life has been unduly miserable."

Every muscle in Fletcher's body tensed as he scowled at the dandy who was not only dancing with Mrs. Whiteside, his hand was rubbing her waist. "Miserable?" he asked, growling despite himself.

"Well, she was in that awful marriage."

"Oh?" Fletcher forced himself to look at the baroness. "After speaking to your daughter, it is my impression that she loved her husband very much."

"An infatuation if you ask me. Yes, he was a brilliant scholar. Mind you, I do not have anything against a man who is poor, but when he is given a fortune and squanders it on his invention at the detriment of hearth and home. Mind you, he couldn't pay his laborer's wages and made my daughter work day and night with no relief whatsoever." Lady Derby snapped her fan shut. "Well, I'll just say he lost my confidence, and I have worried about the dear gel ever since."

"I see." Fletcher watched as Georgiana twirled. How on earth did she think herself clumsy? Her arms swept out like butterfly wings and slowly drifted back to center. But then Fletcher grimaced when she stepped the wrong way. Fortunately, the lady corrected in the nick of time, not missing a step. "She deserves far better."

"I agree."

"Did you choose her gown? It is stunning."

"She picked the color."

"It suits her."

"Yes." Lady Derby, placed a gentle hand on Fletcher's forearm. "My heavens, I'm afraid I'm a tad over-tired this evening."

Shifting his attention to the baroness' face, Fletcher's eyebrows pinched together. "Oh please, my lady, let me help you to a chair."

"I think not. I'd prefer to call for my carriage, but I do hate to spoil Georgiana's evening ever so much. She looks so radiant this eve."

"If it would please you, I will see to it Mrs. White-side arrives safely home."

Lady Derby tapped her gloved fingers to her lips. "You, Your Grace? I wouldn't want to impose."

"It would be no imposition whatsoever. Not in the slightest."

"I don't know." The baroness drummed her fingers on her fan. "I wouldn't want Derby to awake in the morning to find the scandal sheets reporting some egregious affair. He'd never forgive me."

Fletcher sipped the brandy. "I am quite adept at avoiding the scandal mongers when I so desire."

"Truly? You tend to oft be at the center of their gibes."

"Perhaps, but I can attest their reports are seldom accurate."

"Oh? The next time a report comes in question, I'll have to confront you myself." The baroness sighed. "With your assurances, I shall entrust my daughter to your care. After all, the gossips shouldn't be paying too much attention to Georgiana. She's a widow, the poor dear."

"'Tis such a shame for a woman in her prime."

"Oh, you do understand." Lady Derby patted Fletcher's arm. "You are very generous to offer to be her escort. And a gentleman as refined as you will be certain to ensure no harm befalls her."

A tick twitched in his lip—no member of the *ton*

had ever referred to him as refined. "Of course. You can count on me to act as my station warrants."

"Very well." Her Ladyship curtsied. "Please do inform my daughter that I have retired for the evening—and tell her not to worry. I am perfectly well aside from having slept too lightly last eve."

Placing his palm in the small of Lady Derby's back, he escorted her toward the vestibule. "Allow me to speak to the steward and have him call for your carriage."

"Thank you. You are a very kind and generous duke."

Chapter Ten

❧❧❧

While Georgiana promenaded around the ballroom with Mr. Clarkson, an importer of haberdashery, the Duke of Evesham miraculously appeared. He was hard to miss, towering over most everyone, his black hair combed about his crown in a devilish new style that looked wild yet smart; disheveled yet composed.

The air became suddenly charged as if the Prince Regent himself had swept into the hall with a commanding presence. She couldn't help but glance Evesham's way at her every opportunity. He looked striking, exquisite, and fascinating like no one else in all of London.

He scanned the ballroom and when his gaze settled on her, butterflies as enormous as willow warblers took to flight in her stomach. Pretending not to notice, she smiled up at her partner, completely forgetting why she'd come to the ball and why she'd spent the past fortnight rehearsing with Mr. Walpole until blisters plagued her toes.

"The orchestra is marvelous," she chirped—very unlike her to be chirpy.

Mr. Clarkson didn't smile. His features harsh, it appeared as if his frown had been formed in putty and hardened. "I say, you're quite right, madam."

As they turned, Georgiana stole another glance at Evesham. A flash of heat spread across the back of her neck. *What the devil? Is my mother meddling?* And what were they up to now, the pair having a delightful chat while moving away from the crowd?

Pretending not to notice, Georgiana feigned interest in her dancing partner. Thus far, she hadn't stepped on Mr. Clarkson's toes. Thankfully, throughout the evening she'd managed not to embarrass herself. She'd taken Walpole's instruction to heart and kept her movement subdued without flourish. After all, she wasn't out to impress a beau, she was just trying to make acquaintances. Which, by the way, she now possessed a dance card signed by a number of potential investors—according to Eleanor. Who knew her friend could be so enterprising?

In no time, she and Mr. Clarkson had progressed through the line of dancers, growing nearer to the duke and Mama. The co-conspirators' gazes shifted and they both stared directly at her. Was that pity in the way the duke furrowed his brow? What the devil were they talking about and why were they staring as if she were but a forlorn waif?

Georgiana's mind raced. One, two, three, four, five, six. She smiled as they danced past the pair. No falls yet. This once, she dared a graceful flourish of her arms, fully aware of Evesham's gaze on her back with the intensity of a smoldering vat of coal.

Suddenly flustered, she stepped left. Surely she was supposed to turn that way.

No! Drat!

Quickly, Georgiana fell back into step, praying no one had noticed—especially the duke standing against the wall with her mother. She had almost resigned herself to the fact Fletcher Markham wouldn't attend this ball. But now that he'd made an appearance, all the confidence she'd garnered seemed to flit away with those colossal butterflies swarming in her stomach.

Thank the living daylights when, on her next turn around the ballroom, neither her mother nor the duke was in sight. Georgiana double checked. With luck, Evesham had moved to the card room and Mama had gone off to gossip amongst her friends.

When the music finally came to an end, she realized she hadn't mentioned a word to Mr. Clarkson to plant a seed about becoming more invested in battling fires.

Playing the perfect English gentleman, rigid frown, stiff and stilted movement, he bowed. "Thank you for a lovely dance, madam."

She curtsied. "The pleasure is mine, sir. You are quite light on your feet."

The gentleman offered his elbow. "May I escort you off the floor?"

"Thank you." She took his arm, grateful he hadn't sensed her distraction and hastened the other way. "Miss Eleanor tells me you are an importer."

"Indeed, I am."

"I imagine your business is prosperous especially now the war is over."

Mr. Clarkson nodded though Georgiana was convinced his face would shatter if he attempted a grin.

"Do you maintain a warehouse?" she persisted.

"I do. Several, truth be told."

"Several? I am duly impressed." Georgiana stopped as they reached the wall. "I hope you have never suffered a fire in one of your warehouses."

"Fortunately, nothing too disastrous." The gentleman again bowed. "It has been a pleasure, madam."

Clasping her hands, Georgiana smiled after him. Eleanor had been very smart to suggest that a woman do business in a ballroom. She mightn't have had a conversation about the steam pumper, but she had a dance card with the signatures of several affluent gentlemen to whom she had planted a seed about the very real risks of fires. And she fully intended to send each one an information sheet about Daniel's invention. Perhaps she'd remain anonymous in doing so as well—invite them to the Richmond Park demonstration. After all, if any particular person were interested in fighting fires, what did it matter that she was the individual trying to sell the machine?

"Tell me, Mrs. Whiteside," said Mr. Webster, stepping beside her with a thin-lipped grin. "About Mr. Whiteside's drawings, I would be honored to have a look at them."

Her spine straightened. Earlier in the evening, she'd assumed the gentleman disinterested in further conversation about the pumper. She forced a smile. Instead of growing tense, she ought to be overjoyed to have found one of Daniel's former classmates—though she couldn't place him among her late husband's friends. "Oh?"

"Are they here in Town?"

"They are," she said, searching for Eleanor or anyone to help steer the conversation away from the drawings. She did have copies in her father's safe in London, but the originals were secured in the strongbox at Thetford. In the wrong hands, so many years of labor would be lost. And the drawings weren't all Daniel's. After he'd passed away, the machine had engaged like an exploding canon. Georgiana had no recourse but to make changes and perfect the pumper.

"If it would please—"

"Webster, why is it happy people stop smiling whenever you venture past?" Evesham nudged his way into the conversation. "What drivel are you spouting to Mrs. Whiteside?"

"If it isn't the notorious duke," said Mr. Webster with a disrespectful sneer.

Evesham didn't seem to notice. "'Tis Your Grace to you."

"Ah, yes. A windfall for a poor beggar."

"Hmm, I've been poor, but never a beggar." Evesham took Georgiana by the arm and started for the corridor. "If you'll excuse us."

"Good God, you earn a title and suddenly you're better than all your old friends," Webster said loudly enough to be heard by bystanders.

"You've never been my friend," the duke replied over his shoulder.

Once they were out of earshot, Georgiana pulled her arm away from Evesham's grasp. "My word, Your Grace. You were unduly blunt with that poor man. I will not take another step until you tell me what he did to deserve your disdain."

The duke's lips disappeared into a thin line, his eyes fierce. "I knew him as a boy."

"Did you attend university with him?"

"Eton," he clipped. "Fortunately, I studied at Oxford whilst Webster went on to—"

"Cambridge. He knew Daniel."

"That would be right." Evesham rubbed the back of his neck. "I'll say only this. As a boy, Clarence Webster was unkind. As a man, he is a despicable snake. He runs a gaming house with a reputation for trickery, and I bid you keep your distance."

Georgiana glanced back and lowered her voice, "Miss Eleanor said she thought he watered his gin."

"I wouldn't be surprised." Fletcher brushed her cheek with the back of his finger. The coarse knuckle against her skin made a shiver thrum through her. "But enough of that. I do believe the next dance is a waltz."

She consulted her dance card, though she didn't need to do so. She'd kept the later dances open in hopes...

"And do not tell me it is promised to another."

She dared look into those eyes of fury, but this time the fierceness had been replaced by a fire of another sort. "No."

One corner of his lips turned up as he offered his hand. "Madam."

"Your Grace."

Georgiana looked straight ahead as they moved to the floor. But Evesham's gaze remained fixed on her as if he knew exactly where to go without looking. Her skin tingled with self-awareness and something else. Something more visceral.

"Your dancing has been quite well rehearsed," he said as he pulled her into position, settling his hand on her waist.

She gasped at the friction while her fingers began to tremble. She couldn't look him in the eyes. What if she stumbled? What if she stepped on those immaculately polished shoes? "T-thank you."

"Are you nervous?"

"No." She glanced up, catching the intensity of his stare, making her blood thrum through her entire body as if he were able to see through to her soul. "Yes."

He strengthened his grip—not hard, but firm as if he'd never let her fall. "You've no cause to be when you are with me."

"Why is that?"

"Because you stand upon a pedestal all your own." He chose not to explain further as the music began. One, two, three. One, two, three.

Staring at his neckcloth, Georgiana concentrated on the steps. If she just kept it simple and let the tempo of the music flow through her, she might succeed.

"Look at me," Evesham whispered.

It wasn't a request, but a command which Georgiana was powerless to refuse. And as her gaze met his, the room began to swim. In his arms, she felt completely secure, though his eyes were intense and hungry.

Her heart raced. Her mouth grew dry. Her need for him rushed through her body like a raging torrent.

Why was she so drawn to this unconventional man? What power did he wield to make her insides melt? To make her want to do unspeakable things in the dark recesses? In private. In public. Wherever. She wanted his hands on her—to kiss him, to thread her fingers through his ebony hair. To examine how his skin contrasted with hers. Fletcher Markham was exotic and barbaric, masquerading in ducal clothes.

They twirled in time with the crescendo of the music, dancing as if they were on the wisps of a silvery cloud, removed from the crowd. Alone, they shared this moment, neither caring if anyone noticed the magnetism pulling them together.

Why must he look at her that way? She was a widow, a bookish bluestocking. A man like Evesham should never stir her blood, nor she his. Yet Georgiana could not deny the hot desire thrumming through her veins. This man was dangerous and roguish and everything she'd learned to abhor.

And she wanted him.

When the orchestra stopped playing, she stood dumbstruck, her breasts heaving with exertion.

"You are as graceful as a swan swimming on a glassy pond," he said, taking her hand and kissing it. Warm breath seeped through her glove while he lingered.

A hundred responses denying his claim came to mind. *I am as clumsy as they come. No rational man would utter such nonsense.* "What a very considerate thing to say. Thank you."

He led her away. "I think it is time to hail the carriage."

"So soon?" Georgiana's heels clicked the floorboards as she hastened to match his long strides. "But you've only just arrived."

"Yes, but your mother asked me to see you safely home."

She swept a stunned gaze across the hall. "What have you done with Mama?"

"Me? Nothing." Evesham's grip tightened. "But she—"

She stopped and drew her hand away. "I saw the pair of you off whispering. I knew you must be colluding about something."

Those amber eyes grew dark. "I beg your pardon? If you would allow me to finish before you pronounce me guilty, I would be much obliged."

"Very well. Why has my mother asked the Duke of Evesham to see me safely home?" Georgiana looked over her shoulder. Where in the blazes was Eleanor?

"She wanted to retire early—said she'd slept lightly last eve and was overtired."

"Overtired?" Mama had seemed spry enough when they'd left for the ball. And why hadn't she said something to Georgiana? "I hope she isn't suffering an illness."

"She was emphatic that you needn't worry."

Rising onto her toes, again she searched for her friend. No matter how badly she wanted to slip away with the Duke of Evesham, such a thing simply wasn't done. "But what will people think if we're seen leaving together—in the same carriage. It will be *The Scarlet Petticoat's* headline on the morrow. Please, give me a moment and I'll have a word with Miss Eleanor."

"The viscount's daughter is no longer here."

"Truly?"

"I saw her collect her cloak as I was arriving."

"Oh dear."

Georgiana's insides leaped. She was left unescorted at a ball. Widow or nay, she'd been left to her own devices by Mama of all people. Her tongue slipped to the corner of her mouth as she examined the duke. She would be agreeing to leave with him. To create a scandal whether anything happened or not. People would gossip. Though as Eleanor had suggested, the rules had changed. But was Georgiana ready for such a step? What might happen? She'd already kissed him.

Yes. She'd kissed him like a harlot.

And she wanted more.

Her tongue tapped the top of her mouth as her gaze settled on his lips. Pillowy soft, full, incredibly desirable lips. What harm would there be in another tiny little kiss? What might happen in a darkened carriage while it ambled across London?

"Come," he said, leading her to the cloak room. "I might just surprise you."

Georgiana's mind raced with her alternatives...order a hack, ask someone else like Lord Hamilton and his wife to oblige her. She still hadn't decided on a course of action when at the door, Evesham asked the steward to call for his coachman and let him know he would be taking Mrs. Whiteside home, then returning to collect His Grace. "After all, she is a lady and I wouldn't want the gossips to speak ill of her."

"Of course not, Your Grace."

Arching her brows, she gave him a pointed look, but the duke pressed his massive hand in the small of her back and ushered her outside. A bit of a scandal? Be daring? Wonderful. Now she would be riding alone in the Duke of Evesham's carriage. What a memorable rendezvous she'd be having this night.

And blast him for making her feel so...so...so damned flummoxed. She wasn't a passionate person by nature. And he knew it. Once she was gone, he'd most likely have a good laugh with his companions at the card tables. Georgiana would never be able to understand a man like the duke—a man who courted opera singers, who oft had his name emblazoned on the scandal sheets.

London's most notorious rake?

A man like Fletcher Markham would never be interested in a wallflower like Georgiana Whiteside.

Besides, who was she fooling? He was the dandy who had told her to throw her steam engine in the Thames. She must not forget it. Not ever. Moreover, when the Season was over, she would return to her little country cottage and he would go about his ducal responsibilities. There was simply no use wasting her time dreaming about kisses like a silly maid.

He offered his hand to help her into the carriage. "I look forward to when we will meet again, madam."

"Thank you for your generosity, Your Grace. The next time my mother decides to leave early, I shall insist she sends the carriage back for me—which she should have done in the first place."

She plopped onto a velvet seat while the door closed.

"Mrs. Whiteside is in your care, sirs." The duke's voice resonated through the carriage walls. "Please ensure her safety."

"Aye, Your Grace."

Some indecipherable whispers were exchanged, doubtless some sort of sleight. Come morning, she would confront her mother. How dare Mama meddle and put her in such a compromising position—first to think she'd be alone with Evesham, and now faced with being alone, alone. Both scenarios were humiliating. Both might earn her a mention in *The Scarlet Petticoat*. At least the latter would put her in a frumpy, bookish, uninteresting light—the same light she'd been in all her life.

As the coach started away, Georgiana clutched her cloak tightly around her shoulders. She was comfortable being a bluestocking. She would stop thinking about the Duke of Evesham this very instant. No, she hadn't come to London looking for a liaison and she wasn't about to start losing her head over the most notorious rake in the city.

Mind you, a man who thinks "women have no business tinkering with machines."

The problem? No matter how much Georgiana tried to convince herself she didn't want another kiss from the duke, or to feel his arms surround her, she couldn't push away the emptiness stretching her heart.

Chapter Eleven

While the orchestra played on, Fletcher slipped away from the guests and out to the terrace, pretending to enjoy a stroll in the cool night air. He nodded pleasantly to the people there. After casually pattering down the stairs to the garden, he tiptoed past a couple in a passionate embrace and continued on, projecting an air of calm while he made his way along a hedge, walking farther and farther away from the manse. Beneath the cover of an oak, he took a moment to look to all corners and ensure he wasn't being watched. A few people stood on the terrace but, at this distance, their voices were lost on the wind.

Ducking to the other side of the tree, he started off at an easy trot. He loved this part of the chase. Would the gossips whisper about him? Perhaps. But they had no idea what he was truly up to.

It didn't take him long to reach Brook Street where he resumed a casual stroll as if he hadn't a care in the world. Though he did keep his head down. No use being spotted by any passersby when he'd left his hat, cloak and cane with the coachman. In fact, his head felt rather bare.

As Fletcher had hoped, he spotted her as soon as he

reached the northwest corner of Grosvenor Square. He couldn't have timed it better if they had synchronized their timepieces. Continuing diagonally across the park, he met the coach as the driver reined the carriage to a stop at the southwest corner.

The coachman grinned. "Your hat and cloak, Your Grace."

"My thanks," he said, opening the carriage door.

"Stay back. I am armed!"

For a willowy woman, the lady certainly made herself sound ferocious.

Fletcher raised his hands. "Armed with what, madam? A wicked fan?"

"You!" she exclaimed as if he'd taken her by surprise. But then, how could he expect her to know what he'd been planning?

He climbed in and sat across from Mrs. Whiteside. No matter how much he wanted to sit beside her, wrap the woman in his arms and devour her. He'd resolved to let the lady dictate the pace and, regardless of how difficult it was for him to allow her to do so, he vowed to do his best to be a gentleman.

"Do you have any idea how downtrodden you made me feel when the Duke of Evesham's carriage hauled me off in front of all polite society? Alone, mind you. Sir, I may be a bore and a consummate wallflower, but I'll have you know I do have feelings!"

Fletcher cringed. Yes, he'd sensed her disappointment when he'd escorted her into the carriage, but that only served to make him look forward to joining her all the more. He reached out a hand but snapped it back. Blast it all, he should have told her about his damned plan before he hauled off and injured her sensibilities.

The tension in the carriage grew. This wasn't how a liaison was supposed to proceed. "Fie!" he cursed, shoving his hat and cloak beside him.

"I beg your pardon?"

"This muddle is all my bloody fault."

"The fact that you sent me off in shame in your carriage, or that you are now in your carriage creating a scandal—or not creating a scandal, because all of polite society thinks I'm alone?"

He ground his back molars. Why did he always seem to fumble whenever in this woman's presence? "I never intended for you to feel embarrassed. I'd hoped it was a gallant act, sending you off while I remained behind."

"Gallant?" She snorted. "But then slipped away to join me anyway."

"Yes, well, that's part of the whole..." No, he wasn't about to say courtship. "Game, if you will."

"Tell me, what game is it we are playing?"

He sat for a moment, tongue-tied. Had any woman in the entirety of his life ever rendered him at a loss for words?

No.

He drummed his fingers. *How to proceed now that I've clearly piqued her ire?*

"Madam," Fletcher began, wishing he could clearly see her eyes. It was inordinately difficult apologizing to the silhouette of a female sitting across the carriage—a rather alluring female—alluring and irritated. "Please forgive my unorthodox methods, but you were right. If we had left the ball together, all of the *ton* would have been gossiping about our impending nuptials come the morrow."

A wee gasp came from the shadowy figure. "Did you say I was right?"

"I did." He crossed his ankles, letting loose a long breath. "Now tell me, is my person in danger? With what are you armed?"

Metal flashed through the dim light as she held up her slender weapon. "A hairpin."

"I see." At least she wasn't pointing a loaded flintlock at his heart. "Have you ever attacked a man with such a weapon?"

"To be honest, I cannot say I have ever happened upon an occasion to do so."

Leaning forward, he imagined a lock of long hair curling down the side of Georgiana's face. "Has its removal disturbed your coiffeur?"

"Just a bit in the back, I believe."

He held out his palm. "If I may, I might be able to resituate your coiffeur so it will not appear disheveled when you arrive home."

The pin dropped into his hand. "You would do that for me?"

"Why would I not?"

"I don't know," she purred. "You seem more like a man who prefers removing hairpins than applying them."

A low chuckle rumbled from his throat. "You are not wrong there. But it is important to me to deliver you home without looking like you've been ravished."

She chuckled. "Especially when I haven't been."

"May I?"

Skirts rustled as she shifted aside and he moved to her side of the carriage. "You are a quandary to me, Your Grace," she said as she turned away, giving him access to the back of her head.

"Oh?" He smoothed his fingers along her shoulder until he met with hair as soft as the down on a baby duckling. Fletcher couldn't hold in a low growl as a twinge of longing swirled to life deep down where it shouldn't be. "And why is that?"

"Need I say it?"

He drew the tress to his nose and closed his eyes as he inhaled the fragrance so clean it was as if he'd just stepped outside after a cloudburst. He wrapped the curl around his finger while he leaned closer, breathing deeper. "Are you referring to my reputation in the gossip columns?"

"Mm. I'd say after our encounter at *Don Giovani* I have rather first-hand experience upon which to base my opinion."

"Ah, yes." He palmed a tiny dagger he kept hidden in his waistcoat, cut off the end curl and slipped the talisman into his pocket. Then Fletcher applied himself to the task of pinning the lock into place. "I must apologize for my brash behavior."

"Something tells me you're quite accustomed to being brash."

He secured the hairpin, his hands aching to rest on her shoulders. "Not always."

"Truly? But I would think a man who has been a duke for nearly five years is rather accustomed to having things his way—bending the rules to suit himself."

"Is that what you think?"

"I believe you are fond of having things your way."

"And what about you? Do you not wish for things to go your way?"

"Wish it, perhaps. Though I am disappointed most of the time and, like the rest of society, I must accept my lot."

"What would you do if the tides were to change?"

"Oh, please. My path has already been cut before me."

"Has it?" Without touching, he lightly blew warm air across the back of her neck while every nerve in his body came to life. "What do you want, Georgiana? Right here. Right now. When nothing else matters except this very moment?"

She turned her head, her face glowing blue with the moonlight streaming in through the windows. Her eyes wide, her lips parted, her breathing ragged, she slid silken fingers along his jaw and to the back of his neck.

"This."

With Fletcher's next blink, she closed the distance, her mouth clamping over his with a searing, demanding kiss. A torrent of pent up desire burst in his chest as he pulled her onto his lap and met her fervor. The moment her lips met his, his resolve crumbled like a sandcastle being consumed by the sea.

As her fingers plunged into his hair, his hand slipped over the top of her breasts. Unable to stop himself, he slid beneath the thin strip of silk covering Georgiana's breasts and teased her nipple.

Sighing, she threw her head back and arched toward him. "I-I don't know what has come over me."

"Don't think," he growled. "Just feel."

Holy everlasting hell, her body was ripe and full, demanding attention and Fletcher had never been so keen to oblige. His every fiber craved the woman in his arms.

As he worked loose her breast, his mouth claimed it, making love to her taut little nipple. A pillowy, ample breast caressed his cheek. "Never, ever let anyone say that you are a bore."

One hand tugged up her skirts while the other cradled her. Soft silken stockings brushed his fingers, then the satin of her garters. A few more inches and he'd touch flesh. Warm, soft, womanly flesh.

The carriage rocked to a stop. "Mayfair Place, Your Grace," said the coachman, rapping on the carriage wall.

Georgiana jolted to the opposite side as if she'd been stung by a bee. "Good heavens," she whispered. "What was I thinking?"

Fletcher clenched his fists until his nails bit into his palms. "Was I too forward?" Damnation, he was supposed to let the woman dictate the pace, but as soon as she'd kissed him, he turned into a pillaging lunatic.

"I was far too forward. My behavior was shameful."

She adjusted her bodice. "Mercy, now I do look as if I've been ravished."

"Not to worry." He gestured toward the driver's side of the wall with an upturned palm. "I could ask the coachman to take another tour about Town."

"Are you serious? Clearly we cannot be in the same vicinity as each other without losing our minds."

"Is that what you call it?"

"Of course. You and I could not possibly have anything in common."

"I wouldn't say that." Reaching across, he helped her adjust the cloak about her shoulders, covering her from the neck down. "Tell me, madam. How do you like to spend sunny afternoons?"

"Reading." She scooted toward the door. "Or taking long walks in the countryside."

"Both things I enjoy."

"I find that surprising."

"Why?"

"Reading? Please. What was the last book you read?"

"*Frankenstein*, second reading. Finished it on Sunday."

"Well then, I stand corrected. We have two things in common: the enjoyment of long walks and fine novels."

When she reached for the latch, Fletcher beat her to it. "Allow me to walk you to your door."

"Absolutely not. You are supposed to still be at Lady Maxwell's ball."

"Ah, yes." He drew his hand away. "Then please allow me to take you for a long stroll in the countryside tomorrow afternoon."

"Tomorrow?" she asked as if trying to churn up an excuse not to go.

Fletcher pounded on the carriage wall. "Footman!"

Then he took Georgiana's fingers and kissed them. A fierce pulse beat beneath her kid leather glove. "I'll not take no for an answer. Goodnight, madam and sweet dreams."

Chapter Twelve

❦

Seated at her writing desk, Georgiana handed four sealed missives to Roddy. "Please deliver these letters straightaway. But first, you must tell me to whom they are addressed."

The boy examined them. "L~ord Hamilton, Mr. W~wen~t~worrrrth." He glanced up. "Mr. Beaverton?"

"Yes, and the last?"

"Sir Guy. That one was easy." He held up the letters. "Are these about the fire engine?"

"They are. Each of those gentlemen owns property which is at considerable risk should there be a fire."

"Do you reckon they might want to finance your machine operations?"

"Either that or place an order for one."

The lad slapped the missives on his thigh. "Who would have thought attending a fancy ball might help? I sure didn't think it would work."

"Well, one must never discount a new idea until one has tried it." She stowed her wax wafers and seal in the drawer. "Anyway, they may all tell me to throw the pumper into the Thames."

"Only ignorant dukes would say a thing like that. But I would never let you destroy your invention, mistress."

"That's because you're a smart lad." Standing, she gave his shoulder a pat. "Now off with you and let me know straightaway if there is a reply."

"Yes, ma'am."

Sighing, Georgiana washed the ink off her fingers at the bowl and, while she dried her hands, she turned her attention to another matter. It was time to confront Mama about leaving her in the lurch last eve. How dare her own mother corner Evesham like that? Worse, Georgiana scarcely was able look herself in the mirror for the horror of her behavior. How could she have allowed herself to act so wantonly? And she hadn't even imbibed in a libation. At least then she could claim a lack of judgement due to inebriation.

First, Eleanor had planted the seed about being a widow and bending the rules, and then Mama left without so much as a goodbye. Oh, how things changed when one removed herself from the *ton* for six years and returned a widow.

Except the meddling part. Mother has always been a champion meddler.

After descending the stairs, Georgiana stood at the parlor entry. Her father sat in his wingback chair reading the *Gazette* while Mother embroidered. Rasputin hopped to his feet, pattered over and shoved his nose into her palm.

"I see you've been working with the dog, Papa," she said, moving inside. "He didn't jump up, plant his paws on my shoulders, and slurp his tongue across my face."

"He's coming along." The Baron of Derby glanced over the top of his paper. "Though I'd like nothing more than to do away with the remainder of the Season and take him back to Hardwick Hall."

Georgiana gave Rasputin's back a scratch. "I daresay, that would suit everyone."

"Do not be ridiculous." Mama looked up from her

sewing. "We have two months before we must return to that drafty old castle."

Papa frowned. "I never found it drafty."

"Of late, the damp has grown unkind to my rheumatism." Rubbing her knee, Mama smiled. "And how are you this morning, my dear?"

As Papa returned his attention to the news, Georgiana slid onto the settee beside her mother. "Shocked, dismayed, still in disbelief," she whispered. "How could you have left the ball without saying a word?"

Sliding her needle up from the back of her embroidery, Mother projected the picture of calm. "You were dancing, of course. And Evesham gave me his word he would provide a proper escort."

Georgiana collected a skein of silk and shook it. "Never in my life have you left me at the mercy of a single gentleman. Why now?"

"If you do not know why, then you are more ignorant than I ever thought possible."

Groaning, she tossed the silk into the basket. One did not make a point with a coil of limp thread. "You ought to have sent our carriage back."

"Yes, but then the duke wouldn't have needed to protect you." Mama smiled knowingly. "Mind you, men love to play the role of supreme protector of women."

"A lot of protection he provided." Huffing, Georgiana shifted her back against the cushions and crossed her arms. "The duke sent me home in his carriage— with a coachman and two footmen; but he stayed behind just to ensure I would not be the brunt of this morning's scandal columns."

"Well." Mama sniffed as she tied off a knot. "I daresay you could use a bit of drama in your life."

"Hear, hear," Papa agreed from behind the *Gazette*.

Georgiana leaned forward and gaped. So now both her parents were conspiring against her? She wouldn't put it past them both to create a bit of a scandal to force a hasty marriage.

"It's not as if you're an inexperienced young lady." Mother sifted through the basket of silk. "You're a widow."

"And the lines of propriety are somewhat blurred for me?"

Choosing the yellow, Her Ladyship glanced up. "I wouldn't go that far."

"No, of course not. If anyone can speak in riddles, it is you, Mama."

"That's an understatement," Papa's deep voice resounded from his hidey-hole. At least he hadn't completely gone over to Mother's side.

"Perhaps when you have children, you'll understand me better. But when it comes to seeing my daughter happy, I am capable of all manner of rule *bending*. And since you once were married, anything you may do is not as likely to reflect poorly on your parents. In addition, your brother remains happily in the country with his wife and my three grandchildren, so there was absolutely nothing to worry about."

Except for my pride. "I see. It is reassuring to know the extent to which you've thought last night's faux pas through." Georgiana grabbed a pillow and squeezed it atop her midriff. "But why do you insist that I am unhappy?"

"You cannot fool your mother, dear. I remember a girl without a care who loved to climb trees, and paint, and ride her pony. She was smart and loving and filled Hardwick Hall with laughter. She possessed talent few could attain and everything and everyone she touched felt her joy." Mother picked up her needle and used it as a much more effective pointer than the skein of thread. "After you were married, I watched you work your fingers to the bone, all the while I prayed for Daniel's success. But he died...and left you with that hideous machine. Listen to me. It is an anvil around your neck and you will not find peace until you slip from under its noose."

"Ugh!" Throwing out her hands, Georgiana had heard the lecture a dozen times. She pushed to her feet. "Let us focus on one thing at a time, and that is meddling in my affairs. The next time you decide to leave early, please do me the honor of letting me make up my own mind as to whether or not I will stay. Thank you."

"Just remember," Mother called after her. "It is as easy to fall in love with a wealthy man as a poor one."

Georgiana headed for the corridor. "I'm not looking to fall in love."

"But do not discount it, dearest. You're still quite young."

"And furthermore," Georgiana added, speaking over her shoulder. "I have nothing in common with the Duke of Evesham."

"Hmm." Mama situated a monocle over her eye. "But he has something in common with you."

She planted her hand on her hip. "Which is?"

"He is infatuated with you."

Georgiana turned away as her breath caught. She clutched her hands tight beneath her chin. "You couldn't possibly know that."

"I beg your pardon, madam," said Dobbs, looking directly at her, rather than the baroness. "The Duke of Evesham is waiting in the entry."

"Truly?" asked Mother, sounding quite smug while the leaping lords returned to dancing in Georgiana's stomach. "Why am I not surprised?"

৯.

SIMPLY FOLLOW DOBBS OUT TO THE ENTRY AND PRETEND
as if nothing is amiss. If Evesham chooses to remember how I

unabashedly threw myself at him, I will play the innocent and aloof widow and move on to a more appropriate topic.

Before stepping through the corridor, Georgiana took a deep breath. With luck, one of her letters would be successful and then she'd flee back to Thetford posthaste. There she'd forget about dukes and courting and kisses in dimly lit carriages in the middle of the night.

By the time Georgiana reached the entry, she'd nearly built a wall of brick around her resolve. But after taking one look at Evesham's intense amber eyes, all the stones crumbled away.

"Madam." He held out a bouquet of pink roses. "I see you are ready for our stroll."

"Stroll?" she asked, taking the flowers while her entire body felt as if it had begun to levitate. Dash it, if she weren't a grown woman, she might actually be smitten. She drew the roses to her nose and inhaled. "These are lovely, thank you."

He winked. "They suit your coloring, madam, reminiscent of last night's stunning ensemble, I might add."

By the heat spreading across her face, red might have been a better descriptor of her complexion. "A-are you certain you want to trouble?"

"I hear there is a fine orchestra playing at Vauxhall today. I thought it would be pleasant to stroll through the gardens and then enjoy a bite while we listen to the performance."

Georgiana glanced toward the parlor. What else was there to do? She'd written her letters. Why not enjoy the day out of doors, doing something enjoyable? "That does sound diverting." She craned her neck to peer out to the street. "Did you bring your phaeton, perchance?"

"I did."

Thank God. Who knew what tricks her misbehaving heart might play if they were inside an enclosed carriage.

"Very well." She bowed her head. "Allow me to arrange for these to be put into a vase and collect my things, and I'll attend you shortly."

Chapter Thirteen

❧

Fletcher slipped his fingers into his waistcoat pocket. Between his fingers he rubbed the brass locket holding the lock of Mrs. Whiteside's hair—a bit of her he intended to treasure forever. This being the height of summer, the gardens at Vauxhall wafted with heady fragrances of brilliant flowers. The lovely widow bent forward and sampled the fragrance of jasmine blooming on a trellis. Such a delightful view, he happily stood and examined the heart-shaped curve of her bottom beneath unknown layers of fabric. She had a most pleasing figure. One he fully intended to come to know better...as she let him in.

Moving slowly with a woman was foreign but, oddly, he found moving slower invigorating—challenging like a game of chess with a woman who tempted him to the point of distraction, making his every move more difficult and thought-provoking.

Last night when she'd acted out so unabashedly, a voice in the back of his head had warned to stay in control. Under any other circumstance, Fletcher doubted he'd have acted the gentleman. The scoundrel lurking at his core would have surged to the surface and taken his plunder.

But Mrs. Whiteside was different from all the rest.

She made him want to be respectable—or at least to be respected by her.

True, Fletcher could not deny his primal urge to have her. He wanted to keep her, to possess her. And that petrified him to his toes. Was that why only she managed to tame the lurking beast? Last night when she was dancing with Mr. Clarkson, Fletcher had yenned to take the man outside and thrash him just for putting his hand on Georgiana's waist.

She plucked one of the small blooms and straightened while she twirled the flower between her fingertips. "You once told me you hadn't always been a duke. What was your life like before?"

Not one for mulling over his morose past, he shrugged. "I believe you know my father legitimized me on his deathbed."

The blossom continued to twirl as she passed it beneath her nose, her expression contemplative. "I'd heard. How did that make you feel?"

"Empty." Fletcher had rarely expressed his feelings about that night one way or the other, but oddly, his throat didn't tighten this time.

"Goodness, that does sound grave." Together, they moved along the path. "Did you spend time with your father whilst you were growing up?"

"Nary a once."

She glanced his way, her brow furrowing. "Did he tend to your maintenance?"

"I suppose he did." Fletcher had no idea why he wanted to say more, but he couldn't stop himself. "My mother lived in a cottage which was part of the duke's estate. She was of Romany blood, though only half. We didn't fit in with the Gypsies and we were outcast by the English. Mother took in mending and we kept a small herd of goats which provided a living. And when I was seven years of age the duke sent me to Eton."

"So, he saw to your education."

"He did—sent me on to Oxford as well."

"At least he had enough of a conscience to see you well placed. What did you study at university?"

"Engineering. I had a particular interest in the works of James Watt."

Georgiana drew a hand over her mouth and she gasped. "Steam power," she whispered.

"Exactly."

As she lowered her hand, a sad smile played on her lips. "Steam was Daniel's passion as well."

Fletcher bristled at the name of her deceased husband. "The inventor," he mumbled.

"Yes…" She glanced away as her voice trailed off. "He wanted to invent a pumper powerful enough to replace a hand-operated fire pump. Men tire so easily."

"But it's impossible to harness enough pressure."

"Not with Watt's design," she said as if she were well-versed on the subject.

"No."

"Though his cycle speeds were exemplary for the time." She tapped the flower against her chin. "If only he had realized the temperature differential on either side of the piston was too low."

Fletcher stopped, his mouth agape. "Wait a moment. You studied Watt as well?"

She shrugged as if such a feat was nothing remarkable. "In great detail."

"I'm duly impressed. In fact, you might be the only woman I've ever met with a firm grasp of steam power functionality."

"Thank you—but I digress," she said, continuing on. "You were telling me about your past. Where is your mother?"

Fletcher rubbed the back of his neck, reliving the night they awakened him at Eton to tell him his mother had perished. "She passed away. When I was sixteen years of age."

"Oh, how so very dreadful for you. I cannot imagine. And she was your only close relation?"

With the side of his toe, he kicked a stone off the path. "Yes."

"And after, your father didn't have you come live with him?"

"No." Fletcher offered his elbow and continued down the path. "The duke's solicitor paid me a visit and relayed the message that as long as I continued to perform well in school, my tuition and board would be taken care of. After which, I would no longer be entitled to a farthing from the estate. Once I graduated, it was up to me to make a name for myself—and that's how I wanted it, mind you."

"And you prospered?"

He laughed. "I managed. I found a position working on developing a steam-powered pump to keep a copper mine from flooding near Stow-on-the-Wold."

"How long were you there before you were obligated to take up your ducal responsibilities?"

"Four years."

"Did you enjoy working at the mine?"

"Truth be told, I did." Fletcher batted a fragrant clump of lilacs overhead. "At university, I was always an outcast. Being illegitimate and one-quarter Romany doesn't help any young man make friends."

"No friends?"

"Well, there was another with questionable birth like mine. He became a ship's captain and now spends his time sailing the high seas—hardly ever sets foot in England."

"It must be awfully lonely."

Chuckling, he faced her. "The recluse of all people, worried about my loneliness?"

"Yes, obviously I don't mind being alone. But whilst I'm busy at it, in the back of my mind, I know my parents are happily living their lives and any time I please I can pay a visit to them or my brother and his family in Twickenham."

"The future Baron of Derby?"

"Indeed—they all live at Hardwick Hall where I grew up." Georgiana let her jasmine bloom flutter to the ground. "You see, I have family to visit over the holidays and that means ever so much to me."

Fletcher didn't realize he was clenching his fists until his fingernails bit into his palms. "I have no need of holidays."

She patted his arm, her hand consoling. "I'm sorry. How heartless of me to carry on about my family."

"Not to worry. I'm glad you have them."

"Perhaps I ought to speak to Mama about inviting you to Hardwick Hall for Christmas."

Was she inviting him to her family's home because she wanted him in her life, or because she pitied him? "I wouldn't want to impose."

"I think she'd be delighted."

A flicker of a flame spread through his chest as Fletcher caught Georgiana's wrist. "Only your mother?"

Warm, chocolate brown eyes met his. White teeth scraped over a delicate bottom lip. "What is it we are doing, Duke?"

"Why, madam, are we not becoming friends?"

"Friends?"

He brushed an errant curl away from her eyes before he led onward. "Yes. As I recall, on more than one occasion, you told me you were not ready to be courted. It is my desire to honor your wishes, though I can foresee no reason why we cannot come to know each other better."

She gave him a quizzical stare. "But why me?"

The path gave way to the rotunda and Fletcher gestured to an open table. "You, madam, are interesting."

"Me?" she asked, her voice singing with disbelief.

"Surely there are plenty of interesting women in London."

"You'd be surprised at how few there are." He held the chair for her. "And even fewer who are not hunting fortunes."

Beneath her bonnet, the back of her neck turned bright red.

"Have I struck a chord?"

She smiled slightly—a forced smile. "Somewhat. If you may recall, I was married to a pauper."

"Yes, and how did that come about? I find it difficult to believe your mother wouldn't have called foul."

"Oh, she did. Both of my parents were quite boisterous about their discontent. But I refused to hear any argument. I'd found my prince charming."

Fletcher clenched his fists so tight, his knuckles popped.

But Georgiana seemed not to notice his tension as she sighed. "At least I thought I had."

"Your Grace," said a waiter, approaching with a broad smile. "We haven't seen you here in some time."

He nodded with a congenial smile. "Two ham supper boxes and a pint of arrack punch."

"Is Vauxhall's punch as notoriously potent as reports claim?" asked Georgiana.

"Every bit as potent, which is why I only ordered a pint."

"Do you..." She leaned in, lowering her voice. "...intend to make me intoxicated so that you may have your way with me?"

A spark of energy swirled low. Oh, how this woman could catch him off guard at every turn. He replied with a whisper, "I'd be lying if I said the thought hadn't crossed my mind."

Placing her hand on the table beside his, her gloved little finger brushed his ever so lightly. "Do you know what I think?"

The sensation of the tiny bit of friction made her allure all the more enticing. "I have no idea."

Georgiana's brown eyes glistened with mischief. "I think you are not quite the scoundrel everyone makes you out to be."

He increased the friction between their fingers. "Oh, I assure you, I can be the dastardliest scoundrel in all of Britain when I so choose."

"Hmm." She lowered her hand to her lap. "Then you're a scoundrel with a good heart."

"I assure you, 'scoundrel' and 'good heart' cannot be used as descriptors for the same person." Fletcher looked over both shoulders. "Please refrain from speaking your mind too loudly, you might ruin my reputation for the rest of my days."

"You are awful."

"Thank you."

The food arrived and, with it, the curtain in the outdoor theater opened. A small orchestra played while a baritone sang. "I say, isn't that the chap you engaged for your dancing lessons?" Fletcher asked.

"Oh." Georgiana blanched. "Fancy seeing him here."

He snapped his fingers. "What was his name?"

"Mr. Walpole."

"Hm, Walpole. No, the name doesn't ring a bell, but I swear I've seen him somewhere before."

"He's a prominent London actor, surely you've attended the theater when he's been on stage."

"Perhaps that's it." Fletcher examined the man—not a dandy by any means, but there was something about him he disliked. If only he could put his finger on it.

Chapter Fourteen

❧

"Pack the blue and the violet...hmm...the yellow and the pink. And most especially do not forget all the matching accoutrements."

Opening her eyes, Georgiana hoped she'd just had a nightmare, dreaming her mother just swept into her bedchamber with the lady's maid.

"Straightaway, mistress," the maid's high-pitched voice trilled—very unlike a dream and far more like a nightmare.

Ugh, they are truly here. Clutching the bedclothes beneath her chin, Georgiana looked up. "Exactly what are you doing?"

Mama pattered toward the bed, looking as if she'd just been told the Prince Regent was paying a visit. "'Tis time to tell you at last! I've been planning your birthday celebration ever since you decided to stay with us for the Season."

Oh dear. Georgiana was quite certain the stone sinking to the pit of her stomach had nothing to do with excitement. The maid disappeared into the withdrawing room while the hinges of Georgiana's trunk screeched.

But Mama had always paid particular attention to her children's birthdays.

"Exactly why am I supposed to be excited? That I will be seven and twenty on Saturday and you've decided to pack my things and turn me out?"

"No, you silly goose. We're going to Hardwick Hall for a country house party!" Mama tugged away the coverlet. "Come, dearest, there's no time to waste."

Georgiana swung her legs over the side of the bed. "Mama," she moaned. "I cannot possibly attend a house party. At least not this week." She stopped herself from mentioning the show at Richmond Park. Such an utterance would only serve to make her mother more determined to cart her away.

"Rubbish. 'Tis only for a sennight. And just yesterday you and your father discussed how fortuitous it would be to quit the Season and take Rasputin to Hardwick Hall."

"Lud." Georgiana pulled off her nightcap and pushed the linen against her eyes. The fete at Richmond Park was six days away and she would move heaven and hell to be there. On one side, Hardwick Hall was only about a half-hour ride from the fairgrounds. But how could she manage to transport the pumper if she weren't in London?

"Come, don your carriage gown and that lovely pelisse. I've arranged for you to travel with Miss Eleanor if that suits?"

"Eleanor is coming?"

"Of course, she wouldn't miss it."

"Ah yes." Georgiana looked to the velvet canopy above. "So reminiscent of the olden days."

Mama tugged her hand with a matronly smile. "Reminiscent, yes. Old no."

Moving to the washstand, Georgiana splashed water on her face. "How long has Miss Eleanor known about your plans?"

"A fortnight or so." Mother thrust her finger toward

the maid. "Careful how you fold that. India muslin must never be wrinkled."

"Yes, ma'am."

"Who else have you invited?" Georgiana asked, drying her face.

"If I told you, it wouldn't be a surprise, would it?"

She hung the cloth on the rack. "I think I've been sufficiently surprised for one day."

"Nonsense." With a swish of her skirts, Mama strode out the door. "You have an hour to dress and eat breakfast. I suggest you make haste, my dear one."

Georgiana pursed her lips while she watched her mother walk out and close the door. Once she was gone, she glanced to the maid. "Why do I not presently feel like a dear one?"

"I have no idea, mistress. I would think a country house party with lords and ladies milling about would be a dream come true."

Georgiana sighed. What a fraud she felt trapped between two worlds. On one side, she was poor like the masses, yet born into the nobility, which afforded her certain privileges like house parties away from London when she should be attending soirees with Eleanor, meeting potential financiers.

Goodness. I must make arrangements.

With her thought, she hastened to dress, had the maid pin her hair in a simple chignon, and dashed down to the kitchens. "Roddy, I need your assistance."

The young man sprang up from the table. "Yes, mistress?"

She grabbed a crumpet from the board and took a bite. "I must go to Hardwick Hall for the week."

"But what about—"

Mouth full, she thrust up the pastry. "Allow me to finish."

Roddy clamped his lips shut and gave a nod.

"I need you and Mr. Walpole to supervise the trans-

portation of the pumper. I've already made arrangements with a driver who will bring his team here at
dawn on Sunday morning. Can you do that for me?"

"Aye, but how will we give the show if you're not
there?"

"Oh, I'll be at Richmond Park, all right. I shall meet
you there, no matter the odds. Mr. Walpole has been
practicing his lines and you know how to run the machine. I am certain our demonstration will be a monu-
mental success." She clamped a hand over her stomach.
She'd invited Lord Hamilton and a host of other gentlemen to Richmond Park to see the fire engine in action, her mother might thwart her plans for the week,
but the baroness would not stand in the way of Sunday's
long awaited success.

"Ah, there you are, Mrs. Whiteside," said Dobbs as
he stepped into the kitchen. "There's a Mr. Webster
here to see you."

"Webster?" she asked as a pinch jabbed her between
the shoulder blades. "Is he one of Mama's guests?"

"No, not that I'm aware of. I did tell him that you
are preparing for an outing and he said he only needed a
moment of your time."

"Very well. In the parlor, is he?"

"Yes, madam."

Georgiana took a deep breath. After she'd been
warned off by Fletcher, she wasn't certain Clarence
Webster was the type of person she needed for a business associate. But nonetheless, she was growing more
desperate by the day, and if the man truly harbored an
interest in steam-powered fire engines, then she owed it
to herself and Daniel's memory to take him seriously.

She opened the parlor door and smiled. "Mr. Webster, what a surprise to see you again so soon."

The man rose and bowed. "Good morning, madam.
Please forgive my intrusion, but it was such a delight to

meet you—I mean to meet Daniel's wife, I couldn't stay away."

"Please do resume your seat." Georgiana reached for the bell. "Shall I ring for a refreshment?"

"Oh, no. I am aware you haven't much time."

"Indeed. Mother has quite a day planned." She bit her lip, it was best not to mention anything about the country party. It was Mama's affair, and if Webster didn't know about it, he wasn't on the guest list. "How may I be of assistance?"

"If you recall, at Lady Maxwell's ball you mentioned that you are in possession of Mr. Whiteside's drawings."

"Yes."

"Would I be able to see them? Perhaps borrow them for a few days?"

"Hmm. I'll have to think on that, but why are you so interested in the pumper's drawings? I don't recall Daniel ever mentioning you being involved with his work at university."

Glancing toward the window, Mr. Webster drew a hand down his mouth. "I assure you we were best of friends. I-I was wondering how much had changed since he left Cambridge."

"The pumper is vastly different. I can attest to that." When Daniel was at university, the steam pumper had been but a sketch of an idea. Moreover, the stabbing between her shoulder blades hadn't eased. She moved to the edge of her seat, trying to picture Webster among her husband's friends and came up with no recollection. Truly, they couldn't have been as close as the man claimed. "I would be leading you astray if I didn't profess the only person I'll show the drawings to is a business partner."

"Partner?" he asked, his tone somewhat curt.

Georgiana sat ramrod straight. "You heard me correctly. In short, I am looking for financial backing to manufacture Whiteside pumpers en masse—say with an output of two per month."

"Two?"

"Yes. I'm ready to start production forthwith, but I need an investment of fifteen hundred pounds. Is such an investment enticing to you?" Every muscle in Georgiana's body clenched. Never in all her days would she think herself capable of being so brashly forward. But she felt so strongly about the capability of her—of Daniel's design. And if Mr. Webster merely wanted to have a look at the drawings for posterity's sake, he could wait.

"W-well I'd have to see the pumper work first. I'd need some sort of guarantee."

"And you have the money?" she asked, ready to shake on the transaction or leave him in her wake. She had little time and if this man was ready to put up the investment, she must make further inquiries as to his character. "We can proceed as soon as fifteen hundred pounds is deposited into the Whiteside account at the Bank of England. Have you an interest in a partnership, sir?"

"I? Ah...me?" His Adam's apple bobbed. "What you're suggesting would be a small fortune to many."

"I am aware." Georgiana stood. "Perhaps if you would consider coming to Richmond Park, you'll have the opportunity to see the Whiteside pumper demonstration. That might set your mind at ease."

"Yes, a demonstration would be absolutely necessary." He rose as well. "You said the fete was on the twelfth, did you?"

"Yes. I'd love to personally show you all the machinations. It is quite an impressive machine—it has a two hundred gallon holding tank and pumps at one hundred pounds per square inch."

"Unbelievable."

"Believe it, Mr. Webster, for you shall see its power come Sunday."

❧

THE CARRIAGE AMBLED ALONG THE TURNPIKE WHILE Georgiana sat across from Eleanor. "Mother said you've known about this party for a fortnight."

"No." The lovely auburn-haired lass shook her head, making the daisies on her bonnet appear as if they'd been caught by a breeze. "I'd say it couldn't have been any more than a week."

"She always does exaggerate but, still, why didn't you mention it to me?"

Eleanor flicked the tassel holding back the window curtain. "Mention a surprise? I was sworn to secrecy by the all-powerful Baroness of Derby."

"Oh, please."

"When we were growing up, your mother always ensured I behaved like a lady—bless her, especially since I had no other patroness take me under her wing. I'm not complaining, but I've always been a bit afraid of Lady Derby."

Georgiana batted her hand through the air. "Mama is all bark and no bite. She's harmless."

"Oh? Is that why the two of us, who have better things to do, are presently sitting in a carriage on the way to Hardwick Hall at the behest of one such baroness?"

Groaning, Georgiana almost slouched, except her stays prevented such a faux pas. "Honestly, all morning, I've been trying to convince myself that she didn't contrive this house party because she knew about my plans for the Richmond Park fair."

"At least you'll be close by. It oughtn't be difficult to slip away."

"Even if it is, I am an adult and I will see to the

demonstration no matter what dear Mama has planned."

"I'd have thought no less." Eleanor sighed and looked out the window. "However, I must say, her thoughtfulness is endearing."

"Ah, yes." Trying not to roll her eyes, Georgiana glanced down at her hands, now gripping the ties of her reticule in tightly clenched fists. "As long as I'm taking part in an activity she approves of, Mama is quite amenable."

"Mm hmm. And she's allowing you to keep your monstrosity behind the mews."

"I beg your pardon?" Georgiana tossed a velvet carriage cushion at her presumed friend. "So now *you're* calling Daniel's brilliant invention a monstrosity?"

"I'm just saying it's nice to have someone dote on you. I, for one, would very much appreciate having a familial relationship that is not one-sided." Eleanor gave Georgiana's knee a pat. "If only I should be so fortunate. But I move in circles where birthdays are forgotten memories."

Her heart squeezed. "Forgive me for being insensitive to your plight. You always present such a stalwart face, I oft forget the trials you endure. Tell me, what is the prognosis for your father?"

Shrugging, Eleanor looked up, but rather than her stalwart façade, her expression was a bit wounded. "Nothing can be done. Papa is lost in his own mind. Most days he sits and stares out the library window. No one knows what is happening in his thoughts."

"How dreadful. The war ruined him forever."

"It did. At times I think it may have been merciful if he'd died in that battle. But then, who am I to say? There must be a reason for him to exist."

"Perhaps he's thinking of a new invention and, one day, when he has all the details sorted out in his mind, he'll burst forth with a grand pronouncement."

Resuming a pleasant, happy, self-controlled countenance, Eleanor chuckled. "That would be stupendous."

Together, they watched the scenery pass for a time while Eleanor pulled out a skein of wool and a crochet hook.

"What are you making?"

Eleanor held up a gray panel. "A scarf for Papa."

"Lovely. I'm sure he'll like it."

"I doubt he will." The saucy spinster winked. "I think this is number twenty-three. I make them to keep my hands busy, but I've never graduated past scarves."

"Well, if you ever come across pink wool, I'd love for you to make one for me."

"I'll keep that in mind...perhaps next birthday."

Georgiana mentally tried to go through a list of key points for the pumper demonstration, but her mind kept deviating and a few trees would pass by the window, and suddenly she was picturing the Duke of Evesham—in the salon at Almacks, or in the window embrasure at the theater, or how vividly his amber eyes had glistened in Green Park. So many times on their walk at Vauxhall, she thought he might pull her into the foliage and kiss her. But he hadn't. Had she been too forward in the carriage? Had she frightened him away? If so, then why had he bothered to come the next day?

"Eleanor?" she asked.

"Hmm?"

"Do you know who Mama has invited to this house party?"

Holding the wool tightly wound on her finger, Eleanor shook her head. "Not at all. When I asked, she shook her finger under my nose and said it was a surprise."

"Wonderful. My dear mother and her surprises."

"But she did say she'd invited the Dowager Duchess of Ravenscar and her son."

"I should have guessed. Her Grace is one of my

mother's closest friends. But the last time I saw her son, he was fourteen—and had already inherited the title."

The crochet hook moved with lightning speed, whipping three stitches. "Was that six years past?"

"Yes."

"Then he'd be at least twenty, would you say?"

"Twenty." Georgiana snorted. "Still quite young."

"Indeed, though most likely one of the wealthiest men in the kingdom. I say he's rather handsome as well."

"I suppose he spends a great deal of time in London during the Season."

Eleanor drew a length of wool from the skein. "Such is the lot of dukes and their duties to the House of Lords."

What if Mama hadn't invited Evesham? Moreover, what would Georgiana do if he came? How would she be able to keep from attending the fair. Worse, the man who caused her a great deal of disconcertedness would be sleeping under the same roof—though hardly nearby in a castle as palatial as Hardwick Hall.

The confounding fact? Once she and Eleanor arrived at the estate and the guests were assembled for afternoon tea, the Duke of Evesham was nowhere to be found.

Chapter Fifteen

❧

Beneath a dripping sycamore, Fletcher's Gordon Setters, Max and Molly, obediently sat beside him while blinking the rain from their eyes. For the love of God, Georgiana's birthday celebration had already begun and there he stood watching the blacksmith from Datchet as he changed a wheel on his town coach.

This was not what he'd anticipated when he'd decided to take a detour to Colworth to collect the dogs. Only about seven hours for the return journey, he'd figured if he rose at dawn and drove the horses at a steady trot, he'd arrive at Hardwick Hall by midafternoon.

He snapped open his pocket watch and tapped it. Blast, blast and double blast. There was no chance he'd make afternoon tea, and fairly likely he'd miss dinner. And dammit all, he shouldn't care.

But he did.

Fletcher normally abhorred country house parties. In truth, he'd only been invited to one, and that was right after he'd become a duke. Once his notoriety of a scoundrel became known, he hadn't received invitations to grace the halls of any nobleman's country seat. Invitations to balls and soirees came often enough when he was in Town, but rarely when he was in residence at

Colworth. No, no one wanted the Duke of Evesham to make a sham out of their country party.

The irony was his unsavory reputation had come about quite by mistake. He'd been attending his one and only country party when a Miss Maidenblossom had swooned. Walking behind the girl, he'd been minding his own affairs, when suddenly the doughy-faced debutante toppled backward, right into Fletcher's arms.

Once everyone turned, gaped, and assumed the worst, pandemonium ensued. The young lady's mother immediately insisted they wed, as did the damned hostess—even after he explained that he'd had no choice but to catch the girl as she fell. Aghast, he informed all in attendance that he refused to be tricked into marrying Miss Maidenblossom and he resented her mother's inference of his inappropriate behavior—in broad daylight when she was but twenty paces ahead. Worse, when they refused to let the matter lie, Fletcher finally burst a spleen and told the woman that should her daughter ever fall again, he'd step aside and let the spoiled child drop.

Good God, he'd been fortunate to escape the country estate with his cods attached. Perhaps he shouldn't have been so boorish with the "let her drop" comment, but those vicious women had cornered him. It was as if the three vultures had colluded to have the debutante trick him into an unwanted, ill-timed marriage.

Needless to say, since then, he'd heartily embraced his differences with the rest of the nobility. He might be the product of the sixteenth Duke of Evesham's loins, but Fletcher had been raised a commoner. His mother had enjoyed none of the comforts of the wealthy. She cooked, cleaned and mended for the townsfolk and barely eked out a living. Hell, she had no time or use for highborn airs. What he'd learned about polite society had come from attending Eton and Oxford. Though an outcast, Fletcher had spent his days observing his "betters". As a result, he was able to turn on the charm when he so desired, but most often he did not.

Over the years he'd rather enjoyed having a reputation of being a rogue and a rake even though the moniker had been earned in the midst of a misunderstanding. Truly, Fletcher rather liked the fact that most members of the *ton* gave him a wide berth. They left him to his own devices and that's what he wanted. He was born a bastard and no matter what the slip of parchment had said—the one signed by the sixteenth Duke of Evesham on the eve of his death—Fletcher could not escape the reality of his lowly birth.

Except where Mrs. Whiteside played into the equation. He withdrew the locket with the curl he'd snipped, opened it, and drew it to his nose. Her scent still lingered. Closing his eyes, the sensation of the silkiness of her hair tingled on his fingertips while his blood stirred.

When it came to the widow, all of the balance and harmony in his well-organized world distorted into a messy array of...Fletcher pocketed the locket and patted Max on the head. "Well, the woman renders me incapable of rational thought."

Tossing his head, the dog yowled and wagged his tail.

"Perhaps you're right. Attending a country party hosted by Lady Derby is not the act of a sane duke." Why had the baroness taken a liking to him? She wasn't one of those desperate mothers trying to find a match for her daughter before the Season's end. Or was she?

Molly stood, looking at Fletcher expectantly.

"No, that does not mean we'll be turning around and heading back to Colworth." He pointed directly. "Sit."

With his single command, the female Setter joined her mate, keeping vigil beside their master. If only humans could be half as obliging. Earlier that day, the dogs had received Fletcher with vivacious enthusiasm, and doubtless were presently on their best behavior because, at long last, they were out and about on an excursion into the unknown—excited to be reunited with the leader of their pack.

"Beg your pardon, Your Grace," said the smithy, holding what looked to be a piece of the axle.

Fletcher ground his molars. "Do not tell me that is what I think it is."

"She's fractured. Mangled. And I've no better news than to tell you I've naught but to take it to my shop for repairs." The man threw a thumb over his shoulder. "The Hanovers take in boarders. I'm certain Your Grace and your servants can find a warm meal and a place to bed down just yonder."

Fletcher crossed his arms. "Do you aim to repair my mangled piece of iron or replace it with a new one?"

"I can solder it."

"But then the metal will be weakened. It will be far more likely to break."

"A bit weaker, sir, but functional."

"Replace it with new."

"That will take two days, mayhap three."

"Now why does that not surprise me?" Fletcher turned to his coachman. "I'm leaving you in charge of seeing to the carriage repairs. Thank God we brought my horse."

"You're continuing on in this squall, Your Grace? There's at least two hours' journey to Twickenham, and that's only if the roads aren't washed over."

Stay at some hovel in Datchet or ride on for an entertaining evening with Mrs. Whiteside? "I'm fully aware of the hazards. I'll take the dogs with me. The pair of them enjoy the rain more than the sunshine."

ELEANOR SAT ACROSS THE ENORMOUS TABLE AND
spoke quietly with Mr. Greg, the vicar's son. Sighing,
Georgiana pushed bits of pigeon pie around her plate.
The enormous vases of calla lilies and candelabras
adorning the center of the table made conversation
across the way challenging, though not impossible.

"I believe forks were invented to assist in conveying
the food from your plate to your mouth, dear," said
Mother in a controlled but audible tone from the far
end of the table.

"Can you believe Englishmen didn't adopt forks
until the eighteenth century?" Papa held up his dessert
fork and examined it. "And now it seems as though we
have a specialized spearing utensil for every dish."

Chuckling, Georgiana took a bite, thankful her father had directed the attention away from her.

"What say you, madam?" asked the Duke of Ravenscar, seated beside her. "Do you think an array of forks
are necessary in a formal place setting?"

She speared a piece of pigeon meat. "Years ago I
married into a simpler life and I now reside in a cottage
where, when one sits down to dine, there is only one
fork for each person."

"That's logical," agreed her elder brother, Roland.
"After all, a person can only use one fork at a time."

Georgiana gave the future Baron of Derby a smile in
thanks for his practical opinion. The best thing about
the house party was seeing Roland, his wife, Clarice,
and their three children, who were presently away visiting Clarice's sister in Derbyshire.

Mama sniffed and motioned for the footmen to
start the next course. "You and your bent for reason,
Son."

"I do believe a proper selection of forks on the table
is a testament to the style and etiquette of our class,"

said the Dowager Duchess of Ravenscar. "It separates the wheat from the chaff, so to speak."

Beside Her Grace, Mr. Peters raised his glass. "Hear, hear." The gentleman had been introduced as a well-to-do gunsmith and Georgiana had hopes of conversing with him about his potential interest in her pumper. He also seemed to be on quite friendly terms with Ravenscar's mother.

What an interesting group Mama had assembled—nothing at all what Georgiana expected. Mr. Greg was a year or two younger, Miss Peters, Mr. Peters' daughter couldn't be older than twenty and the Duke of Ravenscar had only just graduated from Oxford—and had been talking throughout the meal about his plans to tour the theaters of Europe.

She sipped her wine. At least Mama hadn't conspired to bring a host of guests together for a matchmaking soiree, which would have ended up in a complete disaster.

But Mother had seemed so unusually fond of Evesham. That he wasn't in attendance came more of a surprise. Perhaps Mama had invited the duke and he'd sent his regrets. After all, it wasn't everyone who was able to put their lives on hold and venture to Twickenham for a week-long soiree.

Georgiana took another sip, the warmth spreading through her chest. Perhaps she was a tad disappointed not to see him.

"What do you think of this storm that has rolled in?" asked Ravenscar.

"I'm very glad all of the guests arrived before the thunder and lightning began." Georgiana looked to her mother to see if there would be a comment about guests who had not yet arrived, but Her Ladyship was engaged in conversation with the dowager duchess. "I cannot imagine traveling in such weather."

"I doubt anyone would. When the rain pours as it

has done today, the turnpikes are awash. 'Tis very dangerous."

"Indeed." Georgiana gripped the serviette in her lap and twisted it. Perhaps Evesham was detained and the weather prevented him from coming? *Stop, you dolt. The duke isn't here and Mother hasn't mentioned him. Surely he'll not be coming...and that is definitely a boon considering the fair at Richmond Park.*

After flummery with raspberry sauce was served, Mama announced that once the gentlemen enjoyed their cheroots, their presence would be needed in the music room where the ladies would entertain them with a recital.

Georgiana and Eleanor exchanged panicked looks but waited until the men had moved to the saloon to voice their dissent. "A recital, Mama?"

"I seem to recall the last time you two ladies were in attendance at one of my house parties, you partook in a recital." The baroness looked to Eleanor. "Do you still play the pianoforte, my dear?"

"I do."

"Well then it is settled." Mother looped her elbow through Georgiana's and proceeded to the music room. "Miss Abagail plays the violin, and you certainly have not lost your voice, sweeting."

"I beg your pardon? I haven't sung in ages."

"Balderdash. I heard you singing in the bath only a fortnight past."

"I may sing when I'm alone, but I have not performed before a crowd in ages."

The baroness smiled as if she hadn't a care. "This is hardly a crowd, my dear. And you may as well stop your arguing, lest I be forced to prevail upon Her Grace to play the bagpipes."

"Bagpipes?" The dowager duchess gave a very subtle snort. "My mother would roll over in her grave."

Mama released Georgiana's arm and turned.

"Priscilla, do you not recall in your first Season, you told Lord Sussex that you played the bagpipes?"

"Oh, goodness, I'd forgotten..."

While the two ladies continued reminiscing about Seasons of ages past, Georgiana joined Eleanor and Abagail at the pianoforte. "I'm afraid I'll make the pair of you look awful."

"Nonsense. Do you still remember *My Bonnie Lass She Smileth*?" asked Eleanor.

"Of course."

"And I can play a verse on the violin to give your voice a rest," Abagail volunteered.

"That would acceptable, though I daresay a violin solo would be far more entertaining than listening to me." Georgiana plunked out middle C on the keyboard. "You seem to be polished. Do you have a repertoire perchance?"

Miss Peters looked a tad uncertain. "I plan to play a Bach fugue as well. That should suffice, would you not think?"

"Bach?" asked Eleanor, not hiding her admiration. "You must be a proficient."

"Isn't that why your mother invited me? After all, my father is merely a gunsmith."

Georgiana found the music for *My Bonny Lass She Smileth* and gave it to the violinist. "I understand your father has done very well for himself. You should be proud."

"I couldn't agree more," said Eleanor, taking her seat at the pianoforte. "Let a man—or woman—succeed on merit rather than his or her birth."

By the smiles on all three ladies' faces, they were all in favor.

Miss Eleanor squeezed Georgiana's hand. "Imagine how the fairer sex might succeed if merit were the determinant of success."

Good heavens, if only society could begin to grasp

such forward thinking, peddling her pumper would be so much easier.

From the back of the room, Mama clapped her hands. "Ladies, we'd best rehearse before the gentlemen join us."

Chapter Sixteen

✦

"Your Grace?" exclaimed Dobbs, ushering Fletcher into a long gallery festooned with portraiture of Georgiana's family. "I cannot believe you've been out in this squall throughout the entire day."

Fletcher removed his dripping cloak and handed it to a footman as he spied a full-length picture of Georgiana leading a stately chestnut mare. She looked to be in her late teens, perhaps more carefree. "My carriage threw an axle near Datchet. It will take days to repair. I had little option but to ride on."

"I commend your perseverance. Allow me to show you to your chamber straightaway." Dobbs snapped his fingers at the footman. "See to it a bath is drawn at once."

A chill coursed across Fletcher's skin. Dear God, he must be soaked to the bone. "Thank you. And if you would please send up a lad with an old blanket for my dogs to lie upon and dry before the hearth. The poor devils are as wet and cold as I."

"Straightaway." The butler beckoned him. "Follow me."

Fletcher rubbed his outer arms and gave the butler a nod. "Lead on."

A tune from a pianoforte filled the hall right before a beautiful voice began to sing. Another shiver coursed through Fletcher's entire body but, this time, it had nothing to do with being cold. He knew this voice, though he'd never before heard the woman sing. Leading the dogs away from Dobbs, he soon found the music chamber while the alluring alto continued to mesmerize. Georgiana sounded nothing like Signora Morella. The operatic soprano was practiced and proficient, but Mrs. Whiteside was sultry, raw, and intoxicating.

Forgetting the water dripping from his clothing, the fact he was bone cold, and accompanied by two dogs, he remained at the jamb of the partially open door and peered inside. Georgiana stood beside the pianoforte wearing an India muslin evening gown of ivory. Her shoulders square, the notes of the aria filled the room with pure temptation. As the sequence ended, she took a deep breath, making round, supple breasts strain against her plunging bodice.

Leaning forward along with her inhalation, Fletcher's shoulder nudged the door.

At the creak of the hinges, Georgiana's gaze shifted his way. "Ah!" she gasped, drawing her hands over her mouth.

The music stopped while all heads turned and Rasputin sprang to his feet and barked. Max and Molly lunged against their leads, responding in kind while the Pointer bounded toward them. "Come behind," Fletcher growled, pulling his pair to heel.

"Rasputin!" hollered Lord Derby. At the sound of his master's voice, the overgrown puppy straightened his legs and slid on the floorboards, toenails screeching until the dog stopped and stared, excitedly wagging his tail.

"Ahem." Fletcher patted his chest with a snappy

bow while the baron commanded his dog to return to his mat by the hearth. "Please forgive me. I was on my way above stairs to don some dry clothes and was stopped by the sound of stunningly beautiful music coming from this very chamber."

"Your Grace." Mrs. Whiteside rushed toward him. "Do not tell me you have been out in this weather all evening?"

Fletcher tugged on the leads, bringing the dogs forward. "Yes, well, you see, I thought Max and Molly would enjoy a country party as well, so I took a detour." He looked down at the smelly, dripping Setters. "And then the carriage threw an axle."

"Devil take it, you've ridden all this way?" asked Derby.

"About nine miles," Fletcher explained. "But I daresay the roads are boggy in places and washed away in others."

"My word, you must hasten upstairs straightaway. Where is Dobbs?" asked the baroness. "Has he ordered a warm bath?"

"I have, Your Ladyship." Returning to Fletcher's side, the butler appeared a bit bothered. "And one of the housemaids is fetching a blanket for the dogs."

"Yes, you must change into something warm and dry before you catch your death." Georgiana curtsied. "I'll see to it a warm meal is sent to your chamber directly."

"I would like that very much." Fletcher looked to the other guests. If only the lot of them weren't staring at him, he'd like to tell the lady to bring the tray herself...and serenade him. Hell, forget the tray and just sing. But like the well-behaved duke he was endeavoring to emulate, he bowed. "If you will excuse me."

"I say, Evesham, your Setters are capital," said Derby. "Are you up for a fox hunt? I'm certain Lady Derby has set aside some time during this frolic for a jolly good chase."

Fletcher's gaze slid to the man's daughter. "I'd assume no less. Especially if Mrs. Whiteside would do me the honor of being my second."

Her smile warmed him. "I'd be delighted."

❧

"It is lovely to have you back at Hardwick Hall, mistress," said Mrs. Parsons, wiping her hands on her cook's apron. "The baroness would have sent a footman to the kitchens to order a tray for His Grace. And by rights, you ought to have done so as well, though I do love to see your pretty face ever so."

"You know how much I like to visit down here. As I grew up, I always felt more at home in the kitchens than above stairs." For the past quarter-hour, Georgiana had perched on her favorite stool in the corner. "Besides, I told the duke I would personally see to it a tray was prepared."

Mrs. Parsons pointed after the footman who'd just headed up to Evesham's chamber. "Well, there's enough food on that tray to keep the duke satiated for a sennight."

"Thank you. The man deserves every bite." Georgiana hopped up, opened a canister, and found exactly what she was looking for. Some things never changed. "Did you know he rode nine miles in the rain from Datchet?"

"A duke? Would no one let him a room?" Mrs. Parsons handed her a spoon. "'Tis unheard of."

Georgiana found a pan in the cupboard beneath the countertop. "We were all surprised to see him."

"Can I help you with something?" asked the cook.

"Perhaps some milk?" Georgiana put the pan on the stove and opened the cast iron door to check the fire. "I thought I'd make myself a dish of chocolate."

Mrs. Parsons laughed. "I should have known that's what you were up to."

"Yes, I'm still addicted to warmed chocolate, though I cannot oft afford the luxury."

"No? My, that does make me sad."

"It shouldn't. I've been happy and the country suits me ever so."

"If only..." Mrs. Parsons turned away and poured milk into the pan.

Georgiana could finish the woman's sentence—if only Mr. Whiteside hadn't died. "His passing was a dark time in my life, but I'm coming into my own now. Though when the accident first happened, I never thought I'd be able to survive. Thank heavens, after the passage of time, I am content."

"Though it would be nice if you could remarry—find a well-to-do gentleman who can afford chocolate."

Georgiana stirred the mixture. "Perhaps I'll be able to purchase my own in the future."

"You?"

"Who knows? If Daniel's invention finds the right backing, I'll not only be able to buy chocolate, I'll be able to commission a host of repairs to my cottage in Thetford."

"Well, I wish you great success. Wouldn't it be a boon to see his work amount to something useful? Why, this family would be shocked for certain."

"I think all of Christendom would be shocked and that would be a dream come true."

Georgiana stirred the chocolate while she watched it eventually come to a rolling boil.

"Here's a dish for you, dear." Mrs. Parsons gestured to a tray. "And I've sliced you a bit of cherry tart to help you sleep."

"It looks delicious." She smiled, taking the tray. "Thank you ever so much. Sweet dreams."

Heading up the servant's stairs with the tray, Georgiana forgot to veer off to the south wing and head for her chamber. At least, she told herself it was a slip of her memory. Evesham had been relegated to the second floor of the north wing where the king's guest apartments occupied the entire ell. Hardwick House was a sprawling baronial estate where one could spend an afternoon exploring and end up completely lost—if he or she hadn't grown up there, of course. The castle boasted five stories and the other guests had been appointed chambers in various, secluded parts of the castle.

There were two reasons Georgiana knew Evesham was in the king's apartments. First, he was a duke, but then Ravenscar was also a duke—so that had initially posed a conundrum. However, after venturing down to the kitchens and overseeing the preparation of a tray for His Grace's dinner, the footman had confirmed her assumption. Thanks to the efficiency of the housekeeper, Hardwick Hall's servants always knew where everyone had been appointed.

Quietly, Georgiana tiptoed through the corridors, ensuring no one saw her until she reached Evesham's door. Her stomach squeezed like she'd just hopped down from climbing a tree as she balanced the tray on one hand and raised her hand to knock. Hesitating, she bit her bottom lip. Never in her life had she done anything this scandalous.

As of this morning, the most daring thing she'd done in her entire six and twenty years was kiss Evesham in his carriage. The memory of it still sent tingles throughout her body. She scarcely believed herself capable of such audaciousness. She, Georgiana Whiteside, had thrown propriety out the window and acted like a wanton. Worse, she'd enjoyed every single moment.

Before she lowered her hand, took the tray, and savored a delicious dish of chocolate in the sanctity of her bedchamber, she knocked—a single rap.

Drawing in a sharp inhalation, she held her breath.

If he doesn't respond, I'll be on my way. Perhaps he doesn't care to have company after spending the day out in the storm.

The Setters barked.

"To your rug!" Evesham's deep voice resonated through the timbers. Water trickled. "Come."

Georgiana pulled the latch and slipped inside, quickly closing the door to ensure no passing servants spotted her. "Your Grace, forgive my impertinence, but after your ordeal, I made you a dish of my favorite chocolate...to...to warm your..."

As she spoke, her mouth grew dry, her skin alive with tingles, her body afire. And then she gaped. She couldn't breathe. She couldn't blink. Good glory, Evesham was still in the bath. Water glistened, dripping from the black curls on his chest, shimmering amber with the firelight. Beneath the droplets, the man was solid, well-muscled, and tan-skinned. She licked her lips, her gaze darting to the table. "F-f-forgive me for intruding. I-I'll just set this on the table and leave you to your bath."

"Must you hasten away?" he asked as if he were out for a Sunday stroll while the dogs watched from their place in front of the hearth.

"I certainly cannot stay here whilst you're..." Moving to the table, she set the tray down. She mustn't stare at a naked duke. Before stopping herself, Georgiana's gaze shifted aside. Dash it, she couldn't help but stare! Shaking her head, she covered her face. "Goodness, I shouldn't have come."

"Why did you?" His tone wasn't accusatory, but curious.

"Well..." she began, burying her face in both hands to ensure not to ogle the man once again. "Quite possibly it was an error in judgement on my behalf." Oh dear, oh dear, she sounded as daft as a hen laying an egg.

The water trickled. No. It more than trickled. It rushed. Lord save her, he'd stood. He stepped out. Footsteps approached. Dear God, a wet, naked duke stood not but five feet from her.

"You once told me that you weren't ready to entertain a liaison—courtship, I think is the term you used." His voice was even deeper than usual. Yet, he spoke as if in complete and utter control while he stepped so near, the heat from his body swirled about her—rosemary-scented soap with a masculine essence, powerful enough to render her delirious. "In light of our most arousing carriage ride, and now here where you've so thoughtfully brought me warmed chocolate, I must ask if your conviction has changed."

Her mind raced. A liaison? That was what she wanted, wasn't it? Hadn't Eleanor suggested the rules were different for widows? As long as they took precautions? "No one knows I ventured up here. Even cook thinks I made the chocolate for myself."

He brushed a lock of hair away from her forehead. "I know you're here."

She nodded, peeking through her fingers—amber legs, hips barely covered by a white drying cloth. If a woman could melt, she'd already be a puddle on the floor. "I should be ashamed, but I am not," she whispered. "Perhaps we might share a rendezvous of sorts." Holy everlasting Father, had the words actually escaped her lips?

His palm slid over her shoulder. "Then look at me."

She was experienced and widowed yet there Georgiana stood, hiding her eyes like a child. Gulping, she lowered her hands, forcing her gaze to focus upon his face—his rugged, beautiful, exotic face.

Evesham's eyes glistened as if they could smile. He

traced his little finger along her bottom lip. "There you are, my elusive swan."

"Y-you ought to try the chocolate. Truly, it is very good."

"I'm not interested in chocolate." Dipping his chin, his hands cupped her face as he brushed his lips across hers. "The only thing I want to drink in right now is you."

She gasped while her fingers found their way around his waist.

His breath caressed her face as he neared. Unable to think, she raised her chin, her lips meeting his as if drinking nectar. He tasted like brandy and smelled of primal male and rosemary soap. It only took but a swirl of his tongue to render her defenseless.

He tapped his forehead to hers. "Before I cross the line where I will no longer be a duke in calm and cool control, I must know why you came—and do not say it was to bring me a damned dish of warmed chocolate."

"Eleanor said—"

"Eleanor is not in my arms. Do you want me, Mrs. Whiteside? Do you want me as much as the air you breathe? Do you want me enough to tarnish your pristine reputation? Do you want me to take you to the moon and the stars and the planets beyond?"

With his every word, her blood warmed and coiled into an ache low in her body. She was no stranger to the pull of desire, yet this was a vortex of yearning more powerful than anything she'd ever dreamed possible. "Yes. Dear God, yes!"

As she spoke the words, her bodice fell away. But she didn't care if he'd been loosening the laces behind. She didn't care if he'd already stripped her bare. She shoved her hands down his hips and ripped away the cloth from his loins.

His manhood jutted from black curls, thick as a bedpost—so much larger than...*oh Lord*. She needed this man. Him. Evesham. Deft fingers pulled away strings. His mouth plundered hers while her stays dropped to the floor. With a whoosh, down went her overskirt followed by one, two, three petticoats.

As he slowly drew Georgiana's shift up her legs, she couldn't manage to take in air. Grasping his shoulders, she threw back her head. "Evesham!"

"Fletcher," he growled. "My name is Fletcher."

"Yes, I know. P-please slow down. My head is spinning."

He laughed—a deep, menacing, deliciously seductive laugh. "And I intend to make it spin all the more." In one move, he pulled the shift over her head and cast it aside.

Gripping her hands and holding them out wide, Fletcher stepped back. Parted lips, darkened eyes, a low hum of approval escaped him. "Hellfire and damnation."

Georgiana glanced down. Nothing had been left to the imagination. Her only garments, ivory silk stockings held in place by a pair of garters with pink ribbons. Lower, she tapped new ivory slippers with a modest heel. Her thighs trembled. "I—"

"Hush," he whispered. "I want to gaze upon perfection."

She tried to slip from his grasp and cross her arms over her breasts, but he clamped his hands tighter. "Never cover yourself in front of me. You're so damned beautiful, all the goddesses who have come before you could never compare. No man could ever behold you without falling to his knees and kissing your..."

"Feet?" she ventured, her body afire.

Dropping to his knees, he shifted his hands to her hips. "To hell with feet!"

She threaded his hair through her fingers. "Oh my, oh my. Daniel said—"

"I am not Daniel, and I bid you remember it," he

growled as he spread her legs. His hot tongue licked the sensitive flesh on the inside of her thigh. "There's only one name I want on your lips when you are in my arms and that is Fletcher." He lapped her again. "Say it!"

"Fletcher," she gasped.

"Louder!"

"Fletcher!" Yes, she loved the way it sounded on her tongue. Quivering, Georgiana gripped his hair tighter, his soft, cropped, thick, delicious hair. When he licked her parting, a cry erupted from the depths of her throat. Her legs quivered and threatened to give way beneath her. While her mind tumbled, directed by the waves of pleasure rocking her, Fletcher's grip slid to her bottom, holding her steady while his mouth performed wicked, erotic, wonderful things.

Stars darted through her vision as she fought for control and arched away. Dropping to her knees in front of him, she slid her fingers down his solid chest. "I want to please you, too."

"Not here." In one motion, the duke swept her into his arms and stood.

Georgiana showered him with kisses, swirling her fingers through the downy hair on his chest. And then, as if she weighed no more than a feather, he set her on the bed—the enormous bed, with thick mahogany posts fit for a king.

Her heart raced with a vigorous pulse while her body had come alive with newfound erotic pleasure.

Fletcher crawled over her with one knee between her legs. "Was it touch you wanted?"

Scraping her teeth over her lip she gave a nod, her gaze shifting lower. "I do."

He took her hand and wrapped it around his tool, his fingers closing around hers. Georgiana's mouth ran dry. He was silky smooth and as hard as iron all at once. And in this moment, she couldn't recall anything more virile or alive as he pulsated in her palm.

With a little grin, she strengthened her grip.

Fletcher moaned, thrusting. "You will bring me undone like a bloody youth."

"Me?" The thought made her giggle. Evesham... Fletcher was so unlike Daniel. She shook her head. *No. I'm not going to make any more comparisons.*

But as sure as she was lying naked atop his bed, she'd now ventured into unknown territory.

And she liked it.

Taking charge of the power she only now realized she wielded, she drew him fully over her. "I want you."

"We must take precautions."

"I..." she looked away. She'd never conceived before, why would she assume she might now? "Can you spill outside me?" Good heavens, had those naughty words come from her lips?

"I can, though it is not a surety. But..." He glanced toward his valise. "I have a French letter."

"I beg your pardon?"

He pulled out a small package tied with a blue bow. "Using one of these combined with withdrawing." Returning to the bedside, he rubbed the membrane on her cheek. "Should do the trick."

"I take it you've had practice?"

He grinned and climbed onto the bed alongside her, pushing away the bedclothes. "Does my reputation upset you?"

Quite frankly, it didn't. Georgiana wanted a liaison. For the first time in her life, she was doing something completely wicked. And who better to enjoy the experience with than a notorious rake? Someone who not only knew what a French letter was, he knew how to use it.

"Does *my* reputation put you off?" she asked.

"What reputation?" His mouth found her lips then trailed to her breast, his tongue flicking over the sensitive nipple.

"Wallflower. Bluestocking," she suggested.

"You're neither of those."

Chuckling, she closed her eyes and let herself revel in the delight of his attentions.

"I'd say you are complex. You are modest. You are smarter than most men, and you are the most enchanting, mesmerizing, beautiful woman I have ever seen."

Chapter Seventeen

❧

A youth. That's what Georgiana had reduced him to. If he didn't take her now, he'd spill into the linens.

"Fletcher!" she cried, squirming beneath him. "Please."

He grinned. It seemed he wasn't the only one growing impatient. Long, shiny chestnut hair sprawled over the pillows. When had he pulled it down? God, he couldn't remember. No. He only felt. And right now he felt hot, bloody passion. His ballocks were so tight, they were coiled as tight as a medieval trebuchet.

He dipped his chin and lapped a rosy nipple.

Crying out, she writhed and reached between them.

When lithe fingers wrapped around his cock, a bellow reverberated through his body. On the very precipice of control, he thrust downward. The minx used his momentum to lever him toward her.

Holding very still she gazed into his eyes. "Do you intend to use that French letter, or are you merely teasing me?"

"Oh, I'll use it for certain. And when I do, you'll damned-well know it." He wanted to thrust inside and claim his plunder.

Glistening brown eyes stared up at him. They were

filled with lust, and something far deeper. Did he want to lay claim to this woman? More than anything on this earth. Here. Now. But her enjoyment was far more important than satiating his own desires. If Fletcher's intuition was right, though not a virgin, the widow had a great deal to learn about the pleasures of the boudoir.

Ever so slowly, he slid between her silken, wet folds and breached her with his thick staff. Damnation, she was so tight—much smaller than he'd experienced before. His eyes rolled back as he stanched his urge to thrust.

Georgiana squeezed her eyes shut, sinking her fingers into his buttocks, pulling him into her. Her face contorted as she bared her teeth.

"Look at me," he whispered.

She gasped. God's blood, was she in pain? He had to see her eyes? Was he too large? Was she too small? Or maybe he'd crossed the threshold into insanity because every time he closed his eyes he imagined the sight of his cock entering her...making him need to thrust with every fiber of his body. He needed her now.

"Georgiana, open your eyes!"

Heavy lids rose. Luminous eyes focused, then drifted away. "Please," she pleaded, tugging on his buttocks and wriggling her hips. "I cannot make you go any further!"

Satisfied, he dropped his chin and kissed her, nudging her legs wider with his knees.

"More," she demanded.

But he wanted it to last. Ever so slowly, he slid his body up the length of her, forcing himself to think of anything but thrusting. "Tell me what you need."

Georgiana sank her fingers deeper and rocked back and forth. "This. More. Now!"

Unable to withhold for one more second, Fletcher dropped his face into her hair and thrust into the tightest, hottest, most glorious woman he'd ever imagined.

And Georgiana matched his pace, her roaming fingers wild with desire, her body bucking against his.

"Faster!"

"You want more?" he asked, loving her verve.

"Yes, you devil!"

He drove harder, setting a desperate pace. He fought for control, sweat dripping from his body, but he would see her come first.

Beneath him, Georgiana writhed, tossing her head from side to side. Her body spasmed. Cries of passion erupted from her throat while her fingers continued to grip his arse. "I-I-I...oh dear Lord in heaven!"

As she shattered around him, his hips pumped. Heat roared up his legs and down his spine until it exploded in his balls while pleasure ripped through him in a shattering burst of euphoria.

Weakened, barely able to hold his weight off her, Fletcher grinned. "My God, woman, who in the hell ever christened you a wallflower?"

Chapter Eighteen

***

I n the dining hall, tables had been set up to display an array of pastries and jam, eggs, ham, fruits, toast, tea, coffee, chocolate and a decanter of cherry brandy for any gentlemen who might prefer a morning libation. Georgiana selected a plate and moved in beside Eleanor as she scanned the room. Predictably, Fletcher had not yet made an appearance.

Even Georgiana, who always rose with the sun, felt a bit muddled. It had been after two in the morning when she'd tiptoed through the halls and made her way back to her chamber. Fletcher had insisted on accompanying her but she wouldn't hear of it—doing so was out of the question. She was perfectly capable of moving through her parents' home, the very place where she'd grown up exploring as a child and, furthermore, if anyone saw them together, the entire house would be alerted to their indiscretion. That would have the makings of a complete disaster not shy of the duke being either forced into a proposal or a duel at dawn with her brother.

It hadn't been easy to leave those warm, brawny arms. To leave his kisses. To leave when he'd made her feel like a woman again—alive, filled with passion and desire.

But the night had come to an end. She must return to her bedchamber and her life. She'd had her liaison. Now she needed to lock the experience away and try not to think on it.

The problem was how did a woman stop thinking about the most erotic night of her life?

She sets her sights on what's important, that's how. Georgiana smiled at Eleanor. "Did you sleep well?"

"I did." Reaching for a slice of ham, Eleanor glanced back over her shoulder. "What does your mother have planned for today?"

"Do you think she'd tell me?" Georgiana took a pastry and spooned a bit of mulberry conserve onto her plate. "Oh no. That would give me time to plot a diversion."

"Fancy Evesham isn't up yet."

"He did have an awful ordeal yesterday. Perhaps he has caught a chill." Georgiana's hand trembled as she held a dish for the footman to pour coffee. If the duke had caught a chill, he certainly had cured himself of it by the time she had arrived in his chamber.

Together, they sat nearest the window. "I don't think I thanked you for coming along. It must be rather dreary for you here."

"Not at all." Eleanor cut a bite-sized piece of ham and dipped it in her egg yolk. "I rarely have the chance to spirit away from London. It's like a restful holiday. Later, I hope to slip into your father's library and do some much-needed reading."

"You're beginning to sound like me."

"And who said you were all that bad?"

"Mama for starters. I believe she's the one who coined the phrase 'bluestocking'."

They both chuckled while the lady of the house swept into the dining hall, dressed in pink taffeta and looking as composed and gay as the icing on a wedding cake. "Hello, my dears, I do hope everyone has found the breakfast fare to their liking."

"I believe there is something here for every palate," said Ravenscar, dabbing at the corners of his mouth with a serviette.

Mother rapidly patted her chest as if she were having palpitations. "How kind of you to say, Your Grace."

She held a fist full of papers aloft. "After yesterday's dreadful rain, I am thrilled to see the morning's weather is wonderfully fine. 'Tis as if the good Lord knew I had planned a scavenger hunt for our first excursion."

"Is there treasure hidden?" asked Miss Peters.

Mama gave the lass a sober stare. "After eighteen generations of Derbys, I assure you this entire estate harbors an abundance of treasure." Resuming an air of unflappability, Mama set the stack of documents on the table and picked up the top sheet. "As you see, each team of two will receive a list of items which are located outside Hardwick Hall. When you find—or believe you have found the item, you will pencil in where it is located."

Miss Peters raised her hand. "May we choose—"

"I have assigned the teams as follows..."

Georgiana leaned toward Eleanor and cupped her hand over her mouth before she whispered, "I'd best tell Miss Peters there's no use trying to interject."

"Have you ever known your mother to miss a detail?"

"Rarely, though it has happened."

The spinster and the widow both muffled their laughter.

Mama held out the next note to the vicar's son. "Miss Eleanor and Mr. Greg."

"Lovely," Eleanor whispered. "At least he's only a year younger."

"And a great deal poorer."

"Who says a wealthy spinster, that no one knows is wealthy, cannot marry a poor younger man and provide for him a comfortable life?"

Georgiana tapped her friend with her elbow. "Are you interested in marrying Mr. Greg?"

"Absolutely not."

"Pity. He's a nice man."

"And totally not for me."

"Miss Peters and Ravenscar," Mother continued as if she were an official at a grand ball while she peered around the hall. "Mrs. Whiteside and...oh my, where is Evesham?"

Shrugging, Georgiana affected an expression of innocence. "It is hardly fair for me to play."

"Nonsense." Mama shook the paper. "No couple has the same sheet, and I have ensured yours is the most cryptic."

With no other choice, Georgiana rose and took the paper. "Very well, I'll head out on my own and Dobbs can send His Grace to the gardens after he has arisen. Goodness, after his ordeal last eve, I'll be surprised if he makes an appearance before midday."

Mother gave out the remainder of the assignments while Georgiana rejoined Eleanor. "The winning team will be the toast of tonight's dinner and have their choice of seats as well as their choice of the evening's parlor games."

"Where would you prefer to sit tonight?" asked Eleanor.

Georgiana waved her instructions. "Far away from Hardwick Hall."

"Pity, we've only just arrived."

"The game begins at half past nine," Mama continued. "That will give you plenty of time to finish your meal and collect your hats, gloves and wraps. Have a wonderful time, my lovelies. I have a delightful luncheon planned to which you all can look forward."

Georgiana raised her coffee in toast. "I can scarcely wait." But she couldn't help looking toward the door. Where was Fletcher? Had he realized his mistake, awaken early and fled? She wouldn't blame him if he had. Any man ought to flee after being put upon by her brazen behavior. Surely his opinion of her must have waned.

Good. I cannot ever allow myself to debase myself in such a way again. I should be mortified.

But she wasn't.

However, Georgiana must not lose sight of the pumper and the fact that Evesham hated it just as did everyone in her family. Her life was in Thetford... working with steam-powered fire engines. Evesham was a duke with a life of court and parties and the running of vast estates ahead of him. They were nothing more than two lonely souls whose paths had crossed in the middle of a single night. What they'd shared was glorious, sinful, and very, very secret. But it must go no further.

She finished the last of her coffee and set her cup on the saucer resolutely. *It is best that he didn't come down for breakfast. Seeing him now would be awkward for us both.*

A MISSIVE HAD ARRIVED FROM LONDON REGARDING the home for unwed mothers, reporting that a gang of religious zealots had forced their way inside by hammering down the kitchen door. Fortunately, they'd just come to frighten the poor women, because no one was harmed. But the blackguards had broken every plate and glass in the house to make their message clear. During the attack, they'd called the home a den of prostitution and the inhabitants devil worshipers, none of which was true.

Evesham had immediately ordered iron bars for the

doors and windows, and added another night watchman. Now there would be a guard at both the front and back doors. While he was furiously writing missives, he sent a long explanation to an acquaintance at Bow Street, asking his assistance at keeping the riffraff from the home and indicating the runner's services would be rewarded handsomely.

Devil take it, if Fletcher did one good thing with his vast inheritance, he would ensure he protected the women who lived in the home. They came from all walks of life, destitute, hopeless, thinking their lives were ruined while the men who had ruined them somehow felt they had no responsibility—as if a woman could make herself pregnant and carry the burden throughout the life of the child.

Fletcher had a few modest rules he'd passed to Mrs. Whipple who ran the home: All women were welcomed with no questions asked. Boarders must maintain a high level of cleanliness, were assigned work in the house, and must never steal. Thieves were handed over to the authorities, but there had only been one of those. Women were allowed visitors in the parlor only and were encouraged to seek employment whenever possible.

Lord Derby's valet held up Fletcher's coat. "Shall I bring you a tray, Your Grace?"

He shrugged into it. "No, thank you." He glanced over his shoulder. "Her Ladyship assigned me to go scavenger hunting with Mrs. Whiteside, did you say?"

"Indeed, though she has a head start." The man used a lint brush on the coat's shoulders. "I'd be happy to help you find her."

Fletcher tugged on his cuffs. "What fun would there be in that?"

"I can't say."

"Though you might give me a hint—point me in the right direction."

"Well, when Mrs. Whiteside was a young girl, she liked to stroll through the maze."

"Ah yes, the maze before the pool."

"Mm hmm, but her favorite place is the gazebo in the midst of the overgrown garden."

"Overgrown?"

The man set the boar's hair brush in a silver tray. "Well, it is draped with wisteria and all manner of vines. Supposed to look overgrown it is, though the master gardener says he spends more time there than anywhere else on the estate."

"That would be right." Fletcher turned. "Now tell me, where might I find this hideaway?"

As he preferred, he stealthily headed off to find his quarry with Max and Molly obediently at his heel. Last night had astounded him. Yes, he'd had his suspicions, but the evening had exceeded his every expectation. Mrs. Whiteside was a tiger in sheep's clothing and the more he came to know her, the more he thirsted to learn.

The estate was vast with a five-hundred-yard-long pool in the front, which he had been told was stocked with trout. To the north of the pool grew a maze of massive proportions, and to the south, Fletcher had ridden in on a grand tree-lined drive. But he'd been sent to the back garden. Filled with the fragrance of heady blooms, the presentation was not as stately as the view in the front, but it was more magical. With winding pathways and sculptures of angles and interesting statuary blended into the drapery of tree and fern—a fiddler, a laborer with a wheelbarrow, too many birds to count, and Fletcher swore he spotted a fairy peeping through the foliage of a rosebush.

He confirmed he'd taken the right path when he spotted the dome of a gazebo peeking above a row of lilacs. Changing his gait, and motioning to the Setters to step quietly, Fletcher and his accomplices didn't make a sound as he approached. He stopped as he spotted Georgiana curled up on a bench with her feet tucked beneath her, a book in her hands. Lavender wisteria hung from the gazebo's arches, framing the nymph as if she were in an ethereal painting—a living portrait made real by a slight breeze, a perfect day, the rich song of a nearby woodlark.

For the first time in ages, he stood transfixed. In this moment, there was nothing he'd rather do than watch Georgiana turn a page—or sigh as the corners of her lips curled upward at something amusing. Watch as she tucked an errant wisp of hair beneath her bonnet.

He neared and loudly cleared his throat to alert the lady of his approach.

Georgiana lowered her book. "Who's there?"

"'Tis only me and a pair of excitable hounds."

She smiled, her brows arching as if she hadn't expected him. "Evesham."

"Fletcher," he corrected.

"How did you find me?" Setting the book aside, she swung her feet to the ground. "This is my sanctuary."

"It seems the servants know every hidey-hole on the estate."

She scraped her teeth over her bottom lip and glanced away. "Yes, they do."

"And I understand you are supposed to be out and about on a grand scavenger hunt."

"Mother's idea of a fun morning."

"So you decided not to play?"

She slid her fingers along the bench's armrest. "My assigned partner was nowhere to be found during breakfast."

"Apologies. I had some urgent correspondence to tend."

"Oh?" The lady drew a hand over her chest, her expression changing. "I hope all is well."

He joined her on the bench and motioned for the dogs to lie at his feet. "It is...or at least it will be."

Patting her leg, Georgiana urged the dogs to her side for a welcoming scratch. "I can only imagine how taxing the responsibilities of being a duke must be."

"Wealthy peers only like to complain about their lot. In truth, most of them are bored, spoiled, and self-indulgent."

"Harshly put for a man who is so near the top of the peerage."

"Quite accidentally, I might add."

"Why accidentally?"

"I am a bastard, am I not? If that isn't an accident, I cannot imagine what is."

"Forgive me. I didn't think...ah...it is difficult to imagine your adverse beginnings."

"There's nothing to forgive." Leaning toward her, Fletcher inhaled the fragrance of clean female and linen while he traced his finger along her arm. "I'm happy to discover you here. Alone."

She scooted away slightly. "I didn't expect you to find me."

Within a heartbeat, he tensed. "You are disappointed to have your peace and tranquility interrupted."

The lady's shoulders curved as she clamped her fingers over the cover of her book. "'Tis not that as much as..."

Was the lady having second thoughts? Feelings of remorse? Had he done something to hurt her? Fletcher's gut twisted. "Yes?"

Her knuckles turned white with the pursing of her lips. "Last eve was very special and very wrong. We must both put the incident behind us and act as though it never happened."

This was a declaration more fitting to Georgiana Whiteside, consummate wallflower. What the devil had happened between last night and this moment? Damn, he knew he should have escorted the woman to her chamber. Did she wake with the sickly feeling of remorse? "What have I done to earn your scorn?"

"You, sir?"

"Yes, me. In my opinion, when you left my bedchamber last night, you did so amicably. I had no reason to believe that all you wanted was to use me and cast me aside."

"Use you? Cast you aside?" Shaking her head, she sliced her hands through the air. "No. That is not it at all."

He removed his hat and raked his fingers through his hair. Though he should have expected her reluctance, hearing her declare last night was wrong crushed him. "Then why this complete change of direction?"

"As adults," she explained, drumming the book with her fingers, "we must look at this situation pragmatically. You and I are utterly incompatible."

Repositioning his hat, he sat straighter. After she'd entered his bedchamber, nothing would have convinced him more of their compatibility. "Please explain."

"First of all, I enjoy living a quiet life in Thetford where I mind my own affairs. And you..." She formed a bursting arc with her arms, indicating she believed him ill-suited for her domestic ideals. "You live in London—"

"Only during the Season when parliament is in session, of course."

"True, but you are constantly in the public eye. You're a duke, and a quite interesting one at that. Every time you're discovered with so much as a hair out of place it is reported in the papers."

"Perhaps not every time." At least he'd managed to keep the home for unwed mothers a secret.

"And my dowry is gone."

Money? Georgiana couldn't begin to employ such an

argument. "I care not in the slightest about your dowry."

She waved his comment off. "And women lust after you. It is quite obvious."

Fletcher glanced from side to side. "Where are all these women?"

"Oh, please, *The Scarlet Petticoat* reports them often enough. How can someone like me possibly compete with such a following?"

"And you'd believe the scratchings from some old crone cloistered away in a London attic, writing every imaginable bit of drivel? Since we've met, how often have you seen me with another woman on my arm?" Those words even stunned Fletcher. Good God, since he'd first seen Georgiana at Almacks, he hadn't so much as looked at another woman. Until last night, he'd behaved like a goddamned monk. What the devil had happened to him?

"The crux of the matter is we are simply not suitable—"

Pulling her into his arms, he clamped his mouth over hers and showed her exactly how bloody compatible they were. He wasn't about to back away without a fight. She'd vexed him, she'd transfixed and bewitched him to such an extent, his goddamned heart was about to hammer out of his chest.

"Fletcher," Georgiana said, breathless, as she pulled away and wiped her lips. "It is broad daylight."

"And we're hidden in the midst of the overgrown garden. Who will see us?"

"But it isn't proper."

"And last night was?"

"I-I was reckless and—"

Before she said another word, he took her mouth again, kissing her until she grew limp in his arms, her sighs rumbling through him. With each swirl of his tongue, his determination grew. Her kisses were like ambrosia to his soul. His hands slid up and down her spine, caressing her, showing her how precious she'd become to him.

"See?" Inhaling deeply, he tapped his forehead to hers. "We are not as incompatible as you think. Why must we worry about what tomorrow may bring, Georgiana? For once in your life, stop thinking and let it be."

Her eyes flashed wide as she raised her head. "What did you say?"

"Why not enjoy the week?" He shifted his fingers to her silken cheek. "What harm is there in letting down one's guard?"

"Do you mean to suggest we choose not to think about the future?"

God, yes! "Absolutely. Why not enjoy this respite one day at a time?"

"And you agree whatever happens whilst we are at Hardwick Hall will remain a secret forever?"

"I do like how your mind works, madam." He took her hand and pulled her to her feet. "Come now. We have some exploring to do, you and I."

She pointed as she stumbled after him. "The house is that way."

"Very well, but I'm not heading for the house."

Chapter Nineteen

✦✦✦

Georgiana followed Fletcher through the wood, the two Gordon Setters walking at heel without leads. When they were children, she and her brother had used the path to walk to Twickenham, but it surprised her that the duke might know where it led. "You realize we are headed to town, do you not?"

He glanced at her out of the corner of his eye. "I'd assumed as much."

How a man managed to be entirely desirous with a look, she couldn't fathom. After all, his skill in the art of seduction had never been in question. Just being within ten feet of the man made gooseflesh rise across her skin. "Have you ever taken this path before?"

"No."

And his response had been so cocksure. *Oh, to be so self-confident.* "Then how do you possibly know where it leads?"

"Madam, if a man doesn't develop a sense of direction by the time he reaches his majority, he very well might spend the rest of his days wandering in circles."

Of course he provided a nonsensical answer. Daniel wouldn't have set off walking without first asking if his assumption that the path led to town was correct. Paths never traversed the ground in a straight line.

She twirled her bonnet ribbon around her finger. *Stop it, Georgiana. I vowed to cease comparing Evesham to Daniel, and I'll not tolerate my continuing to do so.*

"Are you averse to going to town?" Fletcher slowed his pace. "Would you rather return to the manse?"

"Heavens no. Forgive me. I was telling myself to forget an old memory." She unraveled her finger and plucked a leaf from a sycamore. "But I am curious as to what you hope to find in Twickenham."

His eyes narrowed as if he harbored a secret he wasn't about to divulge. "Perhaps there is no other reason aside from venturing out on an adventure."

Chuckling, she tossed the leaf into the air and watched as it twirled to the ground. "But nothing exciting ever happens here. Believe me, I know."

"Surely there's an annual parade or two."

The path opened to a paddock with the village right below. "I'll give you that. There's the annual Saint George's Day parade."

When they reached the road, Fletcher attached the leads to the dogs' collars.

Georgiana ran her hand down Molly's coat. "It doesn't seem as if they need to be restrained."

"They don't, but I use the leads as a precaution." He offered his elbow and inclined his head toward town. "What is your favorite shop in Twickenham?"

"One can always find something of interest at the haberdashery. We also have a skilled jeweler in town. Some of his pieces are sold at Rundle and Bridge in London."

"I am duly impressed." The road took a bend as they started past a myriad of shop fronts on either side. "Where might we find this master jeweler?"

A flyer attached to a lamppost broadcasted "Richmond Fair" in enormous letters. Before Fletcher could read it, Georgiana stepped in front of the sign and pointed across the street. "Over there. Matthews Jewelers."

"Capital." He pulled the dogs to his right while they waited for a hay wagon to amble past. "All clear."

"One usually doesn't find London traffic in Twickenham."

In the blink of an eye, he kissed her cheek.

Skittering away, she gaped. "People can see us!"

He gestured up and down the deserted street. "As you said there's no traffic."

"But that didn't mean we should do—do—" She shook her finger at his mouth, positive she'd turned as red as beetroot. "That!"

His lips twisted as he gave a bow of his head. "Forgive me, but it is you who make me behave like a swain."

"You're impossible."

"I try my damnedest."

Such an audacious duke. Pursing her lips, she gave him another finger-shake just for good measure. "No more flirting."

With a tsk of his tongue, he fell into step beside her. "You're no fun."

While Fletcher tied the dogs' leads to a post, Georgiana spotted another flyer for the fair in the window of the shop. She stood in front of the tabloid while looking on. "Do Max and Molly need to be tied?"

"Not really, not especially near Colworth. Though one can never be too cautious when in an unfamiliar place." Fletcher straightened and gestured toward the door. "Shall we?"

"Thank you. I'm sure you'll be duly impressed with Mr. Matthews' work." A bell rang as she stepped inside while the duke held the door. "Are you looking for anything in particular?"

"Not especially."

"Hello, I'll not be but a moment," said a reedy voice from the back.

"Take your time. We'd like to do a bit of browsing." Fletcher tugged Georgiana over to a display. "Is there anything here that takes your fancy?"

"My fancy?" She almost laughed. "I'm afraid I have no use for jewels."

He moved nearer, so close the wool from his coat brushed her arm. The rough pad of his pointer finger traced a line from her earlobe to the base of her throat, making gooseflesh rise across her skin. "I disagree. With beauty as exquisite as yours, I see no better canvas for a work of art such as..." He pointed to an amethyst necklace and matching comb. "This lovely ensemble, for example."

She gave him a nudge with her elbow, mouthing, "no more flirting." Then Georgiana nodded politely when a maid came in with a feather duster.

Clearing her throat, she regarded the piece. "It is beautiful. But I'll have no place to wear it when I return to Thetford."

Fletcher bent over the display. "Ah yes, the cottage your mother refers to as a hovel."

"Mm hmm," she said, examining the amethyst set more closely. Each stone was set in a circle of gold filigree, and there was a pair of earrings to match.

"Or do you prefer the garnet?" he asked as the maid moved behind the display.

Georgiana's gaze slipped to a single necklace with a gold chain, the pendant was, indeed, a teardrop garnet, surrounded by tiny pearls. "It is nice. And a fair bit less ostentatious than the amethysts."

"Am I correct in assuming you prefer simple jewelry?"

Wearing garish paste made Georgiana feel garish and overdone. "Positively."

"Always the practical lady. What about the pearls?"

No, Georgiana wouldn't have been a woman if her breath didn't catch at the sight of the elegant strand of pearls. "Oh my."

Fletcher pointed above the necklace. "Of course no strand of pearls ought to be worn without a matching tiara and earrings."

She cupped a hand over her mouth and whispered, "Those could be worn with nothing at all."

Fletcher's black eyebrows shot up just as the maid dropped her duster and gasped.

Good Lord, Georgiana's face burned so hot, it must have turned as red as rubies. How could she have been so vulgar as to say such a thing...and in a shop of all places?

But the woman wasn't looking at Georgiana. Her enormous eyes regarded Evesham as if she were rapture-struck. "Your Grace," she said, looking left then right. "I know I shouldn't utter a thing, b-but I owe you my life."

Fletcher grew a tad pale.

"Do you know this young lady?" Georgiana asked.

The woman nodded at the duke. "He may not know who I am, but I certainly know of him. If it hadn't been for His Grace, I never would have come into a position working for gentleman such as Mr. Matthews."

Odd. Fletcher didn't know the maid, yet he was responsible for...what appeared to be...a relatively advantageous appointment.

Evesham rocked back on his heels. "I'm glad to hear you've prospered, miss."

"And my son, Jimmy. He's seven now and causes no trouble. Mr. Matthews employs him to fetch wood and run errands about town."

"Marvelous," Fletcher said amicably before returning his attention to the display.

Georgiana touched his elbow. "Exactly how did—"

"Please forgive me. I hope you've found something

that suits your fancy." Mr. Matthews stepped in from the back room. "Mrs. Whiteside is that you?"

She blinked and shifted her gaze to the jeweler. "Indeed. Please allow me to introduce His Grace, the Duke of Evesham."

"Duke?" Mr. Matthews bowed deeply. "It is an honor, Your Grace."

Georgiana couldn't help but puzzle, gape-mouthed while the maid picked up her duster and slipped out the rear door.

"Might we have a closer look at the pearls?" asked Fletcher.

She wrung her hands. "Oh, no. It isn't necessary."

"I rather think they'd complement the lady's complexion stunningly."

"Indeed," agreed Mr. Matthews as he removed a skeleton key and unlocked the back of the display. "Her mother is rather fond of sapphires."

"That is because Mama has blue eyes."

Evesham took the necklace from the jeweler and held it up. "If you would allow me."

She turned. "I suppose it won't hurt to try them on. Don't mind my bonnet."

The pearls were cool against her skin as she ran her fingers across them.

"Lovely choice, madam." Mr. Matthews held up a looking glass. "See for yourself."

No one in all of Christendom would have been able to withhold gasping at such beauty. She drew her fingers along the perfectly matched strand. "Oh my, you do such exquisite work, sir."

"Thank you."

The duke's reflection smiled at her in the glass. "Those were made for you."

No. I cannot allow him to shower me with expensive gifts. "They are magnificent, but they'll have to be saved for someone else."

"Namely me," said Evesham. "I'll take the pearls and the tiara and the matching earrings. Oh, and the sapphire brooch as well, please."

She reached back and unclasped the necklace herself. "But you cannot possibly..."

He gave her a look that insisted he would stand for no argument on the matter. "I can and I will. It hasn't escaped me that someone is having a birthday—Saturday, is it not?"

"Yes, but what will Mama think if you gave me pearls?"

"I should care what your mother thinks?" He winked—still flirting, blast him. "Besides, how can you be certain I am buying these for you?"

"Excuse me but a moment and I'll wrap these for you." Mr. Matthews relocked the display. "And Mrs. Whiteside, I can think of no one in the whole of England who would look more radiant wearing these."

Fletcher snorted.

"He had to say that," she hissed as the jeweler headed to the back room.

"No, he could have said Twickenham rather than England, and that wouldn't have been half the compliment he just paid."

"What about the maid?" Georgiana asked, changing the subject. If she wasn't going to win on one count, he owed her an explanation about the other. "What on earth did you do to help her, and if you were so helpful, why did you not recognize her?"

"'Tis a secret."

"Oh? And you expect me to step out of this shop with you? Either you tell me what happened with that young woman, or I'll demand that Mr. Matthews return the pearls to the display."

He growled, affecting an unconvincing scowl. "Damnation, you are difficult."

"Only when it is absolutely necessary."

"If I tell you, you mustn't utter a word to anyone. And that includes Miss Eleanor."

"Fine. Just tell me this mysterious secret of yours."

"If you must know." Tugging on his cuffs, he exhaled. "I am the financier of the Benevolent Home for Unwed Mothers."

"For—?"

"'Tis on the east end. I wouldn't expect you to have heard of it."

"And the maid—she's received the help from your home?"

"Evidently she has. Mrs. Whipple is the overseer who runs the day-to-day affairs. Most women who shelter there have no idea who their patron is. I was quite taken aback to have Mr. Matthews' maid recognize me. As such, she must have been very close to and trusted by the matron."

"Who would guess?" Georgiana leaned in, placed a hand on his arm, and whispered, "The most notorious rake in all of London is a philanthropist."

❧

"HAVE YOU BEEN AWAY FROM HARDWICK HALL FOR so long, you can no longer find your way back to the house?" Mama asked, clearly annoyed.

"It is my doing," said Fletcher as he escorted Georgiana into the gallery where the guests had assembled. "I'm afraid I led her astray. I've never been to Twickenham before and thought it might be diverting to do a bit of shopping."

"You've been shopping?" Mother asked, sounding aghast, though she did manage to flutter her eyelashes at the duke. "But what of the scavenger hunt? What was so pressing it couldn't wait until this afternoon?"

"Mama, it wouldn't have been fair to the other guests had I partaken in the scavenger hunt."

"You mean to say you didn't even attempt to play?"

"Once again, Your Ladyship, I must take the blame. Mrs. Whiteside did say you would be disappointed if we returned without playing the game. And as such, I was fortuitous to happen upon a Mr. Matthews." Crossing the floor, Fletcher pulled a small box from his waistcoat pocket. "He informed me that you're quite fond of sapphires."

"For me?" All angst fell away from her features, turning into an expression of genuine surprise. Mama accepted the gift and opened the box. "Oh, my, this is exquisite."

Beaming, Fletcher twisted the signet ring on his little finger. "Your daughter mentioned it would match your eyes."

Eleanor shouldered in beside Georgiana. "Saved by jewelry. He is suave, is he not?"

She had no idea. The man could charm a badger into submission. "I did not intend to play her silly game —after all, what would she have done to me if Evesham hadn't given her the brooch? Send me to my chamber without supper?"

Opening her fan and covering her mouth, Eleanor leaned nearer. "What else did the duke purchase in town?"

"Pearls, though it is a quandary who they are for."

"Now that's a tall tale if I ever heard one."

Georgiana jabbed her friend with her elbow. "Hush."

"Thank you, Your Grace. Your generosity exceeds all imaginings and I will forgive you this once." Mother's voice drew back Georgiana's attention. "And you, dear, must haste away and dress for luncheon while the rest of us wait."

"Oh, I wouldn't want the guests to wait because of me."

"Nonsense, it is your birthday week we are celebrating, of course we'll wait."

Eleanor grasped Georgiana by the elbow and started for the grand staircase. "I'll go with you."

"You are a dear."

"Oh no," Eleanor whispered. "I want to hear about your outing with the duke."

"I tried to discourage him."

"Evidently not enough."

Georgiana led the way through her chamber door. "I feel as if I've jumped off a cliff into an abyss with no bottom."

"'Tis that bad?"

After removing her pelisse, she turned for Eleanor to loosen her laces. "Worse."

"And he took you to a jeweler's shop?"

"Purely by accident."

"I'm not sure I believe anything Evesham does is an accident."

She drew in a deep breath as the walking gown fell to the floor. "But he'd never been to Twickenham before."

"All right, let's say your excursion was purely by chance. You said he purchased pearls."

"Yes," Georgiana said over her shoulder, hastening into the withdrawing room. Good Lord, she didn't want Eleanor to see her face.

But her friend followed closely behind. "What else?"

"Nothing." She picked up a pink gown the maid had set out for luncheon. No, she wasn't going to mention the tiara and earrings. "And he made no mention of who they were for."

"Of course not." Eleanor brushed her finger along ribbons hanging from a hook. "And your birthday isn't on Saturday, either. Did you know your mother is planning a grand ball in your honor?"

"A ball? I hate balls! And how am I going to attend a ball on Saturday evening, only to rise at the crack of dawn Sunday and rush off to Richmond Park?" Georgiana dropped to the ottoman. "This entire week is a disaster."

"I think it is rather diverting."

"Do not tell me you fancy Mr. Greg."

Eleanor joined her on the seat. "Not diverting for me, silly. You have won the attentions of a very eligible duke."

"You sound like Mama."

"You truly do not like him?"

"'Tis not a question of like. It is a question of compatibility. Every time I kiss him, I feel like a traitor."

"Why? Because you sprayed a bit of water on him at the start of the Season?"

"A bit? Two hundred gallons, mind you. And, if he knew who I really am, he would be livid to say the least."

"You do not believe him capable of forgiveness?"

"Not in these circumstances."

"So what will you do?"

Georgiana rose and stepped into her dinner gown, tugging it over her shoulders. "This morning, I tried to tell him we weren't compatible."

"And what did he say?"

As heat rushed to her face, she turned away. "He disagreed...quite emphatically."

Eleanor took charge of the laces. "Why am I not surprised."

"But what should I do?"

"Hmm." She tucked the strings inside the skirt. "Here are the facts as I see them: He likes you a great deal. You like him, as well, except for your steam pumper venture."

"Mind you." Georgiana swapped her walking boots for a pair of satin slippers. "That steam pumper has occupied most of my time over the past six years. I cannot just walk away."

"May I give you a tidbit of advice?"

"Why not? The well is certainly dry when it comes to relying on my own advice."

"Roll the dice and see where they lie. It is only Wednesday. Why not enjoy the party, attend the ball and on Sunday, you'll spirit away to the park, do your demonstration and find your financier...then you'll have choices."

A lump swelled in Georgiana's throat. "Right, choose Evesham or choose the steam pumper."

"Why should it be one or the other?"

"Because married women do not run steam-powered fire engine businesses—" Groaning, Georgiana moved to the toilette and examined her hair in the mirror. As usual, her bonnet had smushed the curls around her face.

"I think you're being awfully short sighted."

"What say you?" She used her finger to revive the ringlets. "My feet are planted firmly on the ground and you have stars in your eyes. Perhaps you have been a successful importer for too long. Believe me, my friend, if you found a husband, he would not stand idle and allow you to continue your business dealings—as soon as you say, 'I do', your property becomes his."

"You're right there, which is exactly why I haven't married."

"See?"

"Hmm," Eleanor mussed, pinning a pink bow at the top of Georgiana's chignon. "So, how do you want to proceed?"

"I must tell Evesham he must stop showering me with attention."

"I thought you already tried that."

Chapter Twenty

❧

It hadn't escaped Fletcher's notice when Georgiana led Eleanor to the north wing on her way to change for luncheon. She'd gone the same direction to dress for dinner. Now after eleven, he'd decided to take Max and Molly for a walk...to the north wing, of course. Moreover, after a sneeze during the Derby's parlor games, Mrs. Whiteside had given him a kerchief. Now the lacy piece of muslin needed to be returned.

Hardwick Hall was a sprawling five-story castle, with south, east, and, north wings. The man who'd been appointed his valet had told Fletcher the servant's quarters occupied the top floor, aside from those who had rooms in the basement. He had already deduced that there were no bedchambers on the first floor. Which meant, Georgiana's bedchamber must be somewhere on the second and third floors in the labyrinth of corridors in the north wing. But knocking on the wrong door would be a grand faux pas.

Setters weren't exactly bloodhounds, but Max and Molly had been exposed to scent training. On the second floor landing, he pulled the lady's kerchief from inside his doublet pocket. He gave each dog a good sniff. "Find her."

Max yipped, wagging his tail and spinning in a circle.

Molly started up the steps but stopped and returned to Fletcher's side.

He let them sniff the kerchief again. "This way?"

Max started off, his head down, his long black tail straight up, the fur waving like a flag. Molly fell in beside him as they swiftly walked over the carpeting, zigzagging through the maze of passageways.

Once Fletcher was good and lost, Molly rounded a corner, stopped at a door, and scratched.

"This one?" he asked, letting the pair smell the kerchief one last time.

Max jumped up, his toenails clicking on the timbers.

"Down," he whispered.

"A moment," Georgiana's voice came from inside...at least Fletcher prayed it was she.

He gave each dog a scratch.

"I thought you might come back—" said the woman, her mouth forming an O. "Ah..." She popped her head into the corridor and looked left, then right.

"Were you expecting someone?" he asked.

Georgiana tightened the sash on her dressing gown. "Not really. My maid left her monocle."

"Your maid uses a monocle?"

"She's older—Mama appointed her for the duration of the party. She has been with the family for a long while."

"I see."

"Your presence outside my bedchamber is quite unexpected." She kneeled and gave the dogs a scratch. "Hello, darlings, are you out for a stroll—but you're not out are you?"

Fletcher grinned. After the Green Park incident, it was nice to see the lady growing so fond of his dogs. "I thought I'd do some exploring. With the dogs. And it was Max whose toenails rapped on your door."

"Ah." She smoothed her hand along the dog's coat. "So you are the cause of this impropriety."

"The devil take it."

She straightened. "How convenient to blame the dog."

"Quite." Fletcher held up the conversation cards he'd carefully selected and removed from the deck below stairs. "There were quite a few cards from Question and Answer remaining unturned when your mother called an end to the night's festivities."

"Thank heavens for small mercies."

"You're not fond of conversation cards?"

"I abhor all parlor games and I'm not fond of my mother's attempts to play matchmaker."

"Is that what she's doing?"

Georgiana gave him a pointed look—one that said, "she is and you know it."

Molly yipped, dashed into the bedchamber and grabbed a realistic-looking toy squirrel from a trunk at the foot of the bed. The Setter shook her head, prancing in a circle.

As Max dashed after the deviant, Fletcher groaned and hastened inside, the door closing behind. "Bad dog. Drop it!"

Molly released the squirrel, her tail tucking between her legs. While Max immediately sat and affected an angelic expression.

Fletcher retrieved the sodden toy. "I'm sorry. They don't usually misbehave."

With her pincers, Georgiana returned the squirrel to its place among an assortment of porcelain-faced dolls. "Unless they're gaining access to a widow's bedchamber, yes?"

Glancing back to the closed door, Fletcher brushed a lock of hair from his brow. "My tactics at least seem a tad spontaneous. However, missing the turn to your bedchamber in a house where you grew up and bringing me a cup of chocolate, though much appreciated, I believe my tactics compare."

"I'll grant you that."

He retrieved the borrowed conversation cards from his pocket, admiring the décor, reminiscent of a teenaged girl—frilly pink bedcurtains with matching coverlet and pillows. "Shall we play?"

Georgiana gestured to the settee. "Where are the answer cards?"

"I didn't bother with those...I'd rather hear a candid response."

"Does that not spoil the mystery?"

He sat and crossed his ankles. "Parlor games are meant to introduce unmarried men to unwed women. I think we're well enough acquainted to move on to the next phase."

"Bedchamber games?" she asked, her eyes innocent as if she didn't realize she'd just made his pulse quicken.

Clearing his throat, Fletcher turned over the top card. "I do like your wit, madam."

Adorable, bow-shaped lips formed another O. "And you are a rake."

As he drew his hand away, his little finger brushed the delicate skin on her wrist. "So say the rumors."

Georgiana reached in and took the cards from him. "Then I shall shuffle the deck. Chances are you've already ordered them to suit your fancy."

"I wouldn't dare."

Nonetheless, she efficiently shuffled, cut and repeated, then put the deck on the table in front of them. "How shall we decide who goes first?"

"Let's make it easy. Ladies first, as customary."

"Very well." She took the top card and read. "*Are you true to your word?*"

"Always."

"Truly?"

"What use is there in saying something one doesn't mean?"

Frowning, Georgiana shifted as if his response made her uncomfortable. What had she expected? For him to tell her he was a consummate liar?

Fletcher took the next card. "*May I be bold in my requests?*"

"How bold?"

Fletcher's tongue slipped to the corner of his mouth as he slid his finger beneath the tie on her shift and slowly tugged. "This."

She brushed his hand aside and pulled the bow taut. "Do you aim to seduce me?"

"No more than you did to me last eve."

As she turned away, a blush along her neck betrayed her modesty.

"Did we not agree to take things one day at a time?" he asked.

"We did."

"So, I believe it is your turn to ask the next question."

Complying, the lady drew. "*Do you like to laugh?*"

"Dearly and often." That answer requiring no contemplation, Fletcher took the next card. "*Will your memory of me keep you warm for the winter?*"

Georgiana's gaze met his for a moment, then meandered downward as her tongue licked the corner of her mouth. "Hmm. But that would be predicting the future—time beyond this week."

Unable to resist the temptation, he brushed his lips across hers. "I'll wager there's a bit of fire thrumming through your blood now—just as it is for me."

"That, sir, is not one of the questions and I refrain from providing a reply." Taking in a deep breath, she selected the next card. "*How shall I express my affection?*"

Before he grinned, a warm glow spread throughout his body. "Oh, yes, I so wanted you to pick that one."

He took his time raking his gaze from her face, to her slender neck, to the cinched robe that concealed the delectable treasure beneath. His entire body smoldered as he looked into her soulful brown eyes. He slipped the card from her fingers and let it sail to the floor. "You may express your affection in any way you desire as long as you do it right here, right now."

Before Georgiana blinked, a look of pure seduction crossed her features—slightly parted lips, an intake of breath that caused her chest to heave, and the half-cast fluttering of lashes made her look more tempting than warm chocolate made with fresh cream. But then she looked to her clasped hands. "You must swear you'll never tell a soul," she whispered so softly, Fletcher almost asked the lady to repeat herself.

Almost.

Using the crook of his finger, he lifted her chin. "Did we not agree that whatever happens this week will remain a secret forever?"

"Yes," the word sounded breathless as a bit of amusement returned to her gaze.

Fletcher sat back and spread his knees, resting his hands at his sides—a very vulnerable position for anyone. Yet for a man, such posture expressed confidence and, he hoped, surrender.

Delicate fingers traced up his arm and across his shoulder until she untied his neckcloth with the skill of an efficient valet. Georgiana's eyes grew dark while she slowly pulled the fine muslin away from his throat. "In order to properly express my affection, I believe it is necessary to remove a few garments."

Her teeth scraped over her bottom lip. "I think I like where this is leading."

"I believe you will." When he reached for the sash tying her robe, she brushed his fingers away. "I am expressing affection. Not you."

He moved his hands back to the position of surrender. "As you wish."

She slid a thigh over his lap and straddled him, focusing on his shirt's buttons. "You see, I've never done this before."

Fletcher puzzled. She was a widow and hadn't appeared as a virgin in his bedchamber last eve. "What haven't you done, exactly?"

"I've never...ah...taken charge before."

"Never seduced a man?" The mere thought made him lengthen. God's blood, it took immeasurable self-control not to rip the robe from her shoulders, tear open her shift, and take her on the settee.

"Mm hmm." Nibbling at his neck, she rocked her hips, the softness between her legs slid along his erection.

Fletcher's mind numbed at the friction, but it wasn't enough. Too many layers of clothing were involved, especially the thick, woolen robe wrapped around her body.

She smelled like lavender, honey, and delicious woman. And her tongue...mercy, every sweep of her tongue melted on his skin, stirring the fire within to a blazing furnace. Her hips moved to the side while she spread his shirt open, her mouth continuing on its torturous conquest.

Fletcher lay his head back and moaned. "Are you sure you haven't done this before?"

"Do you not know?" She gave him a knowing grin while flicking the buttons of his falls. "A wife's duty is to lie on her back and endure."

"You believe that?"

"'Tis what Mama told me on my wedding night."

"I see." *What she has been missing all these years.*

Georgiana released the next set of buttons. "But I've always wanted to express affection like this."

"Like what?" he asked, his voice climbing as she slid his cock out from beneath his smalls.

"I've heard the gossip in the servant's quarters. You cannot tell me a man can pleasure a woman with his mouth, yet a woman is unable to reply in kind."

"Many men take their gratification by such means, but not by a gentlewoman." He groaned as she licked him.

"Am I lowering myself by kissing you here?" She slid him into her mouth.

Surrounded by moist warmth, his voice caught between a sigh and a moan. Fletcher's bum muscles clenched as she sucked him. "You are the goddess divine."

Her chuckle rumbled through him, making a surge pulse from the base of his cock all the way to the tip. Fletcher clenched his teeth, willing himself to maintain control.

Her fingers slid up his shaft. "Am I gripping too tightly?"

"Perfect," he growled while lightning flickered at the base of his spine. He clutched her hair while he thrust inside the tight little mouth, the gentle teeth barely stroking him.

Then she swirled her tongue around the tip of his cock. "You are more sensitive here, are you not?"

"Bloody hell, you slay me, woman."

Her sultry chuckle washed over him before she glanced up. "I think I like taking control."

"If you keep milking me with your mouth, you'll bring me undone."

"Is that not the objective?"

"Not until you've been pleasured."

"Why?"

He gathered her into his arms and stood. "Because I aim to prove exactly how much a woman can enjoy lovemaking—not merely endure it."

As he strode across the floor, she rested her head against his shoulder. "Both our bodies bare?"

A bit of seed leaked from the tip of his cock. By the time he reached the bed, his breeches were hanging down around his thighs. It didn't take long to slip out of his clothes or remove her robe and chemise as well.

Once in bed, Georgiana wasn't finished taking charge. She ran her fingers through the hair on his chest, thrusting her mons up against his cock. "You're so..."

"Yes?"

"Virile."

As he lowered his lips to hers, her tongue surged inside his mouth with the same fervor from the settee. Sliding her hands to his shoulders, she rolled him to the mattress, then straddled him. God she was gorgeous. Chestnut locks hung in waves down to her waist, partially covering one eye. Full breasts teased him, but when he cupped one, she shook her head.

"Can I make love to you on top?" she asked.

"Yes." He moved his fingers to her waist. "Have you never been?"

"I've only done it on my back."

Had he died and gone to heaven? "And you'd like to...try new things?"

A flicker of a challenge reflected in her brilliant eyes. "Is that not what we're doing?"

He spread his arms wide. "Your wish is my command, madam."

❦

ENCOURAGED, GEORGIANA MOVED DOWN FLETCHER'S body until she held his manhood in front of her. Of course, she had a fair idea of how to proceed. She liked being in control, yet no matter what he said, Fletcher's pleasuring was more important to Georgiana than her own. Should she ask him, or should she just act?

She ran her fingers up his shaft. A ripple of heat exploded inside her as she watched his face contort with pleasure while he arched and moaned.

"Lower yourself onto me," he growled.

It wasn't a demand, but a request and as he cupped her bottom and guided her upward, she grasped his shoulders and opened for him, swirling her hips until he crowned her entrance. Watching intently, she wanted to draw out the moment and eased downward inch by ravenous inch.

Fletcher's eyes grew dark, his lips parting with the laboring of his breath but his hands remained gently gripping her—as if there to support her if she tired. He seemed to fully understand her desire to explore.

The black curvature of his eyelashes lowered while his eyebrows drew together. A sheen of perspiration gave his face and chest a steamy glow like that of a bronze warrior. He bared his teeth and mumbled a curse—something foreign—something that sounded very dirty.

"What?" she asked.

"I said you were damned beautiful."

Georgiana swirled her hips as she slid all the way down to his root. "Damned?"

He thrust so deep inside her, she gasped. "Kiss me, oh goddess divine."

She leaned forward, her hair covering them in a cocoon of passion. Oh, how stirring to have all that sinewy power beneath her, his robust hips cradled between her thighs.

Fletcher's eyes filled with a challenge while he rocked beneath her.

Georgiana took his cue, bracing her hands and rising and lowering in tandem with his wicked, powerful strokes. As she lay atop his massive chest, he continued to be patient, allowing her to experiment. His heart hammered a fierce rhythm against her breast. Panting, she increased the tempo while spasms of heat rippled inside her. As she pushed up, his mouth caught the tips of her breasts.

He smiled up from the tangle of her hair. "You enjoy tormenting me."

"Yes," she said, barely able to speak.

The hint of a grin vanished as he grasped her buttocks, encouraging her to plunge deeper. Faster—filling herself with him. He answered her demand, stroke for stroke, thrust for thrust. She loved the sight of his half-lidded expression, lost in passion, his head tilted back, his throat exposed.

A storm of searing arousal swept through her. Her thighs shuddered as they clamped around him. Fletcher continued to match her pace, his movements becoming jerky and forceful. And as she watched him, a cry caught in her throat as her climax erupted like a starburst.

"My God," Fletcher boomed as he immediately withdrew and spilled on his stomach.

Trying to catch her breath, Georgiana looked down at the pool of his seed and felt a pang of remorse. But then, this wasn't everlasting love. This was a liaison—something she needed clear to her soul—something secret—something beautiful, yet oh so very taboo.

She rolled off the bed, wrapped herself in her robe and collected a cloth from the washstand. As she caught sight of her reflection in the mirror, she vowed to enjoy every moment alone with Fletcher Markham, then lock it away in her heart for the rest of her days.

Chapter Twenty-One

❧

"Y ou're looking well this morning, madam," said the groom, Tom, as he helped Georgiana ascend the mounting block beside her beloved gelding, Herman. The horse had been a present when she was a young girl, and she adored him.

She hitched her leg over the upper pommel of the sidesaddle and slid her seat into place. "Thank you." After gathering the reins, she combed her fingers through the horse's sorrel mane. "I've missed this fellow ever so."

Tom held up her crop. "I think he's happy to see you as well."

She took it and gave the horse a gentle tap. "Are you, Herman?" He nickered and moved away from the block while the sound of barking dogs approached. "The hounds sound eager."

"Aye," Tom agreed. "The master of the foxhounds said the dogs have known they're about to embark on a hunt for two days now."

"Truly? I wonder what makes them so perceptive."

"I think it is on account of the baron returning from London. He paid the kennel a visit the day he arrived."

"Ah, I should have realized."

The shadow of her father mounted on a fine thoroughbred appeared in the doorway of the stables. "Are you ready, Georgiana? Everyone's waiting."

She grinned at the lad. "Thanks, Tom. I mustn't be the cause of any delay."

Contrary to what her father had said, the hunting party was far from ready to ride. Once outside, Georgiana backed her horse away from the yelping, jumping dogs, their leads in a complete tangle. "Where is Rasputin?"

"In the house, yowling," said Papa. "His training isn't complete by half. Besides, I bought him for birds."

"Such a shame. He must feel awfully dejected."

"A little dejection is good for the young pup."

"Are you pairing up with Evesham?" asked Eleanor, reining her horse to a stop.

Georgiana searched for the duke's broad-shouldered stature among the guests. "I'm not..." Fletcher and his dogs came racing in from the paddock, his top hat managing to remain securely on his head while his black coattails flapped behind. The man expertly handled an enormous bay horse, looking like he'd been born with his feet in a pair of stirrups.

"A picture speaks a thousand words," said Eleanor.

Georgiana sighed. "He is magnificent, is he not?"

"I wasn't referring to the duke. The expression on your face answered every question I could possibly have."

"Oh dear." Cringing, Georgiana regarded her friend. "Is it that obvious?"

Eleanor tugged up her gloves. "'Tis lovely to see you glow with happiness."

"Yes, well, it cannot and will not last beyond Saturday's ball."

Before the lady answered back, Evesham reined his horse to a halt beside them. "It looks as if we're about ready to start."

"Once the master of the foxhounds brings the dogs

under control." Georgiana looked to Max and Molly who obediently stood beside the bay horse with their tongues lolling to the side. "Are you bringing your Setters along?"

"Of course." Fletcher smiled, his eyes shining like obsidian in the sunlight. "They live for the hunt."

She leaned toward him and snorted. "Rasputin has been banished to the house."

"Is that the woeful noise I heard coming from the manse?" Evesham's saddle creaked as he turned to look back. "Not to worry, he'll be leading the pack in a year or two."

Ahead, the foxhounds had been brought under control and the master circled his whistle above his head.

Papa trotted his horse to the forefront. "Let the hunt begin!"

Georgiana gave Herman a tap with her crop. "Walk on."

"Walk?" asked Evesham, leaning forward. "In my experience, you do not seem like the type of woman who'd be satisfied with idleness during a fox hunt."

Eleanor leered out of the corner of her eye, giving a barely-muffled chuckle.

"Sh," Georgiana silenced the duke in a heated whisper, positive she'd just turned as crimson as her riding habit. If he kept talking like that, they'd all think she'd turned into a hellion.

He sat easy in his saddle, regarding her. "I said nothing remotely incriminating."

She used her heel and crop to request a canter. "I thought you were keen for the shooting."

His horse quickly closed the gap. "And what are you keen for, madam?"

"To enjoy the morning's ride. The wind in my face and the thrill of jumping the thicket." Running beside them, Molly barked. "Can the Setters keep pace?"

"Are you jesting?" He patted the musket holstered at the horse's flank. "This is what I brought them for."

She slapped her crop and leaned forward together with her hands. "Then I'll race you to the bottom of the gully!"

"You're on."

Fletcher took the lead, but Georgiana held her own. Good heavens, she'd missed riding. In Thetford, she usually drove a curricle and pony because nearly every time she left the cottage she ventured out to buy supplies.

They were neck and neck at the bottom of the ravine, but Max and Molly had run ahead, leading them away from the hunting party. It didn't matter. Georgiana cared less about chasing a fox. She wanted to ride for hours with the wind in her face and her mind consumed with the reins, and the path, and keeping her seat while coaxing old Herman to run faster than Evesham's beautiful stepper.

"This way," he called, pointing his crop toward the dogs. "They're on a scent."

"But the foxhounds are heading north."

"Who gives a rat's arse?"

She laughed. "If you don't, I most certainly do not."

The dogs leaped over a hedgerow dividing the paddocks as if they'd done it many times before. Fletcher glanced her way. "Would you prefer to ride around?"

"Are you buffle-headed?" She urged Herman faster. "The daughter of the Baron of Derby does not ride around."

"Very well then, ladies first."

Georgiana eyed the hedge and moved her hands low against her gelding's neck. "Are you ready, old boy?"

Seeming to understand, the horse grunted and picked up speed.

As the jump approached, her heartbeat fell into time with Herman's gait. She'd made this jump a hundred times when she was a girl and riding now came as easily as an afternoon stroll. As they approached, Georgiana focused.

Three, two, one.

As the horse leaped, she leaned out over his withers. The thicket passed beneath them in a blur, but she kept her eyes up, looking to the other side.

Until her heart flew to her throat.

Herman's front hoof struck, making him veer to the right. Georgiana countered, leaning further out over his left flank, but the gelding came down askew. Gripping his mane along with the reins, she tried to hold on, but the horse's jerky momentum rendered her helpless. Flung through the air, she shrieked, every muscle in her body tightening as she hurled toward the muddy ground.

Hitting with a thud, her mouth filled with dirt as cold muck enveloped her.

"Georgiana!"

Before she oriented herself, Fletcher already had her in his arms, pulling her out of the mire. "Are you hurt?"

She winced, cradling her arm against her chest. "Only my wrist...I think."

He carried her beneath a tree and sat, steadying her on his lap. "That old gelding is a bit long in the tooth to be taking jumps."

Georgiana's heart squeezed as she looked for her beloved horse. "But I've had him since I was nine years of age." Thank heaven's he'd started grazing only paces away.

"And how long has it been since you've ridden him that hard?"

She groaned. "Six years, mayhap more."

"See what I mean? I doubt your father would have allowed a nine-year-old child on a young horse. I'll wager he's five and twenty if a day. 'Tis a wonder he even tried to make the jump. Now let's have a look at you." Fletcher carefully pulled her arm. "This wrist?"

She hissed. "That hurts."

He pushed up her sleeve and made a tsking sound. "'Tis already swollen."

She dared to look. "Oh, bother."

"Can you move your hand?"

Gritting her teeth, she managed to clench her fingers in a semblance of a fist. "That's a good sign."

"Perhaps, but for you the day's hunt has come to an end." He kissed her forehead and moved her off his lap. "I'll fetch my horse—you can ride with me. I need to take you back to the house straightaway."

"But what about Herman?"

"He seems happy enough. I'll send the groom back to tend him."

"Thank you."

Fletcher returned with his mount, mud splattered across his white riding breeches and dripping from his coat.

"Oh, dear. I've ruined your clothes." Georgiana glanced at her riding habit as she stood. The laundress would never be able to clean it. "And mine as well."

"Clothes are replaceable. Wrists are not." He beckoned her. "I'll lift you."

"Are you jesting? Your horse must be seventeen hands. If you try to hoist me up that high, we'll both be hobbling back to Hardwick Hall with injuries."

"You weigh but a trifle, now come."

He tugged her good wrist, swept her off her feet, and set her across the big thoroughbred's withers. Then he stood back and grinned, opening his arms wide. "As you see, I am perfectly fit."

Yes, she'd seen exactly how fit the duke was. How on earth did he manage it? What were his flaws, aside from being somewhat notorious among polite society? But then, he was single and a duke. The two combined was like possessing a carte blanche granting him permission to act something of a scoundrel. Though she couldn't completely discount his reputation. Dare she forget at Almacks he'd practically tried to seduce her before he'd even asked her name.

⁂

THE BUTLER OPENED THE DOOR AS FLETCHER ARRIVED on the portico with Georgiana in his arms. "Dobbs, tell Lady Derby her daughter has fallen from a horse and injured her wrist. And send someone for the physician straightaway."

"Yes, Your Grace." Dobbs stood aside to let them pass. "Shall I have a footman carry Mrs. Whiteside?"

Georgiana groaned. "I am perfectly able to walk."

"Not until you've been seen." Fletcher continued to the stairs. "Send up some sherry as well. That will take the edge off her pain."

Though Georgiana complained, Fletcher wasn't about to set her down or let her walk or do anything until he was absolutely certain she wasn't suffering more than she let on. He'd watched in horror as the woman he adored was mercilessly thrown from that old gelding. And thank heavens she'd landed in the soft mud, else she might have broken every bone in her body, including her neck.

Only after he entered her bedchamber did he set her down—on a chair. "We must remove your muddy garments."

"We?" she asked. "I do believe you sent for my mother."

The lady's maid popped in. "Do you need assistance, mistress?"

"Yes," said Georgiana, holding up her finger and giving him a look of defiance.

Fletcher pursed his lips. Of course he shouldn't be

the one to remove her clothing, no matter how responsible he felt. But he wasn't about to leave. He beckoned the maid inside. "Please remove Mrs. Whitesides' soiled garments. I shall turn my back until she is dry and cinched tightly in her dressing gown."

The young woman looked to Georgiana. "What happened?"

"Herman missed a jump and I was thrown."

"Heavens, 'tis amazing you didn't crack open your skull."

"Yes, I have a quagmire of mud to thank for that."

Fletcher took off his dirty jacket and draped it over the fire screen before he faced the hearth, clasping his hands behind his back. "Please ensure you exercise utmost care. Until Mrs. Whiteside is seen by the doctor, we cannot be too cautious."

"Yes, Your Grace."

He endured the rustling of clothing to the tune of Georgiana's restrained grunts. She was in more pain than she was letting on, dammit. And she was just the type who would suffer in silence. Why hadn't he been the one to take the fall? She was too fragile, too delicate. Good Lord, what if she'd landed on her head?

His heart twisted into a hundred knots. He'd never be able to look himself in the mirror again. For the first time in his life, he'd met a woman who wasn't only alluring, she was smart and interesting. And she knew something about engineering.

"All done," said the maid.

Fletcher turned. "Let me carry you to the bed."

"No, thank you."

"But you cannot remain in the chair. Not when the doctor is on his way."

"I agree," said Lady Derby from the doorway.

Georgiana groaned once more and stood. "Then I shall walk to the bed myself."

Her Ladyship hastened inside. "Please, dearest, let Evesham help you."

He grasped Georgiana by her good arm. "I agree."

"'Tis just an injured wrist. There's no need for so much fuss."

Lady Derby wrung her hands. "But Dobbs said you were thrown."

The maid drew down the bedclothes.

"She was," said Fletcher. "Quite violently. Where is the sherry I ordered?"

The maid curtsied. "I'll go check on it."

"Thank you," said Lady Derby, moving to the bedside and putting her hand against Georgiana's forehead. "Are you fevered at all?"

"Of course not."

"What a relief. Now let me see your wrist."

She pulled her arm from beneath the linens. "It looks like I swallowed a tennis ball and the silly thing went straight down my arm."

"Oh, that does look rather bad," said the baroness. "What if this had happened whilst you were alone in Thetford?"

"I promise you, I do not go on fox hunts and jump horses in Thetford."

"I should say not. I'll have Cook send up two slices of flan." Lady Derby patted Fletcher's arm and gave him a once-over. "Goodness, Evesham, you look as if you've been thrown as well."

"Just a tad muddied from assisting Mrs. Whiteside, forgive my shirtsleeves." He gestured to his coat. "My jacket bore the brunt of it."

"I am grateful you were there to help her. My daughter believes she is ever so independent, but we all need each other now and again. It isn't natural to live alone."

Georgiana rolled her eyes to the bedcurtains. "We are not having this conversation, Mama."

Fletcher took Lady Derby's hand and escorted her toward the door, giving a wink for good measure. "A slice of flan sounds absolutely delicious. I would be ever so grateful if you would see that someone brings them up."

"Yes, of course. Straightaway."

"Thank you, my lady."

When he turned, Georgiana was giving him a pointed look. "I have a sore wrist. I'll not be treated like an invalid. I'm sure the swelling will go down by tomorrow morning, and I'll be perfectly fine."

He sauntered toward her. "You have experience with wrists swollen to the size of my fist?"

"Not exactly, but this is far from the first time I've sustained an injury."

"I've never seen a woman so fiercely averse to being pampered."

"Well, I do not have time for mollycoddling."

"Whyever not? Because you must return to London and resume your duties accompanying your mother to all the engaging events of the Season?"

She pursed her lips and looked away.

Fletcher's gut squeezed, and not in a pleasurable way. "What else is so pressing you cannot enjoy a bit of attention for a sennight or two?"

"Nothing." She released a heavy sigh. "Perhaps Mama was right."

As a dozen questions filled his head, Lady Derby returned with the physician. He was a wizened man with kind eyes and mentioned he'd known Georgiana since she was a babe. Fletcher stood, looking over the man's shoulder while he methodically asked questions and examined the lady's wrist, then had the wherewithal to have her move her feet and knees and turn her head this way and that before he pronounced that she had a badly sprained wrist and must wear a sling for at least a fortnight—longer if the pain didn't subside.

Once he took his leave, Georgiana swiveled her feet over the edge of the bed. "Well that's that. I cannot attend the ball."

Letting Lady Derby take the lead on the topic, Fletcher poured the sherry which had arrived during the examination along with the flan.

"You are not serious. You are the guest of honor!" Her Ladyship drew her wrist to her forehead as if she were about to swoon. "Clearly you are averse to being bedridden. You cannot even manage to stay put for a single afternoon."

"I refuse to attend a ball wearing a sling."

Fletcher gave the baroness a glass, a bit overfull for good measure. "Perhaps we could fashion something out of lace—or something to match your gown."

Lady Derby took a generous sip. "Oh, I do like that idea. And we can all talk about the hunt and how His Grace rode to the rescue."

Georgiana groaned. "Right, and how incredibly clumsy I am."

Fletcher poured for her. "The fall had nothing to do with you and everything to do with a horse that was too old to be jumping hedges."

The baroness completely emptied her glass. "See? There's plenty of riveting conversation just between the three of us."

"I shall wear gloves—if I can find a pair to fit over this lump. And no sling, otherwise the guest of honor will be elsewhere. And mark me, I will not be dancing."

Fletcher refilled Lady Derby's sherry. "Has your daughter always been this difficult?"

"Always. She's been stubborn since she was in the womb."

"Thank you, Mama. I'm sure His Grace wants to hear stories from your confinement."

He raised his glass. "I'd love to."

"Perhaps another time." Lady Derby sipped as she

backed to the door. "If you don't mind excusing me, I must go check to see if the hunting party has returned. We've quite an afternoon planned."

"More games?" asked Georgiana.

"What would a house party be without games?"

Once they were alone, Fletcher offered his elbow. "Will you join me on the settee for a bite of flan and a glass of sherry?"

"Wine sounds marvelous."

"Then let us drink to your swift recovery."

"You know, you do not need to remain here and keep me company."

"Oh, but I do." He plucked one of her curls and drew it to his nose. Mm, he loved her scent. "You're the reason I'm here."

She used her left hand to take a bite of flan, then licked a morsel from the corner of her mouth. "Remember our agreement. Our *liaison* is for the duration of the week only."

"I see...so you can return to your life as a hermit in what your mother calls a hovel?"

"Mm hmm." She kissed him, her lips sweet. "And you can tend to your far greater responsibilities to king and country."

Not about to let her ease away, Fletcher slipped his fingers behind her neck and plunged in for a proper taste. Sighing, she kissed him with equal fervor, making him chuckle. "So, my self-proclaimed wallflower, you will fade off into the sunset and hide from the world as if this..." Ever so lightly, he brushed his lips over hers. "Never happened?"

Chapter Twenty-Two

❧

"This reminds me of our first ball," said Georgiana from her perch on the settee as she watched Eleanor lightly dab a hint of rouge with her ring finger. "Do you remember?"

"How can I forget? After my first attempt with the rouge pot, I looked as if I had scarlet fever."

"The perils of the forbidden use of beauty treatments on unsuspecting debutantes."

"Of course, anything taboo was all the more alluring. At least the rouge disaster was a lesson quickly learned." Eleanor turned from the mirror. "Are you still planning to go to Richmond Park on the morrow?"

Georgiana smoothed her hand over her wrist. The swelling had gone down a tad, but it still looked as if she was hiding a tennis ball in her glove, not to mention it hurt like the devil. "Absolutely. I'd go even if the fall had broken my leg."

"But how will you manage?"

"I've asked Tom, the groomsman to have a curricle hitched first thing in the morning. He'll take charge of the ribbons."

"Then you have it all planned?"

"I do."

"And Evesham still knows nothing?"

She sighed, but the week had come to an end and so had her affair with the handsome duke, no matter how much her heart ached. "Correct."

"'Tis a pity."

"Why?"

"He's so very fond of you. And you pair enjoy each other's company ever so. Have you given any consideration as to what it would be like to marry him?"

"Marriage?" Georgiana's stomach fluttered, but she drew her fists against her midriff to stanch it. "And walk away from Daniel's dreams?"

"I don't see why you can't just hold forth and tell Evesham about your pumper. I think you're not giving him the benefit of the doubt, my dearest."

The queasiness in her stomach dropped like a lead weight. "Doing so would ruin everything."

Georgiana rose and moved to the window. A light mist was falling, yet the guests would be arriving soon. What if she did tell Fletcher about the pumper? Mayhap she ought to start by showing him the drawings —after all, he'd studied Watt. Once he understood exactly the capabilities of the machine, she could then tell him the story of how disastrous her first demonstration was...and why.

But now wasn't the right time to bare her soul. Perhaps after they returned to London, he might call. If she served tea in the parlor and created an amiable atmosphere, she ought to feel comfortable enough to make such a confession. That would be far preferable to taking such a risk on her birthday—during a ball where she was the guest of honor. Besides, Mama had gone to so much trouble.

Georgiana spotted a carriage approaching and then another.

What if Fletcher didn't storm out when she revealed the truth? What if he laughed and said he knew it was her all along? What if he did propose marriage?

Gooseflesh rose across her skin.

She'd never considered what it might be like to be a duchess. Such a station would be akin to becoming her mother. Georgiana would be called upon to host balls and soirees, to be a benefactor of countless charities... though she wouldn't mind that part. But in no way would she ever be permitted to act the wallflower at any social event. Egad, how on earth could she act the part of social butterfly? The mere thought made her swoon.

A knock came at the door. "May I have a word, Mrs. Whiteside?" Fletcher's deep voice resounded from the corridor.

Eleanor headed across the floor. "I'll see you in the reception line."

"Ah, you look lovely this evening," Fletcher said as the door opened.

Sidling into the corridor, Eleanor gestured across the chamber. "Not as lovely as the guest of honor."*-

Smiling, Georgiana held out her hands. "I do believe if there were a contest for the loveliest, we'd all receive top marks."

Fletcher's gaze met hers with a crackle of energy, so potent, Georgiana scarcely heard the door close. "Must you grow more radiant every time I lay eyes on you?"

A low chuckle rumbled from his throat. "The question is, must *you*?" Evesham looked the part of duke from his wildly stylish hair to the tips of his polished shoes. His neckcloth was pristine, and he wore a black velvet tailcoat over an ivory satin waistcoat. Ivory knee breeches with white stockings, ribbon ties to match his doublet. Good Lord, the man looked as if he might be ready to sit for a portrait.

Stepping before her, he gently raised her injured hand. "And how is your wrist?"

"Since midday?"

He bowed and kissed her hand, then examined her arm. "I do believe none of the guests will notice."

She drew her hand away. "Hopefully no one will be looking at my wrist."

"And what about the reception line?"

"The gentlemen will simply have to kiss my left."

"I'd be happy if they left all the kissing to me." Giving a sly grin, he pulled a box tied with a silk bow from inside his coat. "Happy birthday, love."

Georgiana reached out her hand but didn't quite touch it. Love? The endearment made her knees go weak. But it hadn't been a declaration of undying love, it had just been used in passing. And thank heavens, because the fair was tomorrow. Then everything would change.

And he'd ride off into the sunset, or whatever it was that dukes did after a week of bliss.

She looked up, dozens of warring emotions swirling through her. "You know you shouldn't have."

He pushed the box into her palm. "You have given me a respite I shall never forget. For that, a bit of jewelry seems insufficient."

"Thank you." Why not accept it? He wanted to give her a gift, and Georgiana doubted she'd ever experience another house party, let alone an affair with a man like Fletcher Markham.

She pulled the ribbon, opened the gift, and ran her finger around the exquisite pearls. "They are almost too beautiful to wear."

"Nonsense." Slowly, he drew the necklace from the box and coaxed her to turn around. "And they'll look ideal with your pink satin. Hmm, you even have pearls embroidered into the trim."

Watching in the mirror, Georgiana studied Fletcher's face as he worked—contemplative, gentle, yet angular with a powerful jaw. "You are far too kind to be a scoundrel."

"I believe you are the only person in Britain who feels that way."

"Oh?" She donned the earrings. "What about the maid at the jewelry shop? To her, you are a hero."

"She doesn't count."

"I think she does. And how could you say such a thing? You endured poverty and hardship before you came into your fortune." Georgiana looked at his reflection and paused for a moment. "Or have you forgotten?"

Fletcher reached around and pinned the crown in front of her chignon. "No. Admittedly, I will never forget."

"Then the maid's opinion counts, yes?"

"Yes." As he tugged her into his arms and kissed her, all trepidation of the future melted. "I like your pragmatic ideals. They ground me."

She slid her hands around his waist while delightful kisses wandered along her jaw and down to her neck.

"Are you certain you will not dance this evening?" he asked in a low growl, making her head swim.

"Absolutely not. The only positive thing about the fall is it gave me an excuse to..."

"Mingle with the guests?"

"I suppose Mama will not allow me to retire to the ladies withdrawing room to read."

Georgiana's reply was consumed by a hungry swipe of her lover's tongue.

FOR THE FIRST TIME IN HIS LIFE, FLETCHER DIDN'T mind standing in a receiving queue, though Lady Derby was emphatic about enforcing the aristocratic pecking order. He was introduced first, then Ravenscar and his mother, then the hosts, followed by Georgiana and Miss Eleanor, Mr. Peters, his daughter, and finally the vicar's son, Mr. Greg. A number of guests held up the line when stopping to talk to Mrs. Whiteside, which wasn't unusual considering the ball was in her honor. Though on the other hand, she was a self-professed recluse. How could she possibly know them all?

With every passing day, she wove her tendrils around his heart. In truth, Georgiana was everything he'd ever wanted in a woman—pleasing to the eye, passionate, a sharp mind, yet she didn't take herself too seriously.

And once the guests had all been announced, the object of his affection approached, leading Miss Eleanor by the arm. "Have you a partner for the grand march?"

He waggled his eyebrows. "I thought you might do me the honor."

"I was serious, no dancing for me, not even the march." Georgiana looked to her friend. "Though Miss Eleanor hasn't had an opportunity to have her dance card signed and Mr. Greg is stepping out with Miss Peters."

"Oh, bother." Eleanor fluttered her fan as if she hadn't a care. "I do not need to parade around the ballroom in all my finery. This is your day, Georgiana."

"Yes, and that's why I want to see two of my dearest friends enjoy themselves."

Friends? Fletcher looked to the slender neck he'd just adorned with kisses and pearls. Though he ought to be appreciative of the fact that the lady had referred to him as a dear friend and not just a friend. Heaving a sigh, he offered his elbow. "Madam, I believe we've received our marching orders."

"How apropos." Miss Eleanor smiled at him as he led her to the dance floor. "She likes you."

Such words bolstered his bruised ego. "I'm glad of it."

"Just give her time."

"I'm not certain time is what Mrs. Whiteside needs."

The march began. Fletcher rarely arrived at a ball early enough to partake in the grand march. Which always suited him. Parading around a ballroom like a peacock made him uncomfortable. And yes, everyone was watching. After all, the march was intended for the busybodies to show off their regalia and to gawk without being obvious.

In truth, strutting with Miss Eleanor on his arm made him feel like a pompous boor. Just like two-thirds of the other dandies in their expertly tailored velvet tailcoats.

"Are you heading back to London on the morrow?" asked the lady.

Fletcher hadn't thought much past this evening, but this was the grand finale of Lady Derby's house party. He nodded. "I'll need to take Max and Molly back to Colworth first."

"And then return to court and your duties in the House of Lords?"

"Do not remind me."

Miss Eleanor gracefully swept around the corner. That she was a spinster posed a bit of a quandary. "I think this is the best attended private ball I've ever been to."

"Is it?"

"You do not?"

"I suppose it is—especially since Twickenham is relatively close to London and the turnpike runs nearby."

"And everyone knows the baroness is a fabulous hostess."

"She is—quite amiable as well." Fletcher raised Eleanor's hand to make a bridge for the dancers approaching from the opposite direction to walk beneath. "I wonder why Mrs. Whiteside is so different."

"Oh, I think Georgiana is one of the most good-natured people I know."

"I didn't mean to infer she isn't but, in everything else, she is quite the opposite of her mother."

"I suppose you're right, though if I had to live with one of them, I'd choose the daughter without hesitation."

Fletcher smiled. "Can you imagine being married to Lady Derby? A man would never have a moment's rest."

"I don't know. Lord Derby manages to maintain his sanity quite well."

"That's because he spends a great deal of time at the gentlemen's club, fobbing off his escort duties to his daughter."

Together, they grasped hands and began their passage through the tunnel. "This Season. Mind you," Eleanor replied. "He isn't as scarce when Georgiana is in Thetford."

If the music hadn't stopped, Fletcher would have pursued that topic a bit further. Why was Georgiana so attached to a cottage where she had no family support? Though he'd asked, she hadn't volunteered anything of substance. And though she professed that she was not yet ready to remarry, she lacked no enthusiasm in the bedchamber. In fact, her behavior between the linens was quite extraordinary for a bluestocking...not that Fletcher had anything with which to compare. His past partners had all been rather outgoing—like Signora Morella.

After a gentleman stopped to ask Miss Eleanor to dance, Fletcher found Georgiana in the vestibule engaged in an animated conversation with Lord Hamilton. She smiled and clasped her hands, looking as if she'd just won a horserace with ten-to-one odds.

Fletcher hastened toward her but was stopped by a woman who introduced him to her daughter—a blushing debutante. He tried to be reasonably polite but excused himself directly. By the time he was close enough, Hamilton was bowing over Georgiana's hand. "Thank you ever so much, madam."

"No, no, thank you," she replied.

Fletcher slid in behind her. "It seems Hamilton has made you happy?"

"Possibly. He expressed his interest in some of Daniel's work."

"Oh, that's right. He was an inventor. Odd you've never spoken of his inventions."

"Yes, we've discussed steam engines. He was a fan of Watt just as you were, do you not recall?" Her face turned red, then Lady Derby passed as if she were on a mission. Nonetheless, Georgiana grasped her mother's elbow. "There you are, Mama. Are you planning to waltz with His Grace? Of all the guests, he's the closest to the throne. It wouldn't be proper if the matron of the house did not."

Fletcher gave Georgiana a questioning glance before he bowed and offered his hand. "Of course, I'd be delighted."

He waltzed with Lady Derby and the Dowager Duchess of Ravenscar, and two other matrons of the *ton* before the orchestra finally took a recess.

"My word, Evesham, I'm surprised to see you here," said Lord Saye.

Searching the hall for Georgiana, Fletcher gave the man a bland stare. It was beginning to seem as if everyone present was conspiring to keep him away from the lovely widow. "Why's that?"

The man snorted sarcastically. "What with your reputation, I'd imagine everyone was as shocked as I to see you as the guest of honor of all things."

"Perhaps there are still some members of polite society who believe a man's character is not defined by the gossip columns."

"Oh, please." The earl gave him a once over. "I need no tabloids."

Fletcher had heard it before. He was of ignoble birth and, therefore, an imposter in many men's eyes. But none of them were able to do a damned thing about it. "Unfortunately one cannot choose one's parents."

"Quite."

He watched as the pompous arse sauntered away. Of course, Saye had no idea Fletcher's slight was directed at his father. In no way would he deign to disrespect the memory of his mother. He looked to the refreshment table where, while Fletcher was dancing, Georgiana had been in conversation with not one but three gentlemen, but now she was nowhere to be found. Bless it, if he didn't know better he might think she was deliberately trying to avoid him.

His suspicions mounted tenfold when he arrived at the cardroom and found the lady sitting along the wall in deep conversation with Clarence Webster. That the man had ventured to the cardroom was no surprise, but that the swindler had anything good to say was impossible. Webster had not only bullied Fletcher at Eton, he would cheat a man out of his last farthing, then send his ruffians to rough the poor sop over and collect on any outstanding debts.

In fact, Webster was the initial reason why Fletcher had sought boxing lessons. At Eton, Fletcher had been the smallest boy in his year, oft picked upon by older boys, Webster being the leader of the pack. In one summer, he'd grown an entire foot but the swindling fool had moved on to Cambridge. Nonetheless, if nothing else, his youth taught Fletcher one thing—no one would ever run roughshod over him again.

He cracked his knuckles as he strode into the room, his blood boiling while Georgiana covered her mouth and laughed at something the weasel had said. But his temper completely boiled over when Webster rested his hand on her arm.

"Webster," he growled, stopping in front of the pair,

and jamming his fists into his hips. "Whatever pulled you from your dung hill?"

Georgiana's jaw dropped. "Your Grace!"

The dastard hopped to his feet. "Evesham, you are insolent and insulting."

Drawing in a deep breath, Fletcher's chest expanded. "It is impossible for me to be insolent. I am a duke. And last I checked, you had no title."

The lady rose and stood beside the varlet. "That may be so, but Mr. Webster is a guest—"

"And a swindler," Fletcher added. "I have no idea why he'd be on the guest list."

"Because I suggested Mama invite him. He has expressed interest in Daniel's work."

"Daniel's work? And why is it this groundbreaking invention is suddenly of such import? Aside from this evening, you haven't mentioned it to me."

Webster thrust out his damned chest. Evidently, he still thought he was king of the bloody roost. "Mayhap that's because Mrs. Whiteside knows better than to trust the likes of you."

Fletcher backed the cheat against the wall and pinned him with an arm bar across the throat. "You may have been two years my senior and a foot taller when we were at Eton, but no more. You will stay away from Mrs. Whiteside and her family. If I catch wind that you have gone anywhere near them or embroiled them in your deceit in any way, I will personally see to it you are ruined for the rest of your days."

"Remove your filthy hands," Webster croaked as he threw a knee intended as a strike to the groin.

But Fletcher reacted in time, taking the jab to his thigh. Snarling, he tightened his grip. "You always did fight like a scoundrel."

Webster spat. "Bite my arse."

As Fletcher ducked, the bastard swung a hook, only managing a glancing blow. He countered with a jab, knocking the swindler to the floor. "Don't bother getting up," he growled.

Webster looked a bit dazed as he wiped a trickle of blood from the corner of his mouth.

"Stop it!" Georgiana shouted.

Fletcher backed away, his hands shaking.

Georgiana slapped his face. "How could you?"

Stunned, he stared back. Didn't she realize he was protecting her from a coward, a cheat? "It shouldn't have come to blows. He struck first."

"Only after you threatened him and pinned him against the wall," she seethed, her voice filled with scorn. She took two steps away, then turned and fled from the room.

Webster smirked.

Fletcher gave the man a dead-eyed glare. "If I ever see you in the lady's presence again, I'll show no mercy."

Without a moment to lose, he bounded out to the vestibule, catching sight of Georgiana as she dashed up the steps. She tripped when she reached the landing, barely catching her fall with the banister. A slipper came tumbling toward him as he followed.

"Wait," he called, picking it up.

Reaching the first floor, she stopped and faced him with fire in her eyes. "I have an important conversation with a businessman and you waltz over and pick a fight like a jealous fiend."

"Me? That man wouldn't think twice before he swindled you out of your last farthing."

"Miss Eleanor said he pays her."

"That's because the woman in question is a smuggler—she's nearly as bad as Webster."

Gasping, Georgiana clutched her hands over her chest. "You, sir, have just insulted not only my dearest friend, you have insulted me. Now I know why your character is always in question—"

"You cannot possibly understand."

"No? I think I fully understand. You were a nobody before you fell into a dukedom, and now you exploit your position by demanding everyone bow to your wishes. I will *not* and will *never* be suffocated by a man who forces me to bend to his will."

"Georgiana, I—"

"No!" She unclasped the pearls and threw the strand at him, then did the same with the earrings and tiara. "We are absolutely, unequivocally incompatible!"

As if slapped across the face, Fletcher stooped, gripping the handrail and watching her flee.

What have I done?

Chapter Twenty-Three

The dew on the grass made Georgiana's hem damp, but she hardly noticed. She ought to be ecstatic about today, but her heart felt as dank as the morning's fog. On the positive side, Roddy and Mr. Walpole had arrived at Richmond Park exactly on time and, during the ball last night, Lord Hamilton had purchased the pumper demonstration model sight unseen and would be depositing payment in her bank account on the morrow. Even if today's demonstration was another flop, she had secured at least one buyer for Daniel's invention. Though she wouldn't bring in enough money to establish a factory, she now had the means to return to Thetford and manufacture another prototype and have it finished within two months.

If only she were able summon the joy she ought to be feeling and shove away her ridiculous melancholy.

Miss Eleanor's coach arrived and she hastened to alight with the help of a footman. "Georgiana, why were you not at breakfast?"

"I wasn't about to chance another encounter with Evesham. Did you not hear? He grew enraged when I was speaking to Mr. Webster and the two came to blows."

"I'd heard about the tussle."

Georgiana pursed her lips against the sickness roiling in her stomach. "So, the duke showed his true colors at long last. To be honest, I'm glad. We have no possible future together." She inhaled deeply. "At least this way, we've made a clean break and that's the end of it."

"Oh dear." Eleanor led her away from the growing crowd. They stopped in a quiet spot behind the fire engine. "Perhaps I shouldn't have introduced you to Clarence Webster."

"How can you say such a thing?"

"He doesn't exactly run a well-to-do establishment."

"Are you saying Evesham's accusations are founded?"

"Well, Mr. Webster has never swindled me, but I've heard enough conjecture to believe his card tables are fixed."

Her stomach turned over. Good heavens, she'd been so curt with the duke last eve. "He cheats?"

"I believe he does."

What was done was done—and for the best. Besides, Georgiana mustn't forget that Fletcher had come to blows last night—at her mother's ball of all places. "That still doesn't absolve Evesham for his abhorrent behavior. And I'll tell you true, he not only accused Mr. Webster of being dishonest, he outright said *you* were a smuggler."

Eleanor laughed. "Oh, did he now?"

"You laugh?" Georgiana puzzled at her friend as if she'd grown two heads. "If I were you, I would be outraged not amused."

Winding a red curl around her finger, Eleanor blinked. "He's not entirely wrong on that count either, though I would put my enterprise at no more devious than that of a privateer."

"I beg your pardon?"

"Business is quite good, though it was better during

the war. And you've seen for yourself how I've prospered."

Georgiana clapped her hands over her ears. "Good Lord, I do not want to hear another word. You are my dearest friend and I would hate for anyone to misjudge you."

"Me as well. That's why I put on airs and go to house parties when I have absolutely no interest in finding a husband." Eleanor looked behind her, then lowered her voice. "A gentlewoman must keep up appearances, mind you."

"Please tell me you're not involved in anything dishonest."

"Dishonest? No, I can promise that without a doubt. Though I might *avoid* paying duties to give my customers the best prices possible."

Georgiana thwacked her friend on the arm. "You are shameful."

"Not really. And remember that when you need supplies to build your pumpers."

Hesitating for a moment, Georgiana calculated a list of sums in her head. How much could she save by purchasing through Eleanor? "You can help me acquire supplies?"

"I can help you acquire anything you need...within reason."

"I shall keep that in mind—as long as there is no skullduggery involved."

"Of course not."

Roddy dashed up and climbed onto the pumper's platform. "Good morn, ladies. The fire in the pumper has been lit and it's ready to go."

"And the water?"

"The holding tank is chock full."

"You are a champion, young man." Georgiana waved at Mr. Walpole. "Are you as prepared, sir?"

"Absolutely, madam. I can recite my lines backward if need be."

"I am duly impressed." Georgiana gestured to Eleanor to follow and climbed the steps of the dais. "Thank you for your efforts. I truly appreciate all you have done, both with the dancing and with the fire engine."

After an inspection, Georgiana deemed all in order. The demonstration proceeded without incident. Both Mr. Walpole and Roddy were magnificent. The crowd even applauded and though no one stepped forward to offer to provide the financial backing for Whiteside Pumpers, Georgiana did receive a second request. This one came from Mr. Beaverton. She had met him at Lady Maxwell's ball and she had sent him a letter with information about the fire engine.

Mr. Webster obviously had not been scared off by Evesham's abominable treatment, and he met Georgiana at the machine. "By jove, Daniel did it."

She bit the inside of her cheek, stopping herself from saying she'd perfected the machine. Besides, her late husband deserved all the accolades. He'd lost his life working on the pumper. It had been his dream, not hers.

"If only he were here to see it."

Running his hand over the cast iron, Mr. Webster moved to the rear.. "You have mechanized both the suction and discharge hoses?"

"Absolutely."

"It is amazing you had enough pressure to do both."

She smiled knowingly. "Harnessing enough pressure was our greatest hurdle."

"I'd like to know more."

"Perhaps you'd like to place an order?"

"Hmm. First I'd need to see Daniel's workshop..."

Mr. Webster continued talking, but Georgiana's attention was pulled away when she saw the Duke of Evesham standing beside Mr. Walpole. Except Mr. Walpole looked as if he'd just been slayed and Fletcher's expression was as angry as a rendering of Zeus during a thunderstorm.

Georgiana froze, heat thrumming through her veins at the breakneck pressure of one hundred pounds per square inch. She'd spent over a month trying to conceal the fact that she was responsible for dousing him at the Southwark Fair.

But by the blaze reflected in his eyes, he not only realized who she was, any affection he'd harbored for her had vanished in the blink of an eye.

"Evesham, come off your dunghill to consort with the commoners, have you?" said Mr. Webster, further proving his questionable character.

"This day will not end with another brawl." Georgiana held up her palm. "Please excuse us. I have a matter to discuss with His Grace."

Fletcher barely acknowledged Webster's remark as he sauntered forward. "Now I know why you were familiar. Devil take it, I should have recognized that worthless actor when I saw you with him at Covent Garden."

"Your Grace, I never intended—"

"You lied to me," Evesham growled, his eyes filled with ire, his face red.

Georgiana clutched her arms across her midriff and took a step away. "I didn't exactly lie, I just didn't ever see the point in angering you further."

"But you kept this—" He thrust his hand at the pumper. "This disastrous fire engine a secret while you deceived me into thinking you might actually care for me."

As his words turned her insides to shreds, she pressed praying fingers to her lips. "But I do care for you."

He threw up his hands. "What other secrets have you not told me about?"

"I assure you this is the only one." She dared to take another step closer. "Whiteside Pumpers is Daniel's legacy. I owe it to his memory to see that his ambitions are realized."

A tic twitched in Fletcher's jaw. "And what about your ambitions?"

This was no time to hide the truth, and it stung like falling into a clump of nettles. "Daniel's ambitions are mine as well. That's why I insisted we not make promises—that our liaison only last as long as the house party."

"So you used me—toyed with my affections when you didn't give a damn about how I might feel about you."

She squared her shoulders. "I did not intentionally mislead you. Please, try to understand."

"I understand quite clearly." Fletcher's chin tilted upward with the narrowing of his eyes. "You are in love with a dead man and have no capacity to care for anyone else."

"But—" Reaching out, Georgiana stepped toward him, but he turned his back and strode away, in an aura of fury. His posture reminiscent of the Southwark Fair, she didn't dare follow. Clutching her hands across her ribs, tears stung her eyes while her throat thickened and burned.

What have I done?

Chapter Twenty-Four

❧

For the past three weeks since returning to London, Fletcher had avoided any and everything to do with polite society. In fact, the only time he'd left his town house was for his sparring sessions with Brum or to play cards at a gentlemen's club where he would be sure not to cross paths with females—especially those who were nobly born and single.

He wanted nothing to do with the fairer sex.

Sitting at his writing table, he pored over the books of accounts for his estates as he grumbled to himself about the excesses. And it was nigh time he put an end to a few of them, especially his housekeeper's maddening habit of replacing the draperies every year due to dust. Fletcher might be wealthy, but he wasn't a squanderer. Egad, that's exactly how men lost their fortunes. He reached for his quill and added to his list of changes, *"Henceforth, draperies shall only be replaced if worn or faded."*

"Good morning, Your Grace," said Smith as he entered with a breakfast tray and the *Gazette*.

"It is morning." Fletcher replaced his quill. "Though I daresay I see nothing good about it."

"You might change your mind when you have a look at the news." Smith set the tray beside the books of account on the table. "There's an article about the Earl of Hamilton acquiring a steam-powered fire engine that pumps a whopping two hundred gallons per minute. The report said it's a Whiteside pumper. Have you heard of them? I do not believe I have had the pleasure."

Frowning, Fletcher picked up the paper and handed it back to the butler. "Yes, I can personally attest to the power behind the flow, but I highly doubt that machine can stand up to the rigors of battling a real fire. If you recall, it was but two months ago when I came home soaked from head to toe by a Whiteside calamity."

Smith tucked the *Gazette* under his arm. "Pity. This says Hamilton tested it on an old warehouse in the west end and it out performed a hand-stroked pumper four to one."

Fletcher bit into a crumpet. "Hogwash. Reporters always embellish the truth."

"Indeed, Your Grace." But Smith didn't bow and make himself scarce as usual. "Were you aware that after the inventor's untimely death, his wife, a gentlewoman, mind you, improved the piston and cylinder, more than doubling the amount of steam harnessed by the engine? Perhaps that is the reason you caught the brunt of its discharge though, I daresay, they were very discourteous if they trained the flow on you."

"She improved it did you say?" Fletcher asked, ignoring the discourteous remark.

Smith swatted the paper as if the article contained the biggest news of the year. "I did. Mrs. Whiteside must have a great deal of tenacity. Evidently, the student became the master in this instance."

Tossing the half-eaten crumpet onto the plate, Fletcher pushed his chair back, clenching his fists against his urge to cuff the man with a hook. "Enough. In my opinion, the student became the charlatan."

Smith hesitated for a moment, the expression on his

face falling before he bowed. "Will there be anything else, Your Grace?"

"Just throw that damned *Gazette* in the rubbish bin. I never want to lay eyes on it again."

Beneath his skin, the ire simmered like steam ready to burst while Fletcher waited until the butler left the room. Then he picked up the chintz coffee pot and threw it at the hearth. Blast it all, he didn't want to be reminded of Georgiana Whiteside. Not ever. She may have perfected her steam engine, but she had used him. She'd made him believe her still the grieving widow—too distraught to fall in love—that she was fragile and needed to proceed slowly.

How she must have laughed behind his back while she tricked him—brought him warmed chocolate as if she were thoughtful and dear and kind. Georgiana didn't care about him. She had no intention of continuing their liaison—or falling in love with him.

He'd known it as soon as he saw her at Richmond Park—and her damned mother had told him where to find the woman. Were the pair of them in cahoots? *Let's toy with the Duke of Evesham and make him realize the extent of his unsuitability as a member of the nobility.*

He grabbed a dish and threw it as well.

To hell with the lot of them!

"WITH THE ORDERS THAT HAVE COME IN, THIS meager workshop will not be able to sustain your operation for long," said Miss Eleanor as Roddy ran ahead with her valise.

Georgiana looked to the exposed rafters. The workshop was naught but an old stable, and a small one at that. "No, but it is a start. And if we work on one machine at a time, we ought to manage."

"Definitely in the short term. Thank heavens the foundry agreed to manufacture your cylinders."

Together, they strolled out to the waiting coach. "I have you to thank for that."

Eleanor slid her reticule up her arm. "I only wish I were able to stay longer."

"You've done so much already, I have no idea how I can repay your kindness."

"It has been fun. And if you need anything at all—"

Georgiana grasped Eleanor's hands. "I will be placing all my orders through you, my dearest."

"Thank you." After a kiss on the cheek, Eleanor turned to Roddy. "You take good care of your mistress, young man."

"You know I will." He offered his hand and helped her into the hackney. "She has made me an apprentice. I reckon my ma would be proud were she alive."

Georgiana gave the boy's back a pat as he handed the bag to the footman. "She'd be very proud."

"Yes, mistress. Ah...do you mind if I run to town? The lads invited me to play a game of cricket." Roddy had already made friends with a few of the local boys in town. He fit right in as if he'd grown up in Thetford.

Georgiana waved as she watched the coach start away. "I think you ought to go. We've already put in a good day's work and you deserve to have some fun."

With a youthful grin, he started off. "Thank you, mistress."

"Be home by supper."

Sighing, she walked back through the iron gate, and along the overgrown path to the cottage. There had been so much to do, she had needed the caretaker's help in the workshop every waking hour. And thank heavens for Eleanor. Without her assistance, supplies to fulfill the next two pumper orders would have cost twice as much, and would have taken thrice as long to arrive.

She opened the old door with its medieval black-ened-iron nails and stepped inside. "Mrs. Tees, I've de-cided that tomorrow Mr. Tees must spend some time in the garden," she said softly.

It wasn't necessary to speak loudly in a two-room cottage. But the housekeeper didn't respond. Aside from Roddy, Mr. and Mrs. Tees were the only servants Georgiana employed, and they had both been an immense help after Daniel's death with Mr. Tees taking on the role as her assistant in addition to his caretaking duties.

Alone, Georgiana stood for a moment with her hands folded. The cottage seemed cold and empty without Eleanor. Against the far wall was a meager kitchen with a hob and cooking utensils hanging from a rack suspended from the ceiling. A copper bed warmer and a broom propped in one corner and a rocking chair in the other. There was a table with four chairs, but nothing terribly comfortable aside from the feather mattress on the bed in the back room.

Mr. and Mrs. Tees lived in the caretaker's cottage out the back, which was even smaller. And Georgiana had fashioned a pallet for Roddy in the loft of the workshop. He seemed to like it in Thetford and had been over the moon with glee when she'd asked him to be her apprentice.

As melancholy stretched in her chest, Georgiana moved to the rocker and sat. This was the first time she'd been by herself since arriving home one month past. And nothing had been the same upon her return. The cottage didn't look as cozy as it once had when Daniel had carried her across the threshold. Back then, Georgiana was so young and happy she wouldn't have cared if he'd taken her to a stable to start their married life. She rubbed her hands on the wooden armrests worn smooth by years of use. The chair had been Daniel's mother's, but bless it if she was unable to remember him ever sitting there. Her heart grew heavy as she looked to the table where he oft sat and read. She could no longer picture him there, either.

In his place, she imagined Fletcher sitting in his shirtsleeves. He looked comfortable that way—his dark skin contrasting with the white linen. A lock of black hair dangled over one eye as it often did.

But she'd lost the Duke of Evesham forever. Evesham would never sit at her table, let alone come to Thetford.

Had Georgiana deceived him as he'd accused? A familiar lead weight sank to the pit of her stomach. She'd not meant to deceive him. Furthermore, on that horrid day at Richmond Park, he'd assumed the worst and stormed away before giving her a chance to explain.

I should have told him about the pumper the instant he pulled me out of the pond at Green Park. Or, better, when Dobbs announced Evesham was in the parlor with Mama, I should have gone down, apologized for the incident, and wished him well in his future endeavors.

Curse her ill-begotten mood. She ought to be happy —elated to have orders for the pumpers. No more would she be counting every farthing, worrying about how she might make ends meet. But instead, her insides felt as if the duke had reached in and torn them out.

A sob grated in Georgiana's throat as she leaned forward and buried her face in her hands. All her life, she'd tried so hard to be a good person. She'd tried to be a good wife. She'd tried to make the fire engine work. For what? To save lives and homes and peoples' keepsakes.

Why did she feel like a wretched soul? Why, after all the years of sweating and suffering in the dank, cramped workshop, did she feel as if her life were in shatters?

Her gut wrenched while tears streamed through her fingers.

Bless it all, she'd lost her bloody heart to a duke. She

loved a man she could never have—not a rake, but a man who supported a home for unwed mothers and purchased pearls just to watch a woman smile.

Worst of all? He would never be hers.

Chapter Twenty-Five

❧

The air at Jackson's was filled with enough pipe smoke to make anyone's eyes burn. Fletcher sat at the rear table and glared at a fist full of worthless cards.

"What's your wager?" asked the dealer.

"Aye, Evesham," said Lord Hamilton, who somehow had eluded his wife for the evening. "You haven't had a decent hand all night."

Snorting, Fletcher tossed his cards onto the pile. "Tell me something I do not already know. I'm out."

He sat back and watched the game progress until Brum caught his eye and gave a nod from across the hazy room. Two minutes later, the boxing champion stood beside him. "You look as if we fed you a plate of rancid beef."

Fletcher tapped the stack of coins in front of him. "Your man is quite adept at dealing corrupt cards if you ask me."

Snorting, Brum looked to the dealer. "Mr. Almond is one of our finest."

"I can see why," said Hamilton, gesturing with his pipe. "There's no question he knows how to play for the house."

Grumbling under his breath, Fletcher waved the man's smoke away from his face. "I say, Jackson, you've

229

taken so much of my coin this night, I think you owe me a week of free boxing lessons."

Brum rapped the back of the chair. "A bloody week? You'll ruin me."

Fletcher collected his money and stood just as a man barreled through the door, his eyes wild. "Fire! All hands needed—Windmill Street!"

Ice shot through Fletcher's blood as he locked gazes with Brum.

Hamilton sprang to his feet and motioned to his man. "Come, there may be time to fetch the pumper from the warehouse."

But Fletcher barely noticed the earl. "God's blood, the women's home is on Windmill Street," he growled as he started for the door.

Brum caught his arm and pulled him toward the kitchens. "This way. We'll arrive faster if we go through Percy Mews."

"Good man."

Fletcher followed the boxer through alleyways even he wouldn't dream of visiting in broad daylight, let alone at night. It smelled of piss and rotten food. The place was infested—and not only with rats. He felt hidden eyes upon him. But who in their right mind would set upon a beast like Brumley Jackson and a man nearly as large?

As they raced around the corner, tendrils of smoke seeped through the air like the breath of a dragon.

"Ballocks!" Fletcher shouted as he caught sight of the Benevolent Home for Unwed Mothers. An eerie glow of amber oozed around the building, while smoke billowed from its windows.

"Damn," Brum cursed as they both began to sprint.

A hand-stroke fire engine had been rolled into place, but the stream was barely effective.

"We need more men!" someone shouted.

Onlookers stood as if in shock. Fletcher grabbed a

man by the arm and yanked him toward the machine. "Your job is to ensure there's a steady flow of men pumping. Do you understand?"

"Yes, sir."

"Good man and there will be a reward in it for you if we manage to put out the fire before it spreads."

Fletcher signaled to Brum and raced through the door.

Thick smoke hung in the air as Mrs. Whipple carried two children on her hips as she hastened down the stairs. "Your Grace!"

"Out. Quickly!" Fletcher took the children from her arms and led the way to the street. "What happened?"

"I think it was those varlets who've been threatening us—the same religious zealots who attacked the kitchens with hammers."

"Good God."

"Hurry, ladies!" she shouted, standing on the footpath and counting heads.

"Is everyone accounted for?" he asked, while mothers pulled the children from his arms.

"Where are Angela and Beatrice?" When none of the residents responded, Mrs. Whipple clutched her hands over her heart. "Dear God, their rooms are at the rear!"

Craning his neck, Fletcher caught the flicker of a red flame leap across the roof while black smoke billowed above. "Where, exactly?"

"Third floor—But you cannot possibly go in there, Your Grace. 'Tis far too dangerous."

Fletcher removed his coat and handed it to her. "Give this to anyone who's cold."

Brum did the same. "I'll go with you."

Leading the way, Fletcher headed for the door. "It's the third floor rear rooms. I'll try the stairs. Do you think you can make it around back?"

"If I cannot, then my name's not Jackson."

"Good man." Without another word, Fletcher ran into the house, the smoke twice as thick as it had been only moments ago. Haunting cries from an infant resounded through the eerie silence. His eyes stung and he removed his neckcloth and held it over his nose and mouth while he barreled up the steps.

The infant's cries grew louder as he approached the third floor.

"Help!" a woman shrieked as he stepped out on the landing.

Fletcher wiped the tears from his eyes as he peered through the thick haze. Flames blocked the corridor, making it impossible to reach them. "Stay where you are. Do you have water?"

"Y-yes,"

"Wet a blanket," he shouted. "Wrap it around you and huddle in the hearth."

"But there are four of us!"

"Do it, I say," he bellowed as he dashed into a room, yanked a woolen blanket from a bed, and charged back to the corridor.

Batting the blaze furiously, he snuffed the flames only to watch them rekindle as he drew the blanket away.

"Haste! Please!" the woman screamed, her voice filled with panic.

"Nearly there," he lied, his muscles torturing him from the effort. Dear God, tendrils of fire leaped up the stairs at his rear. If unable to douse the fire now, he'd burn for certain.

But Fletcher wasn't ready to meet his end. Throwing the blanket aside, he dashed back into the bedchamber, grabbed a mattress and threw it into the corridor, sprinting across only seconds before it burst into flames.

The infant's cries screeched so loud Fletcher's inner ears vibrated. He gnashed his teeth against the pain, slamming the door behind him. "Stay down!" he commanded, breaking the window with a chair. Fletcher dropped to his stomach as a burst of flames knocked the door from its hinges. But the oakwood proved strong enough to keep them from being incinerated.

As if the fire drew back to gain momentum before its final attack, Fletcher rose and shoved his head out the gaping window. "Brum!"

"There's a ladder right below the sill," boomed the boxer's deep voice.

Fletcher swept the infant and child into his arms. "Come, ladies!"

One of the mothers dashed to his side. "Please! Take the children first."

He gave her a nod. "You must follow immediately. We only have seconds to spare." He looked to the eldest child. "Wrap your hands around my neck."

As the young lad did as told, Fletcher nudged him onto his back. "Now hold on as tightly as you can, do you hear?"

"Yes, sir." The fear in the little boy's voice made Fletcher's gut twist in a knot the size of a cannonball.

"Here we go," he said, with no time to stop. The infant wailed, sucking gasps of smoky air. "I'll have you down in no time."

Using one hand on the rungs, Fletcher hastened to the ground and stood back. One of the women was right above, the other stood at the window.

"Mama!" called the tiny child above the infant's shrill cries.

Brum helped the woman down and she immediately took the baby from Fletcher's arms.

"'Tis safe!" he shouted to the mother above. "Climb out!"

"I can't!" she cried.

"Mama!" the boy yelled again.

Any moment, the fire would leap through the open window and take the woman with it.

Fletcher swung the child from his back straight into Brum's arms. "I'll not stand here whilst he watches his mother die!"

Without a moment's hesitation, he raced up the ladder. "I'll catch you. You can do it. One leg at a time."

She looked back while smoke billowed behind her, and the deadly red glow of flames crackled only feet away. "I-I'm afraid."

"Do it, I say!"

Her hands trembled as she reached forward.

Acting swiftly, Fletcher grasped her wrist and pulled her screaming over his shoulder. "I have you," he growled while flames leaped from the place where she'd been standing.

It didn't take long to rejoin mother with her son.

"Come, it isn't safe to stay here," Fletcher said, marshalling the group around to Windmill Street. Then he turned to Brum. "Thank God you found the ladder."

"Grabbed it from Hamilton's men as they arrived with the pumper. Word is they've kept the adjoining buildings from going up in smoke as well."

The street was filled with people everywhere, a powerful stream of water blasted from a loud steam engine.

Mrs. Whipple emerged from the crowd, her hands clasped beneath her chin. "Oh, thank the good Lord, you saved them, Your Grace."

"It was touch and go. Thanks to Mr. Jackson, we were able to escape down a ladder."

"Your Grace?" asked the woman he'd pulled from the window. "You're a duke?"

Mrs. Whipple gave her an indignant look. "He's our benefactor."

Brum thwacked Fletcher's shoulder. "I reckon your secret's out of the bag, old friend."

"Where are we going to sleep, Mama?" asked the little boy—a tiny lad, reminiscent of years past.

Fletcher picked him up and propped him on his hip. "I can think of only one place large enough to house the lot of you."

"And where might that be?" asked Mrs. Whipple.

"Hail enough hackneys for everyone and tell the drivers we're going to the Duke of Evesham's town house on Piccadilly." He looked to Brum and laughed. "My butler needs a modicum of upheaval in his life."

The whites of the boxer's eyes looked like saucers in the darkness. "Your butler? What the devil are you planning to do with a house full of unwed mothers and their children?"

Fletcher patted the child's shoulder. "'Tis only until I can find them another home. I'll wager they'll be out of my house in two days."

Brum chuckled. "Now that's a bet upon which I'd place long odds."

Chapter Twenty-Six

❧❧

Thank God Fletcher didn't take Brum up on his wager. Two weeks had passed and Mrs. Whipple and her band of young ladies had completely taken over the town house. The only place Fletcher had any solace was his bedchamber. Even the library was full of beds... and children. Who knew children were so bloody active? And loud. And curious. And hungry. And adorable.

Of course, Fletcher didn't consider a single miniature human comely. That must have come from Smith.

But Christopher, the lad he'd carried down the ladder had become quite the shadow. And with blue eyes nearly as large as his face, the boy was almost impossible to ignore, regardless of how hard Fletcher tried.

In truth, Christopher was no trouble whatsoever.

Aside from his town house being invaded by women and children, his bloody reputation had suffered a serious blow. The papers had embellished his benevolence and made him out to be as heroic as Richard the Lionheart. He sat at his writing desk and stared at an insurmountable pile of invitations to every soiree, ball, and house party from now until eternity. If it weren't for the need to find a new home for the unwed mothers, he'd board a ship and take a tour of the Continent for the rest of his days.

With a knock, Smith stepped into the chamber. "There's a Miss Eleanor Kent come to call, Your Grace. Shall I send her away?"

Fletcher's gut twisted as he looked up. If only Mrs. Whiteside had been announced. Still, the name of Georgiana's friend made a lump the size of Great Gable Mountain swell in his throat.

"Did she say why she is here?"

"Only that she had a donation for the new Benevolent Home for Unwed Mothers and insisted upon presenting it to you herself."

"What makes her think I'm procuring a new building?"

"The *Gazette* reported you were seen looking at a property a week past."

It had, though Fletcher had not asked for charity. In his mind, requesting help when his estate was overflowing with money was akin to blasphemy.

Smith gestured toward the door. "She's waiting in the parlor, if you'd care to entertain her."

Fletcher stood. "The parlor? Isn't there some sort of tea for pregnant mothers or something or other going on there?"

"'Tis a general tea and I've relegated them all to the kitchens."

"The kitchens? You've sent those poor young ladies to the kitchens?"

"I beg your pardon, Your Grace, but they are not nobly born. Most of those women were raised in one-room tenant housing—and some in the gutter. They can very well enjoy their tea at the servant's tables below stairs where, I'll say, all the rest of us take our meals. Mind you, those young ladies have not been slighted in the least."

The butler turned as red as an overripe tomato,

giving Fletcher pause. Good heavens, at times he, himself, preferred to sit at the servant's tables, which were very much the same as the tables that had gone up in cinders. "Forgive me. I by no means meant to insinuate you or any of the servants in this house are beneath our guests. However, they are our guests, and while they are here, I ask that they are treated with respect. I shall visit the kitchens and see to their comfort after I've had a word with the lady."

Fletcher smiled to himself when a great deal of laughter resounded from the kitchens as he opened the door to the parlor and stepped inside. Of course, Smith was right. And why shouldn't a duke receive guests in his parlor where he usually did? He crossed the floor and took Eleanor's hand. "Madam, how lovely to see you."

She nodded pleasantly, her red curls framing the face beneath her bonnet. "Forgive me for coming without prior notice but I have something for you."

Fletcher held up his palm. "I assure you, I am not seeking benefactors for the new women's home."

"Did I mention I wished to make a contribution?"

"Forgive me but..." Fletcher looked back toward the door. *Damn Smith*. "My butler indicated benevolence was the reason for your visit."

She scooted aside and patted the settee. "If you would sit, I'll share with you the reason for my presence."

Clearing his throat, he gestured toward the bell pull. "Shall I ring for tea?"

"I assured your butler that would not be necessary," she said with a bit of an edge to her voice. Had she come to berate him? To plead with him on Georgiana's behalf?

Eyeing her, Fletcher slid onto the seat. "I take it this is not a social call."

The splay of soft freckles across her nose stretched

with her smile. "I am here to give you a note, but it is not from me, because I am not as cordial as some."

"I beg your pardon?"

Miss Eleanor pulled a slip of paper from her reticule and studied it for a moment. "Mrs. Whiteside sent this to me and asked that I give it to the rebuilding fund anonymously."

At the sound of her name, the air whooshed from Fletcher's lungs. "I—"

The lady sliced the note through the air. "Though I am breaking her confidence in doing so, I felt someone needed to speak up for her."

Heat spread across his body—blasting with sparks like the fire he'd battled on the third floor of the women's home. He gulped against the thickening of his throat. For the past few weeks, every time he blinked, he saw Georgiana's face, even more so of late.

"The lady never meant to do you harm. In fact, she was mortified over what happened at Southwark Fair."

"She should have told me."

"Perhaps, but until the house party, she never thought she'd fall in love with you." Eleanor brushed a gloved hand over her skirts. "If she had told you about Southwark, would it have made any difference?"

Fletcher looked up to the portrait of his grandfather and rubbed the back of his neck. There he was sitting in a house filled with ancestors he'd never known—yet with each passing day, he grew more like the upper class he'd once disdained. "No. I had made my judgment."

"Yes, as I witnessed at Richmond Park, you acted judge and jury, which is exactly why Mrs. Whiteside was terrified to tell you about the pumper. Did you know she was there when the cylinder dropped and crushed her husband? Did you know she alone studied and ran test after test perfecting his *monstrosity*, if you will?"

"I..." Fletcher looked to his hands. "No. She did not share any of that with me."

"The papers reported that Lord Hamilton's men arrived at the fire with the Whiteside pumper and kept the neighboring buildings from burning."

"He did."

The woman gave an indignant nod. "And with enough men to man the hose, I take it no innocent bystanders were drenched with water?"

"None that I saw."

"So." Miss Eleanor gave him the note. "After receiving orders for more pumpers, Mrs. Whiteside felt she had enough coin to give *you* a hundred pounds to help with necessities for the new Benevolent Home for Unwed Mothers."

Fletcher ran his fingers over the feminine penmanship—so very lovely—so very like her. "'Tis a great sum." *And such a selfless gesture.*

"It is. And I'll say it is coin she herself needs. Georgiana might have taken a giant step out of poverty, but progress will be slow for her." As Miss Eleanor stood, Fletcher did as well. "I wanted you to know the truth before you damned her to hell."

What? He nearly spat out his front teeth. "Madam?"

"You know who I am and what I do. And if I cannot speak with you bluntly, no one will. Mrs. Whiteside isn't only my friend, she is the sweetest, most decent person with whom I have the pleasure of being acquainted." Eleanor pulled the stings on her reticule, while she pursed her lips so tightly, they turned white. "Furthermore, it is my steadfast opinion that you do not deserve her."

Fletcher bowed his head, words refusing to form on his lips. Everything the lady had said was true, especially the last jibe.

"I'll show myself out."

"STEADY UP THERE," GEORGIANA SAID, HOLDING THE ladder for Roddy while Mr. Tees manned the cable reel.

The boy grinned down, but even his smile did nothing to ease her jitters. She didn't like seeing anyone up so high. It was too dangerous. But this new rope was twenty times stronger than the one that had snapped.

Roddy leaned over, feet on the second-highest rung and one arm around the rafters while he threaded the cable through the pully. "I nearly have it."

Every muscle in Georgiana's body tensed as she prayed nothing would go awry. "Careful."

"I'm always careful." Roddy pulled the rope and grinned as he drew it downward. "See? All done."

"Perfect!" She clapped her hands. "Now climb down before my heart gives out."

Mr. Tees came over with the cast-iron hook. "I reckon this will hold up to anything."

"Miss Eleanor says it is the strongest available—the same cable they use on the tall ships."

While Roddy hopped down from the ladder, Mrs. Tees stepped into the workshop. "There's a gentleman caller for you, madam."

Georgiana wiped her hands on her apron. With all the supplies she'd purchased, there had been a number of callers of late—all wanting to sell her more than necessary. "Who is it this time?"

"He didn't give his name—said it would spoil the surprise."

For a fleeting moment, her stomach fluttered. But she swiped a hand over her mouth and looked away. The Duke of Evesham had walked out of her life forever. *How many times must I remind myself of that fact?*

On a sigh, she looked to the three dear people who were helping her to make Daniel's dream a reality. They were all she needed to care about. "It has been a day of good work. Why not shut up shop a bit early?"

"Beauty!" Roddy spun in a circle. "There's another cricket game and if I go now, I'll not miss it."

"Very well, but I want you to read before you turn in this night."

"I promise I will," he said, heading out.

After bidding good afternoon to Mr. and Mrs. Tees, Georgiana straightened her lace muslin cap and left for the cottage.

A tall, fair-haired man dressed in a tailcoat looked out the front window as she entered through the rear door. "I'm sorry to have kept you waiting, Mr..."

He turned. "Mrs. Whiteside, surely you have not forgotten me already." The man's gaze was hard, his mouth turned up only at one corner.

"Mr. Webster." She glanced back, wishing she hadn't dismissed Mrs. Tees. "I am so very surprised to see you here."

"Is that so? Did you not invite me to see your pumper?"

"Ah...I recall inviting you to Richmond Park. And you were there."

"Yes." Thank heavens his smile seemed more genuine. "Though we didn't have a chance to talk at the time. Evesham seemed to have made a calamity of the day and afterward didn't seem the appropriate time to discuss Whiteside's invention."

"I can see where you'd be dissuaded given his behavior from the previous evening." She gestured to the table. "Can I offer you a cup of tea and a biscuit?"

"That would be lovely, thank you." While Georgiana busied herself putting on the kettle, Mr. Webster opted not to sit but strolled around the chamber, inspecting everything. "I expected Whiteside to have done better for himself."

She opened the cast-iron door of the hob and added a stick of wood to the fire. "Truly? Generally, inventors start out poor."

The man pulled back the lace curtain and peered out the window. "And some never rise above it."

How dare he saunter around her cottage as if he were familiar? She'd asked him to sit and he'd ignored her. Dash it, his tone and his behavior made her feel as if he suspected her of some vile misdeed. She squared her shoulders. "Tell me, what was your relationship with Daniel?"

He continued with his inspection. "We were partners—in engineering class. We developed the idea for the steam-powered fire engine together."

"Together? I find that odd. Truly, I met his classmates in London—back when we were courting. And you were not among them. I most definitely would have remembered a partner, but he never mentioned you."

From the bookshelf, Webster selected the volume of *Experiments and Observations on Electricity* by Benjamin Franklin and thumbed through the pages. "Unfortunately, I didn't graduate."

"I'm sorry." Georgiana's shoulders tensed as she watched the pages turn. Could she find out more? "Was there a family calamity of sorts?"

"No." He set the book on the table and stepped nearer, the look in his eyes hard once more. "You might say I was deprived of my education, and thus deprived of a vocation—a share in your dead husband's invention."

The hair on the back of Georgiana's neck stood on end as she swallowed against the constricting of her throat. "But most of Daniel's work came after he left university. And then I—"

As she shrieked, Mr. Webster lunged and grabbed her wrist. Searing pain shot up her arm as she tried to wrench free. No match for the man's strength, he brutally yanked her into him, clutching an arm around her neck as he twisted her wrist up her spine. "I don't care about that bastard."

Georgiana thrashed and twisted, struggling against the man's iron grip. "Unhand me this instant!"

But fighting only made him yank her arm higher up her back. "I want those drawings," he seethed.

"To do what?" she cried, sweat streaming down the side of her face while she fought to keep her arm from breaking. "I-I've already sold the first model and-and have orders for more."

Lowering his lips to her ear, he scoffed, "Do you really think yourself capable of manufacturing more than one?"

Her mind racing, there was only one thing sure to appease him. "If you want the drawings, release me and I'll get them for you."

The beast laughed—a sickening, hateful cackle. "You're the type of woman who'd fight if I let you go. Tell me where they are."

Her eyes shifted toward the bedchamber. "They're in the workshop of course." If she spirited him out the back, the Tees might hear her scream.

"Liar!" He dragged her toward the door. "Whiteside owed me. I was dismissed from Cambridge for stealing —and that damned bastard refused to vouch for my character. Then he took our idea and went on to live the life I should have led."

Cringing with the pain, she dragged her feet, trying to resist. "He died for his invention."

He hauled her into the room. "That's because he was careless."

"How can you say such a thing?"

"Enough talk." Mr. Webster pushed her with such force, Georgiana hit her head on the bed's footboard.

"Help!" she shouted as she fell to the floor.

"Shut up!" He drew a knife and waved it in front of her face. "This is for you, wench. I want those drawings. Now!"

Georgiana kept her gaze on his face, refusing to

allow a shift of her eyes to give away the hiding place of the strongbox. "I said they were in the warehouse."

He slapped her with a backhand. "I've had enough of your lies. Tell me where they are, or I'll bury this blade in your heart and tear this place apart until I find what I'm after."

Staring at the sharp point of the dagger, she had no doubt he would kill her. "It's too late. Everyone knows Daniel's story. It was in the papers."

"Papers oft err in their reports. And no one will doubt a man's word when I step forward and tell the world that you stole my idea. *My* work."

Her entire body trembled. "You're mad."

"No, but I'm going to be very rich." Mr. Webster grabbed the back of her neck and pressed the point of the dagger into her throat. "This is your last chance. Where. Are. They?"

"Beneath us," she whispered, her heart slamming against her chest.

With the ease of his grip, Georgiana scooted away, the coppery glean of the bedwarmer catching her eye. "Just pull back the rug. I'm not strong enough to lever up the trapdoor without help."

It was a fib, but convincing enough. He gave her a dead-eyed stare. "If you move from that spot, it will be the last thing you do."

Georgiana didn't doubt him. What would Webster do after he collected his drawings? Kill her? File a grievance and challenge her in the courts?

As the hinges of the trapdoor creaked, she lunged for the bedwarmer, grabbed the long wooden handle, and smashed it atop the blackguard's head. "You are a vile man!"

"Dammit!" he bellowed, falling into the gaping hole. "I'll kill you!"

Casting the warmer aside, Georgiana fled past him. "Help! Help!"

Webster's thudding footsteps pounded the floorboards behind her. "I'll bloody help you, wench."

She didn't look back as she wrapped her hand around the latch and pulled.

A thick, heavy arm clutched around her midriff so hard, the air whooshed from her lungs. "Now you've done it," he growled.

Georgiana kicked and screamed while he dragged her back into the kitchen. "Stop this madness!"

He shoved her down face first on the table, pinning his body over hers and trapping her arms above her head. "Hold still," he growled in her ear while a hand grappled with her skirts.

She bucked, stars crossing her vision. "Never!"

The front door burst open revealing the Duke of Evesham brandishing a pistol. "Remove your hands from my woman!"

"Fletcher!"

The duke moved forward, his eyes blacker than midnight. "I always knew you were a fiend. If it is a fight you want, throw down your knife and face me like a man."

Georgiana's heart raced as the wicked cur chuckled. "You first."

Fletcher's brow furrowed as his gaze shot to Georgiana. "Fie," he cursed, lowering his weapon. "Now you."

"Put it on the floor and slide it over here."

"Very well." Fletcher released the flintlock's cock, then slowly bent his knees and placed the pistol on the floor but he only slid it halfway—not close enough for Webster to reach. Then the duke raised his fists like a boxer. "Let us finish what we began at Hardwick Hall."

Webster sneered. "You always were soft—more so now that you're impersonating a nobleman."

"Ah yes." Fletcher beckoned him. "And where are your manners, Webster? Not once have you bowed. In light of your disdain, I think you should bow to me now, do you not agree, madam?"

Georgiana threw her elbow, gaining enough room to slip from Webster's grasp. She skittered toward the wall. "I think he should fall on his knees and worship you."

Webster sauntered toward Evesham, the dagger still firm in his grip. "I'll slit you from ear to ear, then I'll bugger your wench before I send her to hell."

The pistol lay on the floor just out of reach. Splaying her fingers, Georgiana took a step toward it.

Webster whipped the knife her way. "Stay where you are."

As the blackguard moved, Fletcher kicked the knife from Webster's hand. With the duke's momentum, he slammed a fist across the varlet's jaw. Webster fell to his side and rolled away, then hopped to his feet with his fists raised. "You'll not take me down so easily, you half-breed bastard."

A shadow passed over Fletcher's face as he grunted —almost laughed, but not quite. "I'm a quarter-breed and damned proud to be my mother's son."

The scoundrel took a swing at the air. "She got what was coming—the whore."

Any other man would have blindly lashed out, but not the Duke of Evesham. He circled silently.

Blood streamed from the corner of Webster's mouth as he turned in place. He swung his right and, as his guard opened, Fletcher bobbed to the side and threw an uppercut straight into the man's jaw. As Webster's head snapped back, Fletcher let loose, throwing strikes to the solar plexus, the face, the chin. Webster's arms flailed as he tried to block the merciless attack.

"Stop." The word slipped through Georgiana's lips as the villain toppled to the floor.

Fletcher stood over him, ready for another bout, but the evil man lay unconscious.

Trembling, she watched Fletcher remove his neck-cloth and tie the man's feet and wrists behind his back like a hog.

When he faced her, his expression had changed to one of defeat. "My God, I wanted to kill him when I saw him bending you over the table."

She rubbed her arms as shame crept through her. "I-I'm sorry."

"No!" In two steps, he surrounded her in his embrace. "That man will rue this day for the rest of his life because death is too good for him."

A sob burst from Georgiana's throat as she curled into his warmth, his comfort, his strength. "I'm s-sorry f-for everythiiiiiing."

He smoothed his hand over her hair. "My love, it is I who am sorry."

Lord in heaven, his arms felt so good surrounding her. If only she could stay there cocooned in his embrace forever. Tears streamed from her eyes as she tried to gain control over her gasping breath. "I-I-I never meant to decieeeeeeeeve you!"

"Hush." Gentle lips pressed to her forehead. "I know that now, my love."

"I loved you...a-and I threw it all away!"

"Because you wanted to honor the memory of someone you also cared for very deeply."

Fletcher's soft voice whispered in her ear and, through her bleary tears, she saw a smile in those fathomless amber eyes. Merciful Lord! Was there a chance?

Chapter Twenty-Seven

After the magistrate took Webster away, Fletcher stood in Georgiana's cottage, facing the woman who had tortured his dreams for months. There was so much to say, but she rendered him dumb staring and wondering where to begin. He'd rehearsed an apology over and over along his ride from London to Thetford. But he hadn't anticipated Webster's attack or the outpouring of emotion once it was over.

Now, as the lady stood with her shoulders back, her head held high, yet wringing her hands, he wanted nothing more than to vow to promise to protect her for the rest of his days.

If she'll have me.

Even Fletcher knew she wouldn't want him to assume she was his—not before he begged for forgiveness. "I behaved like an ass from the very beginning."

A tear slipped onto her cheek as she covered her mouth. "No. From the beginning, I misunderstood you. True, your methods were a tad uncouth and, that, combined with your reputation, made me mistakenly believe I might be only a number in a line of conquests."

"Never." With a step forward, he grasped her hands. "From the moment I saw you, I knew you were not like all the others. You're quiet and principled and thoughtful. And though it took me time to cast aside my devilish ways, when I am with you I want to be a better man."

Another tear dropped to her cheek. "Oh, Fletcher, you *are* a good man. Look at all you have done for the unwed mothers. You care so very deeply but are afraid to let it show. If only people knew who you are on the inside."

He drew her hands to his lips and kissed them. "I think the fire cured me of that inhibition."

Her smile filled the room with light. "But why are you here? You have so many responsibilities."

"Perhaps, though not a one can usurp the love I harbor in my heart for you. You must know I love you with my every breath. I live because of you, it just took thirty years to find you."

"And I you. I didn't know how much until...until you were no longer there." Georgiana cupped his cheek, her lips quivering. "But now what will we do? I have orders to manufacture more fire engines than I can make in a year."

Turning his head, he kissed her palm. "As I understand it, you need a financier...and I happen to be intimately acquainted with a wealthy duke."

Lovely white teeth gleamed with her smile. "Wealthy, did you say?"

"Mm hmm, and interestingly, he is the proud owner of a mill which is presently being used to store his late father's collection of rickety old carriages."

"A mill?" Her eyes lit up. "And how large might this old mill be?"

"I'd say 'tis about fifty feet long by forty feet wide."

"Oh my. And your duke friend will not be averse to joining in partnership with a woman?"

"On the contrary. I believe he would be overjoyed... as long as certain agreements are granted."

A slender chestnut eyebrow arched. "Such as?"

Taking Georgiana's hand, Fletcher bent his knee and looked up at the only face he wanted to gaze upon for the rest of his days. "I have behaved badly, but I vow on my life that I will never doubt you again. I will honor you every day as long as I shall live and I promise you will want for nothing. Please, please. Will you marry me?"

Her head bobbed as she inhaled with a stuttered gasp. "Yes," she said breathlessly. "I will."

Rising, he gathered her into his arms—soft and warm and oh so very dear. His heart swelled as he captured her mouth in a slow kiss. Soft and unhurried, they joined in a dance where their bodies touched with reverence unfamiliar in all Fletcher's years. He took a breath and rested his forehead against hers. "I do not know what I would have done if you had refused me."

Her fingers found their way around his waist. "And I still cannot believe you are here. Thank you for being my knight in shining armor."

"You must know I would stand against an army for you, love."

"Love." She sighed, her face more beautiful now than ever. "How I like to hear you say it."

"The word is reserved only for you." He kissed her once more then took a step back, removing the hundred pound note from his doublet. "The women's home owes you a debt of thanks as well."

Georgiana's eyes popped wide with her gasp. "You weren't supposed to know."

"It seems Miss Eleanor disagreed."

"Eleanor? Curse her—"

"I think not. She gave me the boot up the backside I needed to shed my foolish pride, seek you out, and beg for forgiveness."

"Truly? In that case, I shall forgive her."

The note fluttered to the floor as he brushed a wisp of hair away from her cheek. "Me as well?"

She grasped his fingers and drew them to her lips. "Where you are concerned there is nothing to forgive."

Fletcher swirled his palm over hers. Georgiana's hand was so much smaller, it made his heart stretch with an eternal need to protect her. To have and to hold this woman and never let her go. "I lost my mother in a fire." The words blurted from his lips as if uttered without prior thought.

"Oh dear, I'm so sorry."

He swallowed, blinking away a sting at the back of his eyes. "I was away at Eton. The cottage burned to cinders. I think that's why I reacted so vehemently at the Southwark Fair. I desperately wanted to find a steam-powered fire engine, but after so many failures, I never thought anyone would make a machine with enough power."

Georgiana chuckled, her laugh infectious. "I'm surprised the force behind my pumper didn't dawn on you after you were deluged in the back. At the time, I couldn't believe you remained standing."

"And I was too hot under the collar to realize I'd been hit with a miracle—two miracles, you and your pumper, Georgiana. You finished it. The fire engine is as much yours as anyone's."

She blushed crimson as she lowered her gaze. "Yes, I did finish it, but it wasn't *my* dream—not at first."

"Tell me, my love. Are you truly ready to move on?"

"With you?"

His throat constricted so taut, he barely uttered, "Yes."

Her chocolaty eyes sparkled. "I cannot imagine taking another breath without you."

Fletcher's entire body tingled with her words. At long last, he'd found someone who cared for him—not because of money or title, but she loved him for the man he wanted to be. God willing, he would make every effort to live up to her ideals, her morals, her values. He dallied kisses along her neck, inhaling the intoxicating fragrance he craved.

"Make love to me," he whispered in her ear as he lifted her into his arms and strode into a tiny bedchamber. Stark, the bed filled most of the space, with a cedar chest at the foot. The only other furniture—a wooden chair in the corner. After spending so much time with this woman in the midst of polite society, Fletcher never imagined she might be comfortable in such modest accommodations. Georgiana was truly the partner for whom he'd been searching—charming, intelligent, unassuming, and generous. And gorgeous. Stunning. An angel sent from heaven.

No, Fletcher did not deserve this woman, but he would spend the rest of his days earning the right to love her.

As he set her on her feet, she rested her head on his chest. "I'm so happy."

His fingers glided down her back and released the bow of her apron. Slowly, carefully, he drew it over her head and, with it, the ridiculous doily hiding her chestnut locks. "Your hair is like polished mahogany."

She chuckled, unfastening the buttons of his waistcoat. "Oh my, you've a tear."

He didn't give a fig. "The perils of fighting dastardly villains."

She shoved both doublet and waistcoat from his shoulders. "I was so afraid."

With a few flicks of his fingers, her dress sailed to the floor. "But so brave."

"'Tis true what they say, courage is the ability to face one's fears." Rising on her toes, she kissed him while unfastening his falls. "You were heroic, but I never want to see you confront such danger again."

As their mouths joined, the remainder of their garments shed away and Georgiana pulled him to the mattress. "Let me express my appreciation. My adoration. My love."

Completely naked, he rolled to his back and spread his arms wide. "I am yours."

Pushing herself up on one arm, she trailed her fingertip down the center of his torso. "My vigorous hero."

Certain he'd died and gone to heaven, Fletcher closed his eyes and savored the gentle touches to his body—the moist heat of her mouth, the tip of her tongue stroking places that made him tremble.

Unabashedly, she toyed with the curls above his cock, then teasing and stroking his member with her fingers and tongue. Moaning, Fletcher swirled his hips in tandem with her seduction. He'd had many women in his life, but all paled in comparison, bringing on a powerful rush of desire swelling through his insides like nothing he'd ever experienced.

Unable to resist, he gathered her into his arms and rolled atop her, running his fingers through her silky hair. Almost roughly, he drove his hands over her, finding the sensitive paths on her skin. With her every purr of pleasure, desire coiled tighter in his loins. Lower and lower he swept his mouth, until urging her thighs apart. As he licked the wickedly sensitive bud, he caught her nipple between his thumb and forefinger, lightly pinching in a rhythm to match the tempo of his tongue.

Georgiana's sighs came faster, her fingers digging into his shoulders, until she clutched him tight. "I can wait no longer!"

Neither could he. Covering her, his cock slipped to her moist core and he slid himself along her channel. "Is this what you want?"

She grasped his buttocks and pulled him inside. Her inner walls gripped him, sending his mind into a maelstrom of raw passion—greedy and demanding. He searched for her mouth as he slid so deep inside her, it took every ounce of self-control he possessed not to explode. She jerked and writhed beneath him until she arched, her fingers forcing him faster. "Now! Come now!"

Throwing his head back, in two powerful thrusts, his seed burst, filling her with his molten desire. "I love you!"

Chapter Twenty-Eight

COLWORTH THE SEAT OF THE DUKE
OF EVESHAM, THREE MONTHS LATER

❧

Georgiana stretched, opening her eyes to velvet royal blue bedcurtains. Colworth was even grander than Hardwick Hall with not only a lake, but a fountain surrounded by a circular drive. Four stories in total, the original manor had been added on to since medieval times, and now sported four hundred and seventy-five rooms.

Stretching, she reached for her husband but cold linens swept beneath her fingers.

"Good morning, love," his deep voice rumbled from across the chamber. Since moving to his estate, they had decided against sleeping in separate rooms, though hers had an adjoining door where she kept her clothing and toilette.

She scooted up and propped against the pillows. "You've risen early."

"Have I?" He crossed the floor, sat beside her, took her hand and kissed her knuckles. "Miss Eleanor is expected today. I wanted to ensure Mr. Richards has a comprehensive list for her."

"You mean we need to ensure our new engineer has a comprehensive list."

"Forgive me." He kissed her lips. "I misspoke, Your Grace, Madam Chairman."

With proper financial backing, it hadn't taken long to convert the mill into a manufacturing facility. Georgiana and Fletcher had agreed on most things—the hiring of Oxford graduate, Mr. Richards, to oversee the operations, the appointment of Roderick Toombs as the engineer's apprentice, except when their now official ward, Roddy, was away at school. For their years of service, Mr. and Mrs. Tees were given Georgiana's cottage in Thetford. And most of all, Mama was overjoyed—so much so, she put up little fuss when the couple announced their wedding would be in a small chapel on the Colworth estate.

Fletcher waved a paper through the air. "We've had a mention in *The Scarlet Petticoat*."

With a scoff, she rolled her eyes. "Oh, please, do not tell me they've sent someone to spy on us all the way out here in Maidenhead."

"Actually, the article states that Miss Peters mentioned something about seeing me wandering the halls of Hardwick Hall with my dogs...and now she knows why."

"Dear Miss Peters. Did the paper mention anything about her prospects?"

"Evidently there's hearsay about a carriage ride with the Earl of Saye...but whether or not there's a courtship underway is pure speculation."

Georgiana pushed away the coverlet and swung her legs over the side of the enormous state bed. "Someone ought to put an end to that vile compilation of lies."

"And ruin forever the gossip of dozens of bored Londoners?"

"Anyone who reads that balderdash is sorely misguided."

"Here, here." Fletcher offered his hand. "Would you like some toast and a spot of tea before you ring for your lady's maid?"

Her stomach churned at the mention of food. "Perhaps it is still a bit early."

An eyebrow arched as he gave her a knowing look. "Perhaps I ought to send for the doctor."

"Whatever do you mean? I'm not ill."

"No." He slid his palm over her abdomen. "But you might be with child."

"Harrumph." As she began to object, an odd fluttering sensation rose inside, just beneath Fletcher's hand. She gasped. "What was that?"

Those bold eyebrows pinched together. "Hmm?"

"I swear I felt a tiny movement...like bubbles." She tapped his fingers. "Right there."

His eyes grew enormous along with his grin. "See? Just as I suspected."

Georgiana had never conceived in her first marriage —and her courses weren't always timely. "But it cannot be possible."

He drew her hand to his lips and kissed. "My love, with us, *anything* is possible."

And it was. Seven months later, they welcomed Joshua into their arms, a new and very legitimate heir to the Dukedom of Evesham. Aside from being a tad fairer than his father, Josh looked like a miniature version of Fletcher with black hair and a cry loud enough to rattle the windows in the nursery.

And as her husband cradled the wee babe in his arms, Georgiana rose on her toes and kissed him. "You have made me the happiest woman alive."

Afterword

Thank you for reading *The Duke's Untamed Desire*! The next book in the series will be *The Duke's Privateer* about Lady Eleanor (of course) but, first, have you read *The Duke's Fallen Angel*, the prelude to the Devilish Duke's series? Here's a sample...

Also by Amy Jarecki

The MacGalloways
A Duke by Scot

The King's Outlaws
Highland Warlord
Highland Raider
Highland Beast

Highland Defender
The Valiant Highlander
The Fearless Highlander
The Highlander's Iron Will

Highland Force:
Captured by the Pirate Laird
The Highland Henchman
Beauty and the Barbarian
Return of the Highland Laird

Guardian of Scotland
Rise of a Legend
In the Kingdom's Name
The Time Traveler's Destiny

Highland Dynasty
Knight in Highland Armor
A Highland Knight's Desire
A Highland Knight to Remember

Highland Knight of Rapture

Highland Knight of Dreams

Devilish Dukes

The Duke's Fallen Angel

The Duke's Untamed Desire

ICE

Hunt for Evil

Body Shot

Mach One

Celtic Fire

Rescued by the Celtic Warrior

Deceived by the Celtic Spy

Lords of the Highlands series:

The Highland Duke

The Highland Commander

The Highland Guardian

The Highland Chieftain

The Highland Renegade

The Highland Earl

The Highland Rogue

The Highland Laird

The Chihuahua Affair

Virtue: A Cruise Dancer Romance

Boy Man Chief

Time Warriors

About the Author

Known for her action-packed, passionate historical romances, Amy Jarecki has received reader and critical praise throughout her writing career. She won the prestigious 2018 RT Reviewers' Choice award for *The Highland Duke* and the 2016 RONE award from InD'tale Magazine for BEST TIME TRAVEL for her novel *Rise of a Legend*. In addition, she hit Amazon's Top 100 Bestseller List and earned designation as an Amazon All Star Author. Readers also chose her Scottish historical romance, *A Highland Knight's Desire*, as the winning title through Amazon's Kindle Scout Program. Amy holds an MBA from Heriot-Watt University in Edinburgh, Scotland and now resides in Southwest Utah with her husband where she writes sexy, immersive historical romances. Become a part of her world and learn more about Amy's books on amyjarecki.com.

About the Author

Known for her action-packed
page-turners   featuring   a
soldier, Amy Jarecki has received readers' and critical
acclaim throughout her writing
career. She won the prestigious 2016 RTT Reviewers'
Choice award for The Highlander's Ransom, received a
RONE award Finalist Medal
Magazine for BEST TIME
TRAVEL for her novel Rise of
a Legend in addition to the

Amazon's line. The Bestseller list, and earned designation as an Amazon All Star Author through not one
but three relationships through Amazon's Kindle Select
Program. Amy holds an MBA from Heriot-Watt University in Edinburgh, Scotland and now resides in
southwest Utah with her husband where she writes
heart-throbbing historical romance. Become a part of
her world and learn more about Amy's books on
AmyJarecki.com.

9 781648 392160